W9-BNF-642

The Houseguest

Novels by Thomas Berger

The Houseguest (1988)
Being Invisible (1987)
Nowhere (1985)
The Feud (1983)
Reinhart's Women (1981)
Neighbors (1980)
Arthur Rex (1978)
Who Is Teddy Villanova? (1977)
Sneaky People (1975)
Regiment of Women (1973)
Vital Parts (1970)
Killing Time (1967)
Little Big Man (1964)
Reinhart in Love (1962)
Crazy in Berlin (1958)

The Houseguest

A NOVEL BY
THOMAS BERGER

LITTLE, BROWN AND COMPANY

BOSTON   TORONTO

COPYRIGHT © 1988 BY THOMAS BERGER

ALL RIGHTS RESERVED. NO PART OF THIS BOOK MAY BE REPRODUCED
IN ANY FORM OR BY ANY ELECTRONIC OR MECHANICAL MEANS,
INCLUDING INFORMATION STORAGE AND RETRIEVAL SYSTEMS,
WITHOUT PERMISSION IN WRITING FROM THE PUBLISHER, EXCEPT
BY A REVIEWER WHO MAY QUOTE BRIEF PASSAGES IN A REVIEW.

FIRST EDITION

Library of Congress Cataloging-in-Publication Data

Berger, Thomas, 1924–
  The houseguest: a novel/by Thomas Berger.—1st ed.
    p.   cm.
  ISBN 0-316-09163-4
  I. Title.
  PS3552.E719H67   1988
  813'.54—dc19   87-26108
                                                      CIP

            10 9 8 7 6 5 4 3 2 1

FG

Published simultaneously in Canada
by Little, Brown, & Company (Canada) Limited

PRINTED IN THE UNITED STATES OF AMERICA

To Don Congdon

The Houseguest

§ 1 §

The process that led to the decision to kill Chuck Burgoyne, who for the first week of his visit had proved the perfect houseguest, began on the Sunday when, though he had promised to prepare breakfast for all (he was a superb cook), he had not yet appeared in the kitchen by half past noon.

"I'm beginning to be really worried," said Audrey, wife of Douglass D. B. Graves and mother of Bobby, who was newly married to Lydia née Di Salvo, whose father, though prosperous enough by reason of his refuse-disposal business to send her to the expensive university at which she met Bobby Graves, was a thick-chested, coarse man who shouted at table, whereas her father-in-law, an attorney for a family corporation in the city, had gray sideburns and was impeccably attired even on an island weekend, in the flawless taste of the old school: a long-sleeved shirt in very small navy checks and white duck trousers, to which at mealtimes he would add a summer blazer of classic navy hopsack. He was now out for a walk on the beach below.

Again Audrey addressed her daughter-in-law. They were in a sitting room just off a wide deck that overlooked the ocean. "Do you think we'd be justified in tapping at his door? It's going on twenty to one."

"Oh, I think so," said Lydia.

Audrey had very good skin indeed, but wincing unearthed some lines the existence of which could not have been suspected. "We're awfully private in this family. It really goes against the grain to intrude, especially on a guest."

"Yes, I am aware of that," said Lydia. "And I really like it." In her own family sometimes not even the frail lock on the bathroom door was a hindrance to a self-concerned brother who came home full of beer and had a grievous need to pee. "But I'd call this a special situation."

"We might just go and have some toast," said Audrey. "But that might seem rude when Chuck came out, all fired up to make his omelettes, which are really *good,* which I think has not that much to do with a technique that could be learned. He just has the touch. Chuck has a natural, uh, nonchalance of hand that eggs seem to respond to." She smiled suddenly with a show of teeth that were surely capped to look so brilliant at her age. Her hair too was lustrous, without a strand of gray. Bobby would be twenty-three in a month.

He was sitting in the basket chair near the wide glass door to the deck, his big, sandaled feet separated by a yard of polished floor. He wore a Mediterranean sailor's collarless shirt, striped horizontally in red and white, and shorts that were almost indecently tight in the crotch when he sat as he did now, his long thighs (he was six-three) making an obtuse angle. He had been reading a city paper published the day before; to get the Sunday edition someone would have to drive to the village. Bobby was apparently not suffering from a want of breakfast, but he had been up and around only since noon, Lydia, his roommate for a year and these five weeks his wife, having finally gone in and hauled him out. There seemed no limit to how long Bobby could sleep, whereas Lydia herself was sporadically insomniac.

Bobby now lowered the sheaf of newsprint, crumpling it slightly, and said, with a familiar twitch of the fleshy underlip that Lydia found both endearing and slightly repulsive, "He'll be along any minute now." He rose and stretched elaborately. He was hipless, a tube from armpits to knees. As it happened, Lydia found that kind of male build, conjoined with lank blond hair, to be sexually provocative. She had a carnal appetite that was robust. Had they been in their bedroom now, she might well have been tugging at his shorts. But when in the presence of others she was notably modest: she seldom even touched his shoulder or forearm, let alone held hands or snuggled in the public fashion of young couples of the milieu in which she had been raised.

"I'm not worried about eating," said Audrey. "I'm just wondering if something might be wrong with Chuck."

Bobby moued. "Why not go and see?"

Lydia protested. "*Bobby!* Why don't *you* do that for your mother?"

"It's not me that's worried," said he with a slack-limbed shrug and stepped out into the midday sun on the deck, where, fair as he was, he radiated light.

"*I'll* be glad to go," Lydia offered sincerely. It seemed the least she could do. Bobby was habitually rude to his parents, who were nice people insofar as Lydia could tell, though true enough she was not all that close to them nor was likely to be, given the polite conditions that were standard in this family. For example, none of them even spoke much about Chuck when he was not present. After a week of his residence, Lydia was not quite sure what his connection was to the Graveses, and she suspected it would be bad taste to ask to have it defined.

Not that she was unduly curious about Chuck Burgoyne, for whom her admiration was not nearly so ardent as that of her family-in-law. As to breakfast, her practice if let alone would have been to eat fruit exclusively, and in fact earlier this morning, before anyone else was up, she had discreetly enjoyed a banana during a long stroll on the beach. As to Chuck's reputed charm, wit, and energy, Lydia could not see that they were so remarkable as to give him the distinction he enjoyed amongst the Graveses. Yet she was sufficiently balanced to recognize that her feelings might not be devoid of envy: obviously, Chuck had known these people, including her husband, longer than she, and was in a fundamental sense less of a stranger than she in this household.

She was not even quite sure where Chuck's room could be found. The house, of glass and that kind of wood that looks already handsomely weathered when new, had been built to accommodate rather than dominate the bedrock that swelled here and there above the surface of the ground: there were unexpected wings, and likely a bird's-eye view would have revealed no attempt at symmetry. Lydia and Bobby had his former bachelor quarters, down a corridor off the lesser of the two sitting rooms (in one of which Audrey remained now, that which faced the bay), and Bobby's parents lived remotely in the rear, against the hillside, with no view at all. "But it's always cool back there," said Audrey, "and serene and quiet."

But where was Chuck? Lydia could have asked, but she was sensitive about revealing her lack of familiarity with the terrain: it would be still more confirmation that she was out of place. Not to mention that the search would give her the perfect motive to explore the house, through which no Graves, including her husband, had given her a formal tour, and once again, she would not have asked. People of this sort probably did not do that kind of thing, whereas her father not only dragged all visitors to his newly installed sauna (amongst them even the laundryman and the fellow who read the electric meter), but informed one and all of the outlandish price he had paid for it.

Lydia had already left the room when Bobby, speaking through the screen, hand cupped at his eyes, said, "Lyd, hand me my sunglasses?"

He was answered by his mother. "She's gone to look for Chuck. Where *are* your glasses? I don't see them anywhere."

Bobby groaned and turned away, squinting. He plodded down the stairway at the end of the deck: this ended at an interim point on the bluff above the beach; if you wanted to go on down to the water, you took the little flight of steps that consisted of a sequence of bark-on logs set into cuts in the hillside. Bobby now lingered on the topmost of these, for he saw his father heading homeward just below. If he went down there, he knew by experience that his father would feel a need to make conversation without personal substance, wondering whether what seemed the eroding of the shore was rather an illusion or noting that the sun seemed laggard this year in its morning chore of burning off the fog at the mouth of the bay. On what seemed an absolute principle, throughout Bobby's life thus far his father had never failed to avoid any subject of the least value to his son, even when there was reason to believe they shared in certain interests, for example, baseball: if Bobby entered a room in which his father sat watching a game the TV was soon extinguished, as if it had been on only by accident, and there was something in the son that obstructed him from stating forthwith that he too keenly followed the sport. Perhaps he even would inadvertently sneer at the screen. This was one of the many situations in which he was unable to represent himself truly and with justice to all. Was it not then ridiculous that his intention was to become a trial lawyer?

Not at all, said Lydia, beginning her second year as the source of his moral strength: it may well be that the ideal advocate for others is someone who cannot speak effectively for himself — he has no distractions. Bobby's self-assessment was balanced: he knew he was not brilliant, but believed he was both kind and fair.

Though his father continued past the bottom of the steps without looking up and one could now have descended with impunity and walked in the other direction, Bobby decided instead to resist the weak impulse that had directed him to the beach, where he had no actual business, and at least consider going to the club for a few sets of tennis — that is, if the question of breakfast could ever be resolved to the general satisfaction.

He watched the slowly retreating form of his father, who was shorter than he but still a tall man and with much better posture. His father had screwed at least two of the girlfriends Bobby had brought as houseguests throughout the years, which would seem to be in violation of an old principle of human culture, but such matters could be complicated — was not an Eskimo head-of-household constrained to offer his wife to the male stranger benighted in his igloo? All the same, Bobby believed his father would be likely to respect a legal marriage and make no advances towards Lydia. But should he be in error, he had disclosed to her all the relevant facts, as well as some supposition (that, given the sexual adventuring of three decades, his father might well have contracted a venereal disease). Anyway, he and Lydia shared the same bed, which situation would rule out his father's usual tactic of appearing in the wee hours in the room in which the girl slept alone and imposing himself upon her: not exactly rape, but perhaps the next best, or worst, thing, and it had taken Bobby two days in one case to persuade the victim not to go to the police, his most effective argument of course being that his father was a lawyer. Beyond that fact, he could not imagine the obsequious bumpkins of the island police acting adversely to his father were they to observe him committing cold-blooded murder. At least one of the local cops had worked at the house as yardman.

Bobby climbed back to the deck and looked through the screen into the sitting room. Lydia had not yet returned from her quest of Chuck — unless all of them were in the kitchen or dining room, for his mother was gone now. He entered and sat down in the chair he had occupied earlier. Now that he was alone, he could steal a seated nap. On summer Sundays, unless engaged in a game of some sort, he was sleepy all day however late he rose.

Having herself, from the front windows, observed that Doug was trudging westward along the beach, Audrey Graves had decided to take advantage of his absence and search her husband's room for data on his current mistresses; he usually had more than one at a time and sometimes more than two. His preferred practice seemed to be playing one off against the other, all against all, though often not every participant in this competition was aware she was a player. Sometimes none were. All of them tended to assume that Audrey's role was quite different from what it was and erroneously believed her to be their adversary, but then Doug's taste was ever for the kind of woman so stupid as to think herself shrewd, in other words the easiest sort to manipulate by cliché. He would use his familial responsibilities as an excuse not to see Miss X on Christmas, then spend the day with Ms. Y. If this year he was regularly flying to the island on Friday night to stay the weekend, it was surely because, not being as young as he once had been, he needed a rest from his sexual enterprises on weekdays in the city, where, from Memorial Day to the celebration of Labor in early September, he was denied the residential protection of his wife. Audrey was smugly aware of her invaluable use to him. That his cunts were unaware of the extent to which he and she were tacit collaborators was her great satisfaction, probably the only such at this late date, though she had once herself known a genuine passion for the man and could well understand what other women saw in him.

Through long experience Audrey had established that Doug never carried anything of a compromising nature on his person, not so much as an address book containing the numbers at which his sexual partners could be reached. He was too prudent for that, and thus had nothing to fear should he be felled publicly by accident or sudden illness, taken to a hospital and stripped. He was probably right in thinking that the thick sheaf of legal papers to be found in his attaché case was sacrosanct to most of the world by reason of its high potential for bringing boredom. Surely not even the most greedy of thieves would thumb through that bundle. Audrey's patience was no doubt unique, but then what she was seeking could not be called something so superficial or so readily available as material gain.

It was amidst his professional documents that Doug invariably filed souvenirs of his current sexual activities. Not only was this a place of nearly perfect concealment — for the black-leather case was clasped by a combination lock that would be proof against even the innocent intrusion of office assistants — but the practice also could be considered an expression of her husband's wit with regard to erotic activity, indeed the only area of such manifestation, for it would probably not have been unfair to characterize Doug as virtually humorless elsewhere in life. Thus what a surprise when, on their own first date, in fact before they had finished their coffee, the until then staid young man had displayed, down on the seat of the banquette, below the line of vision of fellow diners, a little rubber monkey that when squeezed simulated masturbating a pneumatic pink phallus. Audrey would have been appalled by this and subsequent antics had she not been captivated by the sheer incongruity between the premature fogeyism displayed by Doug when his fly was closed and his capability for the outrageous act when it was open. Once when, as an affianced couple, they had dined with his old half-blind aunt, he reached below the tablecloth and brought Audrey's hand over to bear upon that which jutted from his crotch — this while, bending over his plate, on the other side, was the young maidservant, whom, as Audrey realized only many years later, Doug had surely already enjoyed, for in remembering the incident she could recall that the girl, a newly emigrated Pole, had still been blushing when she reached Audrey with the peas, and probably not, as Audrey had then assumed, because she had seen what was happening in Doug's lap but rather because he had simultaneously put his other hand up the girl's skirt. He was only too capable of such a trick, and was to pull far worse. In years to come Audrey was to read an almost dementedly indecent note written to him by Didi Montrose, once her best friend, in which reference was made to what Doug had been doing to her as the back end of the comic horse they formed together at the mock circus for the children's hospital fund — and not just as they waited in the wings: he had persisted in his dirty work, keeping Didi in a state of ecstasy, even as they cavorted under the spotlights.

Whereas Doug might sit in silence throughout the most comic of plays, and even scowl if the humor verged remotely on the sexually suggestive.

Audrey now entered her husband's quarters, which were beyond her own and at the very end of the hallway. Corresponding to her own little dressing room was a small study for him, with a leather-topped desk over which hung an antique map, with its quaint distortions, of the then known world. To the left of the pristine blue blotter in its black leather holder was a flat box of polished oak containing a working telephone as well as an answering machine. This instrument was used exclusively for communications from Doug's girls, who assumed, no doubt on his assurances, that all such would be confidential and were unaware of Audrey's regular monitoring.

She now opened the lid of the box to see that the machine's little red light was signaling that it had recorded at least one message. Having rewound the tape and played it back, she determined that not one but three women had telephoned Doug since he had last collected his messages, which must have been only an hour or so earlier, unless he was now so disaffected as not to be moved to action by a winking red light and had allowed the calls to collect: not out of the question, for Doug could be ruthless with the overimportunate, and one of the callers, all but shrieking in resentment and self-pity, claimed to have been seeking him unsuccessfully since late Friday. Whether or not hers was a serious emergency was impossible to tell at this point, this being a new voice to Audrey, but there could be little doubt that if her style remained hysterical, whatever the legitimacy of her pains, the woman would be dumped, perhaps already had been. Doug would not tolerate emotional excess. What he provided in return was an extraordinary sexual endurance, which according to the unsolicited testimony of so many partners he retained even at the age of fifty-four. Indeed, on the very tape at hand one of the women alluded to his powers in starkly obscene language — and she too might well be a candidate for dismissal: even in private Doug was bluenosed with regard to language.

The case of one Barbara Rentzel was remembered: a travel agent whose wont apparently was to scream filth in Doug's face as he took her through multiple climaxes. The story had been recorded in the desperate letters she wrote him after being discarded, each of which he carried for a time deep within the legal papers in the attaché case, because he either enjoyed rereading accounts of anguish or wished to give his wife sufficient time to find them.

For it had lately occurred to Audrey that Doug must by now not only be aware of the surveillance she had maintained on him for many years, but be at some pains to abet it. In any event, that suspicion served her amour propre.

The remaining voice on the tape would seem to be that of a winner, at least amongst the trio at hand. For one, she had the thin soprano tones and the tentative phrasing of the grown-woman-as-schoolgirl that Doug preferred; for another, she had the sense to ask nothing, not even a return call, and to express only her longing for him and in romantic not carnal language. She sounded about fourteen, but as Doug was no longer attracted to jailbait, she was certain to be mature and could be even as old as forty-odd.

Audrey carefully left the tape at the point at which the last message ended. Had she been at all malicious, nothing could have been easier than to erase it, and there had been a time when she would certainly have done so. Perhaps it was just as well that Doug in those days did not yet possess an answering machine: nothing could have resulted from such an exercise of spite but the loss of the impeccable moral status by means of which she survived. Such an action could not but be succeeded by others of the same character, each more bitter and thus even less effectual than the former, for pride can never be served by negative means. Not to mention that Audrey was by nature an ironist who was capable of seeing in the rain that fell on a picnic, the staining of one's special dress an hour before the start of whichever memorable event, and like calamities not altogether unwelcome confirmations of her basic pessimism. In contrast, Doug habitually entertained favorable expectations. He and she were fundamentally well matched.

She found the key to the large drawer at the bottom of the desk's left pedestal, a key that was conveniently kept amidst the paper clips in a little leather-covered open drum on the desktop, next to a larger one that held freshly sharpened pencils. She unlocked and opened the drawer and removed the attaché case from it. Though Doug could be erotically ingenious, his powers of invention were notably banal in other areas of life, and the first time Audrey encountered the little cylinders of the combination lock she had no hesitation in moving them to represent the month, day, and year of his birth, and the hasp popped open on the instant. That had been three attaché cases ago, as of this time, yet the same maneuver was still as valid.

But today, for the first time ever, there was nothing in the case, not even any legal papers. Audrey was hard hit by this discovery, as she had never been by the occasional item of flimsy lingerie tucked into the pocket in the lining of beige suede. Moving by sheer habit, she replaced the case in the locked drawer and returned the key to a paper-clip burial before sitting down to deliberate on the edge of Doug's bed. She might have remained there until her husband returned from his walk, in flagrant violation of their tacit agreement, had not the tone of the telephone, so thin in timbre yet so piercing, sounded at that moment, restoring her self-possession.

She snatched the instrument from the box and said, "You have reached Douglass Graves's number."

As she expected, the caller was surprised by this greeting and for a long moment preserved the silence. But when the voice finally came on the line it was not a woman's but hoarse and coarse.

"Get Charlie for me."

Audrey knew an odd emotion which could have been either relief or regret. She answered sweetly, "I'm afraid you have the wrong number."

The caller rudely contested her assertion. "Don't gimme that. You just go and get Charlie."

During such an exchange with a person who was evidently her social inferior Audrey usually felt if not wholly in the wrong to be anyway on an uncertain footing. Therefore she now applied some cogitation to the matter and, after an instant during which she was conscious of the heavy, menacing breaths at the other end of the wire, came up with a possibility.

"Could you mean Chuck, Chuck Burgoyne?"

The question was received with a grating utterance between a grunt and a chuckle. Then, in manifest derision: "You just tell Chucky-wucky to call Tedesco, see?"

"Yes, Mr. Tedesco. Do you want to leave a number?" But, with an uncompromising click, the line was dead.

Audrey took a sharpened pencil from the leather cup, then looked through the desk in vain for a piece of paper. Though she had been taken aback by the current emptiness of the attaché case, she was not astonished to find that the drawers were barren as well. Doug did no work at the island house; he did little enough at the office. The job was a sinecure in a family-owned firm, which employed serious attorneys for the serious work. Doug had barely squeaked through law school in his day, and his passing of the bar exam had been a mystery the investigation of which would surely serve no one's interest at this late date.

She returned the pencil to its place with the rest of those which would through lack of use stay sharp eternally. The message was simple enough, the name easily remembered: *call Tedesco*. No doubt the derisive "Chucky-wucky" should be omitted. In her experience this was the first message of any kind that Chuck had received from the outside world since his arrival. But then, she neither monitored the incoming phone calls nor was always first to get the mail.

There had been no calls or letters in recent days. It was

one of those periods in which one's usually attentive friends, suddenly and as if in concert, forget one's existence. This was far from being unprecedented, yet it was unusual this early in the season. A certain general disaffection usually appeared along about the third week in August, as if in preparation for the complex emotions of the imminent Labor Day, at once another end and another beginning, but as of early June the summer was still new, with many people yet to arrive — but perhaps that was the explanation.

The phone rang again: no doubt Mr. Tedesco, with a revision or addition to the earlier message. But even before the receiver reached her ear the female caller was speaking, in a peculiarly ugly whine.

". . . this to me? I've been sitting here crying all weekend. You're hateful, absolutely hateful. I didn't realize you could be so cruel. You're a shit, a complete shit! . . . I didn't mean that. Please answer. . . . You're there, I know you're there."

"Yes I am, you whore," said Audrey, hanging up. She was really more impatient than angry.

Doug naturally had seen his son at the top of the steps to the beach; there was nothing wrong with his peripheral vision. In fact, he had no physical disabilities whatever, unless some were so subtle as to elude the thorough examination he underwent annually, not to forget that he reported promptly to his doctor at the first appearance of the symptoms of even a common cold. He drank no more, and often less, than two glasses of wine a day and had never smoked. On each day of the island weekends he walked two miles of shoreline; in town he worked out three mornings per week in the gym at his club. He had lived more than half a century, and he was still the man his son would never be. If Bobby had any character at all, he would have shouted down to him. Not only was Bobby's the superior perspective, but all of nature ordained that the younger man was the one with the obligation to take the initiative in such a case.

The moral question aside, Doug was grateful to Bobby for staying mute. He had never been able to speak easily to his son. Audrey provided security, but Bobby made him feel vulnerable. Perhaps it was unfair of him to blame Bobby for the scandal at the Wilmot School, his son having been one of the underaged victims of the male faculty members, pederasts to a man (with the ironic exception of Hargrave Bond, English master and poet with an international reputation, the only one of them to display effeminate ways), but neither was it his own fault that the boy was so passive as to suffer such use for months without complaint — if indeed Bobby had not enjoyed it! Doug himself, age fourteen, had first punched the golf pro who once made advances to him in an otherwise deserted country-club locker room. "All right for you," chided the hairy man, with a simper, and then Doug kicked him in the testicles and went promptly to have him fired. The experience had given him a prejudice against golf, but as it happened when the time came Bobby chose it as his own favorite sport and placed high and often first in junior tournaments: another example of their profound difference, each from each, which went to the bone and could not be called the product of Bobby's conscious defiance. There was no means by which he could have known of his father's experience with the invert. Doug had never revealed this to anyone. His discretion as to sexual matters was absolute, and he went to many pains to keep it so. He had only contempt for those whose greatest satisfaction came from revealing what should have been their secrets.

Doug had been coming to the island all his life. The land on which his house stood had been in his family for three generations. Yet he had not been in or on the ocean for more than four decades. His younger brother had drowned in a boating accident when they both were children, and he had thought of the sea ever since as an enemy and had ignored it insofar as that could be done when it was so close at hand. Most of the island's seasonal residents were boating people, and there were friends of Audrey's who sought to lure him on board their craft, but he successfully resisted all such importunities. Fortunately, Chuck Burgoyne had proved landlocked, indeed had seldom left the house since his arrival: that alone was enough reason to think well of the young man. He embodied Doug's idea of a perfect house-guest in all ways: he was genial; he was self-sufficient, needed no tending. He was not a zealot. Nor did he fall into moods. Above all, he was not vulgar.

But what Doug found inexplicable was that Chuck would be a friend of Bobby's: what in the world did he see in him? Lydia obviously was out to rise in the world, but what could a fellow like Chuck gain from an association with Bobby? As to Lydia, Doug did not find her sexually attractive. He had had his moments with some of the other female houseguests brought by Bobby throughout the decade past (though sometimes, in the earliest years, when the girls might not yet have reached the age of consent, nothing more occurred than fondling), but Bobby had chosen another type to marry than those he had previously dated. Lydia's scholastic accomplishments had earned her four free years at the university to which Doug had to pay a fortune to send Bobby, and the irony of this state of affairs was that her father was if anything more prosperous than Doug, who in his own opinion was a poor man, for the real money was in a trust from which he was provided with only a modest annual stipend, his own father having had no higher regard for him than he for Bobby. With the inconsequential salary paid him by the firm controlled by his uncle and cousins, his yearly income from all sources was not nearly sufficient to support his own tastes, not to mention what was spent by Audrey over and above her own modest independent income and that needed to maintain Bobby.

He now checked the mileage on the pedometer at his belt, even though he had walked this route every Saturday and Sunday morning for many summers, but consulting the instrument was what distinguished exercise from mere stroll: precision was always a value well worth honoring. By now he had worked up quite an appetite. If Chuck was not up and about when he returned, Doug really would be disappointed in him, unless of course the poor fellow was ill, but how tiresome that would be with a guest, especially on a Sunday.

Lydia encountered her mother-in-law in one of the hallways.

"Believe it or not," said she, "I'm still looking for Chuck's room."

"Bobby hasn't given you the tour yet?" Audrey assumed a smirk.

"I haven't ever thought to ask," said Lydia. "Until now I've known how to get anyplace I wanted to go."

"Well, this is our part of the world, Doug's and mine." Audrey threw a hand towards her own shoulder, but she made no offer to show the rooms behind her. "The guest rooms are on out the hall you're in. Go on past your room and through the door at the end."

"Gosh, is there more of the house out there? I thought that door went outside."

"It does," said Audrey. "Or rather, onto a little open-sided but roofed passage called by some, I believe, by that awful word breezeway. The guest rooms are back there."

"Aha," said Lydia. "Separated."

"We thought that was nice and private." Audrey frowned. "It can be inconvenient when rain is blowing in off the ocean. I should in all honesty say that like everything else it was Peter's idea . . . Peter DeVilbiss, the architect."

"Oh yes," Lydia said hastily. "It's a remarkable piece of work. It certainly makes the most of all the features of the property." She despised herself for speaking in this fashion, but there were times when doing otherwise seemed impossible. She continued now through several more banalities, concluding with a reference to "both sea and forest."

"Doug dislikes sleeping in a room that looks out on water," said Audrey. "Hence his faces the hillside. But that's what he wanted."

Fortunately Lydia had never till now found herself alone with her mother-in-law. Audrey was quite as uneasy as she. "Very good, then, I'll be on my way to find Chuck." She walked backwards a way so as not to seem rude.

Audrey made a frowning mouth. "I do hope he's all right. But if he is, we certainly won't want to chide him for oversleeping, will we?"

Lydia was offended by this warning. Why should Chuck be sacrosanct? That it would be rude to kid someone about a little excess sacktime was preposterous. The things that mattered to people who did nothing useful in life!

But now she at last felt free to turn her back on Audrey and stride away, back to the central vestibule or whatever it should be termed in such a structure, from which place she chose the corridor, as directed, off which was Bobby's former bedroom and bath, now shared by her. After a week of nights there, she still felt as though she were an adolescent sleeping over, screwing surreptitiously, as in fact she had done when she was seventeen, as houseguest of a boy in more modest circumstances, so modest indeed that he had to sleep on the living-room couch while she occupied his bedroom. He was supposed to stay out there, but as it happened, when the house was quiet he stole in and slipped between the sheets alongside her and, before she was altogether awake, had aroused her to the degree that when fully conscious she was as eager to proceed as he. This boy was the first of the only three lovers she had had before meeting Bobby; she had had no other since.

For some reason once she had passed their room now and gone through the door at the corridor's end and into a kind of outdoors — for not only was the breezeway roofed, but a fence of shrubs grew close by on the inland side — Lydia was suddenly conscious of her bare thighs. Perhaps it was the sea breeze. She wore shorts, but they were conservative enough, a fit that could be called neat, certainly not undecorous, and made of blue-and-white seersucker. She wore a simple white blouse above and sockless sandals below. With Bobby she had checked this costume for appropriateness and received his unqualified okay. True, he might have done as much had she appeared in a cerise playsuit, but she insisted that he remember that this was not her native milieu and asked him to be serious. Lydia by no means felt inferior when amongst the Graveses, but she abhorred nothing more than being conspicuously out of order, which was discourteous. Crude as they were, her own family had a tradition of courtesy. "If you're served fish, Johnny, then you *eat* fish," were her mother's instructions to her older brother when he was first invited out on his own to dinner as a teenager, and her father continued to slap him for lapses in table manners till he had graduated from high school. Lydia herself had been admonished for wearing jeans so tight they showed the outline of her underpants and thus violated accepted manners. "It's ugly, Lyd, not nice to others," her mother had said. "We all have to live in the world together. Who wants to see what covers your bare behind, for heaven's sake?"

In any event, it occurred now to Lydia that she was on her way to the isolated domain of a man she hardly knew, dressed in attire that could be called skimpy, for there was nothing beneath the shirt and shorts but a ribbonlike garment for which briefs was perhaps too substantial a term. The underwear had even evoked an amazed question from Bobby, "How come you wear something like that?" "*So my pants won't show,*" said she. Of course another taboo of her mother's concerned visible evidence of nipples, but Lydia was not weighty on top and the white shirt was not only opaque but outsized.

Even so she felt vaguely indecent as she reached the door at the end of the breezeway, opened it, and entered a hallway of a series of pale-blue doors, all of them closed but one halfway along on the side that faced the sea. As she had no means of knowing which belonged to the guest room occupied by Chuck Burgoyne, it was most convenient for her first to look into the doorway that was open.

When she did so, there he was, apparently sleeping soundly, in the supine position in or rather on the bed, even the sheet drawn away though the morning was not, back here in this shaded wing, cooled by the ocean breeze, really hot enough to justify that, but perhaps it was a matter of personal metabolism, for not only was he not under bedclothes, he wore no pajamas. He was in the state her father for some reason called "buck naked." And he had a blatant erection.

Lydia remained just long enough to determine that he was genuinely asleep. He seemed to be.

§ 2 §

Somehow Audrey had foreseen that when Chuck finally appeared in the main house, he would not refer to breakfast.

Instead he looked sternly at her and asked whether there had been a telephone call for him.

She answered guiltily. "In fact, there was." It was fortunate that Doug remained away on his walk. "On Doug's private phone. It was just by chance that I —"

"It wasn't Perlmutter?" Chuck's bright blue eyes seemed to show an unparticularized resentment.

"Actually, someone named Tedesco. He didn't leave a number. He said —"

"I can imagine what he said." Chuck was a man of slightly under medium height, of average-to-slight figure. He had a ruddy face that anyone would have called handsome, below neatly cut, straight, very dark hair. "If he calls again, tell him I've left."

"It's not likely I'll be the one to answer if he uses that number. It's really Doug's private one. He doesn't like others to use it. I wonder how Mr. Tedes——" But Audrey stopped here; she would not be rude.

Chuck sat down in the chair that Bobby had earlier

vacated in favor of the deck. Parts of the newspaper lay where they had been dropped. Chuck retrieved them, stacked them on his lap, but did not so much as glance at the headlines.

"Tedesco's not a man to trifle with," said he. "If anybody is looking for trouble, Tedesco will supply it."

Why then would he have given the man Doug's private number? was the question that persisted with Audrey. But she could neither ask it nor mention the subject tabooed by the law of hospitality: namely, were the plans for breakfast now definitely shelved?

"He called you Charley," she said at last, and when Chuck looked at her as if puzzled, she added, "Mr. Tedesco."

Chuck, who had seemed to be brooding, now brightened. "It's a matter of choice. The name you're called by others is not exactly your own property, is it? Charley, Chuck, Chaz. It's the name you can do that with. But Audrey is not, I think?" Chuck took the matter seriously. It was this sort of thing that made him so ingratiating.

"Actually, Audrey's not my first name, as it happens," said his hostess. "I don't like it much but it's preferable to Wilhelmina, which is one of those names one is given to please some relative who might leave money to a younger person of the same name."

Chuck leaned towards her. He still held the newspapers, which he had stacked, she assumed, merely to serve his sense of order. He wore leather loafers, with socks, and apparently had not brought along a pair of sports shoes of any kind, nor jeans or shorts. He provided quite a contrast with Bobby's style, and not only in clothing. "You're a desirable woman, Willie," he said in a voice of intensity but low volume. Having made that startling speech, he rose and left the room at a smart pace, carrying with him the stack of newspapers.

Audry had assumed she had forgotten how to blush, so long had it been, perhaps even since the days of the squint. While Doug's courtship antics had shocked her, she had never been embarrassed by them, but the difference there was that she had been a participant, a collaborator even if involuntarily. At the moment she had been given no role, and sat alone with her blazing face. Whether it was cruel or considerate of Chuck to leave so decisively would have been difficult to say. She was fifty-one and he might be somewhat older than her son but was still under thirty. With another intonation, his words now might well have been interpreted indecently. As it was, they sounded almost businesslike. His departure suggested ruthlessness. With no supporting evidence Audrey might have applied to Chuck what he had said of his friend or perhaps enemy named Tedesco, who should not be trifled with nor frequented unless one was looking for trouble. That certainly had never been true of Audrey. Her style was to avoid conflict, and thus, unlike almost everyone else she knew, she was still on her first marriage.

Lydia too had colored by reason of Chuck Burgoyne, but her flush represented anger. Only a scoundrel would sleep naked with an open bedroom door, even if quartered in the remotest part of the house. The weekday house-keeper, Mrs. Finch, surely went back there routinely as did the team of cleaning women who made regular Monday and Friday visits, not to mention those persons on missions such as that of Lydia only just concluded, or mere wanderers-through-hallways. But what infuriated her most was her inability to decide whether in so establishing the opportunity for self-exhibition Chuck was showing insolent indifference or narcissistic intent. Each would have been offensive, but perhaps the first was the more obnoxious.

Lydia could not abide inconsiderate persons, those who performed as if they were alone in the universe. But until now it could never have been said of Chuck Burgoyne that he operated with indifference to those around him: he was all too aware of others. He was always manipulating the Graveses, inducing them to alter practices that had apparently been lifelong, e.g., it had been their custom to breakfast severally and not collect around the table as a family so early in the day. He was singlehandedly responsible for the canceling of the traditional cocktail party with which the family had celebrated the opening of the season each year for the last seventy-odd, if the count began with Doug's grandfather, whose enormous house had not been at the shore, which in those days was considered too remote a site for a residence, but rather in the town overlooking the harbor. But it had been Audrey, not Doug, who cared about tradition, and the latter made no vocal objection when she announced that, as Chuck had rightly pointed out, the party when seen unsentimentally was no more than, when the time for planning and preparing was included, many dollars of expense and days of hard work for a few hours of tedium.

On the other hand, if it were Chuck's intention to exhibit himself, it could have been supposed that he would have done so under conditions more propitious for success. How could he have assumed that anyone would go back that way on a Sunday? And then what if the visitor had been Bobby or Doug? Presumably the sight would not have been so shocking to another man, certainly not to Bobby, who had told her of some of the contests that had gone on in his day as an adolescent in the locker rooms of the club. Males then actually did concern themselves with size, as she noted derisively. Ah, said he, then women are indifferent to measurements of breast and butt and thigh? He professed not to understand the fundamental difference involved.

To Lydia the sight of Chuck's tumid organ was anything but erotic. It simply represented the ultimate in effrontery.

She had stopped off at her own quarters to collect herself. A bright sitting room faced the sea; the bedroom, behind it on the land side, was always cool and dark and tranquil. The house had been built just as Bobby entered prep school, and his tennis and golf trophies from those years to the present stood on a teak shelving system that had probably been designed for books. Bobby owned few of the latter, being no reader, but with Lydia's assistance he had when necessary summoned up sufficient intellectual effort to get passing grades in his college courses, though they would probably not have been high enough to get him accepted by a law school not heavily endowed by his great-grandfather. All three of the Graveses known to Lydia considered themselves virtually impoverished because they did not have the grand estate of his forebear, with its scores of servants, a property that today had long been a monastery, with grounds ever dwindling as the monkish order, in need of funds in an impious era, sold more of the acreage for tract houses and a shopping mall.

Lydia stood before the big window and sought to be calmed by the sight of the expanse of water: the ocean was a great flat gray sheet at the moment. It was perhaps incongruous to seek emotional balance by gazing at such a potentially violent medium, but this measure never failed even in a storm. Presumably a hurricane might provide a different story, but anything less, if one were safe behind plate glass, did not fail to bring — well, reassurance might be the name for it: what did not seem petty in view of that liquid magnitude?

Lydia was a superb swimmer, but riding on the surface of the sea was another thing. She was the poorest of sailors on her father's big cabin cruiser, large enough for ocean-roaming but used by him exclusively on the meagerly proportioned and rather brackish Lake Winkeemaug, if not altogether a manmade body of water, then at least enhanced by dredge. Aboard that vessel the pubescent Lydia was capable of getting the vapors before the anchor was hoisted, and spent much of any voyage in the toilet, whose door, needless to say, was labeled "The Head."

The two men Lydia loved the most were the same for whom she felt the most contempt: her father and her husband. But perhaps this was normal enough.

Had his daughter-in-law moved closer to the glass she could have seen Doug returning from his walk, ascending the steps from the beach. She would have been in an ideal situation from which to admire the fecundity of his scalp, on which the hair grew as thick as when he had been a boy.

He now had decided that there could be no more waiting for Chuck's appearance: he was too hungry. And if the houseguest did subsequently, belatedly, arise and prepare breakfast, it would be within one's capacity to eat twice: the salt air would see to that. Therefore, having entered by one of the doors which in a conventional dwellingplace would have been more obviously assigned to tradesmen, he was in the kitchen.

Here he stood bewildered for a moment before the large brushed-steel refrigerator that the designer had obtained, if memory served, from a firm whose routine clients were commercial restaurants. It was easy to assume that one could just go ahead and feed oneself, but aside from pouring cornflakes from a box, splitting a muffin and buttering it, and applying mustard to layered ham and cheese, Doug had never his life long been personally responsible for the preparing of that which he chewed and swallowed, and thus he found himself on alien terrain at the moment, without a legible map. He had never even tried frying a slice of bacon, and had an idea, based on scenes in comic movies, that it could seldom be performed by a beginner. To prepare his favorite form of egg, poached, divine intervention was probably to be implored, for even those of his women who were adepts at cookery made cloudy, oysterish messes unless they cheated and brought into play those little steaming-cups from which the eggs came looking as if effigies molded in rubber.

But Chuck's poached eggs were as though formed in God's hand, translucent, veiled, quivering, scarcely over the threshold of solidity. Dammit, where was the fellow now?

Right there: he came out of the butler's pantry.

"Chuck!" Doug cried in happy surprise and frank affection.

The houseguest failed to reply in kind. He frowned and scraped his lower lip with chisel-teeth. He carried two slices of white bread, inserted them into the twin slots of the toaster. Apparently this was to constitute his breakfast-making today.

Chuck asked, "Bobby went to the club?"

"I saw him outside a little while ago."

Chuck made it a statement this time. "He went to the club."

Doug rubbed his hands together. "Toast looks like a good idea. I've been up for hours but haven't yet eaten a bite." He gave his speech a rising inflection so as to imply that this denial had been his own idea.

With excessive force Chuck pulled one of the chairs away from the kitchen table and dropped into it. "Have a seat," he said to Doug. "The womenfolk are elsewhere."

It occurred to Doug that Chuck sometimes used quaint terms, especially with respect to females, had heard him actually say "gentler sex" once.

He took a chair as asked. He could not remember having previously sat in this kitchen; on his brief visits he was wont to lean against a counter.

Chuck put a fist on the tabletop between them. "I don't know whether you're aware, Connie's got to the point at which she's threatening to make real trouble."

Doug felt a reaction at the base of his skull, as if he had been seized, with pliers, at the nape. "Connie?"

"Cunningham," Chuck said impatiently. "I've talked with her. Obviously it's my intention to be discreet — else I wouldn't be sitting here."

Connie Cunningham was a divorcee with whom Doug had lately had some six weeks of ardent sexual encounters. She was skinny, almost emaciated, with breasts consisting of little more than nipples, and her behind was flat, but her vulva could only be called inexhaustible. Indeed, the trouble had apparently been that none of her three husbands had been able to maintain the pace she demanded. Only Doug, eight to ten years older than the eldest of these men, had ever been her match. Anyway so she had assured him, and at first this news proved aphrodisiac. Lately it had been anything but, and as the weeks passed, Connie became ever rougher, seizing him painfully at the crotch on his entry into her apartment, in bed nipping at his glans with her horsey front teeth, riding him as if he were a recalcitrant bronco, bruising his ribs.

Connie had not yet accepted the truth that she had been dumped: hence the anguished telephone messages on the tape in his answering machines at island and city addresses. Fortunately she had never learned the name of the firm; nowadays he routinely kept that a secret when he could. In the past he had too often been embarrassed before his relatives, who usually managed to make a spy of his secretary, for after all, they and not he held the effective power in the firm. "For God's sake, Douglass," said his uncle Whitson K. T. Graves III, who in addition to being on the boards of universities and hospitals had once been a wartime commanding officer of an elite regiment of the National Guard as well as, for the final eighteen months of one administration, ambassador to a little authoritarian state in Latin America. "Douglass, we all wet our whackers now and again, but we don't wave them out the window!"

"I had gone back to look for you," said Chuck. "When the phone rang I answered it. I hadn't been given any special instructions." He stared at Doug. "She assumed I was you, and gave me quite a earful."

Doug raised his chin. "You see, I —"

"Look," said Chuck, "it's better it happened this way.

I gather you've given this person the boot, but she's resisting."

"I —"

The houseguest raised his slender hand, making it into a pistol, the muzzle of the index finger pointed at Doug's chin. "This is something that requires no effort at all on your part. I'll see it's taken care of."

"Oh," said Doug, "that won't be —"

"Please," said Chuck, waving the hand that was still extended. "It's the least I can do." A bell sounded at the toaster, followed by a clicking metallic noise. The houseguest went to the counter.

Doug's embarrassment continued to grow. That he had no clear sense of what Chuck was proposing made it worse. And while Chuck was not as young as Bobby, he had yet to be born when Doug first had carnal knowledge of a female. With all respect to the young man, it did not seem right that he would assume authority in this matter — even though he might well be competent enough.

Chuck returned along a route that included the refrigerator, from which he took a covered butter dish of thick glass.

"She's making too much of it," said Doug.

Chuck had reclaimed his seat and, working neatly, knifed shavings of butter off the firm stick and put them to melt on each piece of toast. "You don't need that sort of thing, Doug: a man in your position." He smiled. "Let's drop the subject. It's been taken care of."

This was news. Just a moment earlier he had put the statement in the future tense. What had happened since?

"I'm not sure I understand," said Doug. "You've said something to Connie?"

Chuck shook his head. "Not me," he said. "I just

arrange things. I'm an idea man or maybe a diagnostician."
He crunched his teeth into the buttered toast. It was
probably not his place to offer the other piece to Doug, for
after all it was Doug's kitchen, Doug who owned all the
bread on the premises.

Before another attempt could be made to get to the
truth of the matter at hand, Audrey entered the kitchen.

"Here you are," said she, and it could be taken to refer
to either one of them or both. "Golly, the toast smells
goood." She marched to the refrigerator. "How about some
scrambled eggs to go with it?"

Doug considered this to be one of the great suggestions
of the era, but Chuck said, "A little late in the day for me,
Audrey, but you go right ahead."

That was enough to discourage her even from preparing
toast for herself and Doug. She sat down at the table,
making a trio that might seem to the onlooker to be
positively familial. "Well, what have you fellows been up
to?" she asked as if jovially.

Chuck had already devoured the first piece of toast.
"Oh," said he, and took time to lick several fingertips,
though with a certain grace that seemed boyish, not
coarse, "oh, Doug and I are involved in a conspiracy." He
grinned at his so-called partner. "And it wouldn't be a
conspiracy if we told *you*." Perhaps because the emphasis
seemed rude in retrospect, he added, after a pause,
"Boy-talk."

But so far as Doug was concerned, that note made it
worse. Said he to his wife, "Sports. Baseball. That's the
secret. It's not as if we're plotting a murder."

Chuck raised his eyebrows inscrutably.

"I predict," Audrey said suddenly, "that this will be a
twenty-win year for the Soldier Boy."

"You might be right," replied Chuck. "It's certainly within the range of possibility, if that bone-chip problem can be licked."

It seemed to Doug as though they had begun to converse in a code for the reason of discomfiting him: he who was still shaken by Chuck's being privy to the matter of Connie Cunningham.

"Since when," he indignantly asked Audrey, "have you been interested in baseball?"

"Oh, I don't know I can name a date. And I still haven't actually ever seen a game except on television."

Doug wondered whether he should be offended: this was news to him. He was not the sort of man who liked women who were keen on sports, even if simply as spectators. Of course female athletes, drenched with sweat, were out of the question.

Audrey asked Chuck, "Think the Bulldog will be swinging a big bat again this season?"

"Probably time for an off-year," he said immediately. "Always happens after the signing of a big new contract."

What in the world could Chuck have meant when he said Connie had been taken care of? Despite his previous favorable opinion of the young man, Doug found a suggestion of arrogance in the suggestion.

He rose from the chair and rubbed his hands together. He now had sufficient justification to announce he was hungry, in which statement there was a definite implication that was critical of Chuck. "I haven't had anything to eat since dinner last night. Does *anybody* have *any* plans for lunch?"

Audrey seemed to quail, but after a moment Chuck threw up his arms and cried genially, "Couldn't sleep, so

I came out early and made a big breakfast. This toast has taken care of me till dinnertime."

Doug was now provoked to reveal his annoyance. "I really was looking forward to your pancakes."

Chuck raised one eyebrow. "You don't remember? We all agreed last night we'd each be on his own this morning?"

Audrey remained serenely silent. She could not be looked to for assistance.

After a moment Doug shook his head and said expressionlessly, "My mistake." He walked to the casement window over the sink and stared out to the parking area, a graveled place below tall pines. Seeing which car remained, he asked, without purpose, "Bobby went to the club?" He slowly came to the table. "I think I'll run in to the village and catch a sandwich at the diner."

"It's closed," said Audrey. "All day Sunday."

Smirking, Chuck strolled to the refrigerator, swung open the door, and while peering into the interior said, "A man's got a square meal coming under his own roof. I'll rustle up something."

All at once Doug had lost his sense of hurt. "Mighty nice of you, Chuck old boy. I wouldn't mind it at all. You've spoiled us with your culinary prowess." He had intended, on the route to the village, to stop at a roadside phone booth and call Connie Cunningham in the city: it was too risky to try that on his private telephone in the house, what with people wandering through the hallways. But he now had an excuse not to perform this chore, at least not promptly, and that was just as well, for he was sure to be wrong in feeling any apprehension as to her welfare: the result would be only to postpone, for more painful days, the necessary end to their association, for Connie was currently in the mood to see a routine hello as evidence of his revived passion.

Audrey protested hypocritically to Chuck, "It's really me who should be doing that. You're our guest!"

"I'd rather be useful than sit around," said Chuck. "You know that."

But good as he had previously been at the stove, today he produced fried eggs with hard yolks and brown edges, and burned the bacon, yet he served this fare to his hosts with the same air of confidence he had justifiably displayed with fine meals.

But one should probably not judge him harshly on the basis of a unique off-day.

Audrey was about to sit down to the plate Chuck had prepared for her when she said, "Oh, I guess I'd better tell Lydia we're eating."

"No," said Chuck, "you sit down while it's hot. I'll find her."

When the houseguest had left the kitchen, Doug asked Audrey, "Know anything about Chuck's family?"

She shrugged. "Not really. I think he hails from out West somewhere. Ask Lydia. I gather she's the one knew him first, introduced him to Bobby."

"He's an awfully agreeable guy," said Doug, munching some bacon, the char-bittered taste of which was actually stimulating to his palate. "I hope he's able to stay for some days to come."

Audrey agreed. "He's nice to have around the house. You know when Mrs. Finch is here he never comes into the kitchen. He's that delicate."

Unlike his wife, Doug had never seen their weekday housekeeper as charmingly quaint. He had been coming to the island all his life and had yet to find a local he either trusted or liked.

"I wonder if Chuck would like to audit her accounts," he said to Audrey. "I doubt they'd pass muster." Members of the Finch family owned the nearest grocery, the gas station, the liquor store, and supplied the cleaning women, and the island postmaster was an in-law. In Doug's experience they were all lazy, surly, and unscrupulous throughout the generations. In appearance most of them shared a potato-face, though now and again a Finch had a foxlike snout: long nose and undershot jaw.

"Oh, Doug," Audrey chided. "You're hardly ever here when she is."

"I will be tomorrow," said he. "I'm not going back this evening."

His wife lowered her knife and fork. "Not flying back?"

"Nor driving. Nor going. I'm staying on for a couple of days for a change. Is it that amazing?"

Audrey made a little gesture. "Well, it's unprecedented."

"You weren't expecting guests?" he asked sardonically. "I can keep my room?"

"Then how long will you be staying?"

"I trust I'm welcome?"

"You'll have more than Mrs. Finch to contend with: the cleaning crew comes again on Monday."

These women, three or sometimes four of them, were also essentially Finches, at least second cousins or perhaps a near neighbor who probably had some of the same blood, so interbred were the island folk.

"You've forgotten. I've been coming here since I was a baby. I know how to handle myself with that tribe."

"Well, I'm just pointing it out. And remember not to leave anything lying around that you want to find afterwards. They put away everything loose, any article of clothing, jewelry, papers, ashtrays, everything movable, so they can dust a room all at once. Trouble is where they put the things: never places I would choose. They'll shove one shoe into a dresser drawer and throw its mate on a closet shelf."

"Genetic deficiencies have been passed on from generation to generation," Doug pointed out. "Necessarily: any breeding done on the island has to be incest. These are essentially the same people that came here three centuries ago. Nobody leaves and no new blood has been added."

Audrey herself could freely criticize the Finches, but of course when Doug added his observations she came to their defense.

"You exaggerate," she said now. "They're probably as good or maybe even better than the usual people found in such a place as this, with a part-time population so different from the human beings who live here all year — to whom the permanent residents are merely servants."

Lydia had composed herself by now and had only just left her room when she encountered Chuck, of all people, in the hall.

For no apparent reason he was positively ebullient. "Hi!" he cried. "You're quite the slugabed today."

If she knew the term at all, it was but distantly, perhaps from some childhood book written in the century past but still read to little girls in her day. It went with "counterpane." Despite these innocent associations she was having a struggle with herself to keep from making a wisecrack with reference to the state in which she had last seen him.

"I've been up and about for hours. You're the one who overslept today." And not being burdened with Audrey's obligations as hostess, she added, "We naturally assumed you'd be up to make breakfast, and waited and waited."

Chuck did not admit a hint of failure. "Where *were* you?" he asked aggressively. "I did cook, and everybody else has eaten long since." His front teeth, now on gleaming display, were perfect. He was not at all her type, but there could be no argument as to his good looks.

He went on. "That's why I came to fetch you. It's so late now there won't be another meal till evening. Better come along and eat some eggs." He turned and strolled along the hall for a few paces, then stopped and spun around to face her again. At first it seemed odd that he would not have waited till she was at closer range to say such a thing, but in retrospect she understood that it was his game to unsettle prospective prey by the use of special effects. "Just as well you're up," said he. "Can't tell what I might have done if I found you still in bed."

Had she had time to reflect, Lydia would have seen that the only effective response here would have been none whatever. As it was, inexperienced at this kind of contest, she answered with some asperity.

"Oh. I can take care of myself."

His grin was triumphant. "I would be counting on that."

She realized she was now in the uncomfortable and in fact preposterous situation of fearing that he might believe she was afraid of him.

The car conked out not long before Bobby would have emerged from the private lane to join the cross-island road: simply coughed twice and stopped. He obstinately tried for a while to start it, angrily failing to comprehend how an engine that was running well could quit without warning and did not at least "miss" for a mile or two. But finally he climbed out and began to walk the quarter mile back to the house. The lane was one car wide, unpaved, and deeply grooved by wheels that had traveled it in wet weather. This was no place for anything but utilitarian vehicles. Not to mention that the salt air pitted any finish within months. The Graveses kept two cars at hand, a station wagon of some capacity and the rusty compact that had just given out on Bobby. These machines were regularly maintained during the summer by the Finches who operated the local garage and then when autumn came "winterized" by them and stored in one of the barns at the disposal of that family. But it was more than possible that, as his father routinely suspected of anything managed by the Finches, this job was poorly done. If so, Bobby did not want to be the one who told them so, for his childhood bête noire, Dewey Finch, now ran the automotive branch of the Finch enterprises. Once when Bobby was twelve and Dewey fourteen or fifteen and much thicker-set than he, the brutal islander had cornered the rich kid in the gas-station toilet and forced the younger boy to masturbate him, after the performance of which degrading act he predicted that Bobby would be far too humiliated to report it, and of course he was right.

Dewey had obviously not forgotten that episode, for he still smirked today if Bobby was so careless as to gas up one of the cars when his enemy was on duty.

On the walk back he saw a red squirrel that looked no bigger than a good-sized mouse and heard the sounds made by a larger animal he could not see but had set to flight amidst the trees. Many beasts lived in these woods. Deer were not uncommon. A gardener when Bobby was a boy, of course another Finch, scared him with tales of wandering bears, but in later years he determined that there had been no bear-sightings locally since the turn of the century.

As he was approaching the house, Chuck came around the wing nearest the parking area.

"Out for a constitutional?" asked the houseguest. Chuck wore his habitual uniform: khaki trousers, navy knitted shirt, and leather loafers. Apparently he had brought little else. Since it was not likely he was poor, this was perhaps an expression of his austere tastes. But Bobby really couldn't understand how anyone would want to stay out of shorts in this season.

He groaned now. "Car broke down, just stopped in its tracks. Sunday the garage is closed, so I guess what I'll have to do is take the wagon out there and pull the car back. Mind steering the car, Chuck?"

"Why don't you let me walk out and see whether I can get it started?" Chuck asked. "I know a few tricks." He held out his hand for the ignition keys that Bobby had been swinging on an index finger.

Bobby felt a great sense of relief. He hated to have trouble with cars, for even the simplest matter pertaining to the internal-combustion engine was mysterious to him: he really had no idea of what, say, a distributor did.

"God, I'd be grateful," said he, surrendering the keys. "I'll go get the keys to the wagon, just in case."

"No," Chuck said evenly. "Let me see first." He started off up the lane in his usual brisk, regular, almost military stride. Bobby would have liked to go along with him on this very male mission, but he had the definite sense that Chuck did not require his company. Also, he was hungry and assumed that now Chuck was up, some provision had been made for a meal.

He found a door that was reasonably near the kitchen and entered the house. In the kitchen he found Lydia eating an open-faced grilled-cheese sandwich with knife and fork. She also had a tall glass of what looked like grapefruit juice.

He told her what had happened. She frowned and lowered her fork. "He certainly makes himself indispensable around here," said she. "I gather Chuck is a longtime friend of the family."

Bobby shrugged. "I guess so. My parents are probably friends of his." The molten cheese looked delicious. "Say, Lyd, make me one of those, will you?"

"You mean you don't know him?"

"Only since he came, last week."

"You never saw him before?"

"Not that I can remember," said Bobby. "I don't think he's ever stayed here before. Hey, how about it: grill me a cheese?"

Lydia pointed with her fork. "See that gadget on the counter, Bobby? That's a toaster-oven. You just take the cheese from the fridge and bread from the breadbox. You put the cheese on the bread and the bread in the tray of the toaster, then you press down the lever on the side. You watch through the window, and when it's done you take it out."

"I know how to do it," said he. "I just thought it might be nice and generous and kind of you to fix it for me."

"You mean," she asked with an expression that favored one eye, "it's some kind of test of my regard for you?"

She could be derisive in the kitchen, but when they were in bed, *he* would be the one who would be expected to perform, whatever the state of his own ardor at the time, and it never quite matched hers.

"I'll have something else, then," he said, expecting her to capitulate, but she did not, so he had to go to the refrigerator and root around. As it happened, he never did come across the cheese. Instead he found one of the many packages of frankfurters for the lunch Mrs. Finch prepared every third day: hotdogs, canned baked beans, and the cole slaw sold in plastic containers at her family's grocery. Unable to breach the tough plastic without a tool, Bobby whined to Lydia, and she gave him the knife she had been eating with.

"For God's sake, this is *dirty,*" said he. "Also, it's blunt." He gave it back, sighing. "I don't have any fingernails." This was true: he trimmed them so short he could not pick up a fallen coin.

Lydia groaned and pointed to the conspicuous hardwood block with slots for many knives, all of them filled. It took him a while to find the littlest one. By the time the hotdogs were available to him, he lacked the energy and patience to cook them, and ate a couple cold, from his fingers, then reached over Lydia's shoulders and stole her grapefruit juice.

She was finished by now, anyway. She took her plate to the dishwasher, and while there looked out the window that gave onto the parking area.

"Huh, Chuck's brought the car back. He seems to have had no trouble with it."

Bobby came to join her. "How about that," said he. "He was right."

"Right?"

"He said he knew a few tricks about cars."

"And not just about cars," Lydia said sourly. "He's a pretty tricky guy in general."

Bobby frowned with his forehead, letting his long jaw hang loose. "He knows how to do everything. Maybe I should take a few lessons from him."

Lydia seized him around the waist. "No, you *shouldn't,*" she said fiercely.

"I really ought to learn something about cars," said Bobby. He found the hug slightly painful: he had a sensitive rib. "I've been driving since I was twelve or thirteen."

"Speaking of cars," Lydia said, releasing him, "where's Chuck's? How'd he get here?"

But Bobby was distracted, watching Chuck lock the door of the car he had just returned to its place. There was no need for that up here: robbery of any kind was virtually unknown during the season. When the summer people were away, however, their houses were fair game — unless they hired the Finches, at quite a healthy fee, to keep an eye on the property. It was his father's theory that this constituted a "protection" racket of the kind operated in the cities by mobsters: namely, that the people who could be hired as guards were, unless given such employment, the selfsame who ransacked the houses — though naturally this would have been hard to prove. Even old General Lewis Mickelberg, former supreme commander of the armed services, had a healthy respect for them, as did other summer residents who were people of power in the real world, e.g., Nelson T. Boonforth, chairman of the board of the third largest bank in the country; and celebrated defense attorney Hartman Anthony Johncock, whose eldest son was Bobby's principal rival on the tennis courts.

Chuck was heading in a direction that would have taken him out of sight had not Bobby leaned across the counter and shouted through the screened casement.

"I'm in the kitchen!"

Chuck halted.

"You got it started?" Bobby asked. "Did it run okay?"

Chuck nodded.

"What the devil was the problem?" asked Bobby.

"Flooded," Chuck answered laconically. He walked away.

Lydia lifted her upper lip. "Don't you think that's rude?"

"I guess it was dumb of me," Bobby said. "But if you

don't keep trying to get the motor started, how's it going to start? Yet if you do, you flood it."

"I notice he's keeping the keys," Lydia pointed out.

"Well, we know where to find them." Bobby yawned, crucifying his arms. "Anyway, the moment has passed for going to the club. I can hardly keep my eyes open."

"Are there extra sets of car keys?"

"Sure," said Bobby. "On the hook inside the door of the cabinet in the utility room, next to the washer-dryer. Why? Going someplace?"

Lydia shrugged. "Good to know such things."

Bobby grinned lazily. "We don't get tidal waves here. Sometimes there's the tail end of a hurricane, but you're safer inside this house than out where you could get hit by falling trees."

"You didn't happen to check the tailpipe after the car stopped?"

"Why should I have done that?"

"Oh," said Lydia, "I was just thinking if something, some foreign object, had been stuck in there, the result would have been just about what happened. The engine would stop if the exhaust was blocked."

He smiled smugly. "You're as knowledgeable as Chuck. No, I wouldn't have thought of that. But Chuck already said it was flooded: that's something else entirely, though, isn't it?"

"Looks like you're headed for a nap," Lydia observed, changing the subject. "Mind if I join you?"

"No, but I really am drowsy."

"You mean I should keep my hands to myself?"

He laughed helplessly. It *was* flattering to him to be always in such demand.

§ 3 §

After the belated (and, in truth, rotten) breakfast Doug told Audrey that he must repair to his study forthwith for the purpose of catching up on some work, in the course of which he might well be telephoning business associates in the city.

"The private line certainly comes in handy," said his wife. He narrowed his eyes at her. "Otherwise," she hastily explained, "somebody might tie up one phone with mere chatter." She rippled the surface of her forehead. "Though, it's true that I haven't heard from anybody for *ever* so long. You'd think nobody had gotten here yet. Since we decided to cancel the party I don't want to call anyone else first, or they'll assume I'm calling to invite them, you see, and then I'll have to explain, and I would have to do that again with every person I called. Better just to stay silent until someone gets in touch with me. I had expected someone would by now. After all, the party was an institution. But then, it's only been a few days. The inquiries will come next week."

"I'm sure wrists will be slashed all over the island," said Doug as he left. When he reached his study he locked the door behind him. It had been unfortunate that Chuck had found such easy access to the place at just the moment Connie phoned. In his years of venery he had never been caught out in such a fashion.

Connie was a real pain, but never would he have wanted any harm to come to her, or in any event, none for which he had somehow set the stage. He was troubled by what Chuck had said, ridiculous as it was to find sinister implications in the sympathetic response of a houseguest and friend of the family to an intimate matter concerning the head of that family. Chuck would hardly be under this roof were he capable of criminality.

And yet Doug found himself doing now that which would have been most unlikely in any other situation: namely, phoning a woman whom he had determined to discard.

She answered on the second ring, simultaneously relieving him and putting him under a new threat. Her voice sounded normal enough. If he identified himself, he would be right back in the soup. He silently hung up and consulted his pocket address book for a number at which he could reach Chrissy Milhaven, who was some sort of distant cousin of his on his mother's side. He had read an announcement of her forthcoming marriage in Friday's newspaper, in town. Whether he and Audrey would be invited to this ceremony was doubtful: he had had no association with that branch of the family for years and had not seen Chrissy since she was a very plain thirteen. But the photograph in the paper showed the comely face of a person of twenty-three. It seemed worth his while to renew old ties of blood.

He called the number he had for Chrissy's parents, for apparently she still lived at home, in the vast apartment they maintained in the city, with its roof garden that went around three sides of the building.

Luckily a maid answered, so he did not have to speak with Millicent, Chrissy's mother, an acerb woman with whom he had simply never hit it off.

"Hi, cousin," said he when Chrissy came on the telephone. He identified himself. "Just saw your announcement." He answered some commonplace, lackluster questions. "Yes, fine. Yes, everybody. That's right, he did get married, privately. Very privately; some country courthouse. Uh-huh. She's from — out of town. But say, Chrissy, I must say you've become quite a beauty since we last got together. We have some catching up to do before you tie the knot, I should say. It's been too long." He suggested they have a drink when he was back in town, middle of the week.

"You'll like Stephen," said Chrissy, with the slight lisp she had retained over the years.

Doug had always felt superior to a man with impedimented speech, but he found it erotic in a female. Also, he was unusually attracted to women who were soon to be married, and there was something special with a person he could remember as an almost ugly little girl. Finally, that he was at least remotely related to her added its own excitement. The result was a growing lust for Chrissy. He was never gross in a situation of this kind: the force of his passion would be exerted subliminally, concealed within or beneath banalities, but if she were the right subject, she would receive these messages with clarity and make an appropriate response. If not, then no harm was done: she might not even be certain that an overture had been made. In his career of lechery Doug had to date made perhaps a half dozen such attempts on the virtue of a newly created fiancée. He had been successful only once, but even he considered it astonishing that nobody amongst these young women had apparently been offended by his attentions. Two pretended not to understand him, but three professed to be flattered. As to his successful project, it continued throughout the first year of the bride's marriage, for the husband while an amiable companion proved intimately enervate.

"I thought just the two of us," Doug said now, "you and me, for old times' sake, to catch up on things. After all, we're family. Then comes Steve."

His intonation was that of near levity. But Chrissy's response proved humorless.

"As you might expect, I'm *awfully* rushed these days. When we get back from abroad we'll have you and Audrey over for a sip or a bite."

As if the general rudeness was not sufficient to discourage him, he despised women who employed such little phrases. Also, it was really difficult to suppose that in only a few years she had been transformed from that repulsive child into an attractive woman. He regretted having called her, the probable result of which would be that he and Audrey would now get an invitation to the wedding.

He heard a splash outside, and went to the high little window in the alcove to look out at the pool, the northern half of which could be seen from this perspective. Audrey, not he, had wanted this house of unorthodox perspectives: she had had a crush on the architect, an imperious, leonine-headed man who was a celebrity in his field and charged an appropriate fee.

Suddenly a swimsuited girl with an exquisite behind walked into his field of view. For a moment Doug had no idea whatever of who she was, even found himself hoping she might be a trespasser, perhaps one of the young female Finches, of whom there was always a new supply, probably dim-witted owing to the poor genes circulated throughout generations of intermarriage. Doug had seen such youthful slatterns over the summers since his own pubescence, but owing to his fear of the males of their blood, and also a certain delicacy of taste that gave preference to flesh of better breeding, he had not had a struggle with himself to abstain from making a personal approach.

But this one, whoever she could be, was on his property.

Then she turned her face so that it could be identified, within its tight white bathing cap, in profile, and of all people this person was his daughter-in-law. How had he failed until this moment to notice that she had the cutest little ass on the island? Because she habitually wore loose skirts or oversized shorts, and he had never before seen her attired for swimming.

He decided to join her at poolside, but before he could leave the room the telephone produced an electronic tone within the polished wooden box in which it was kept. There were only two such tones before the answering machine took over. Chuck's story of happening to be present when Connie Cunningham called and surrendering to the typically human impulse to answer a ringing phone was difficult to accept: to reach the instrument before the machine was activated, he would have had to work quickly for one who was presumably a stranger to Doug's communications center.

Doug now manipulated the volume control on the answering device, so that he could listen to the voice of the caller, if indeed any came, for one of the useful functions of the machine in dealing with the likes of Connie Cunningham was to discourage them from leaving any message or even an identification.

But the voice proved to be that of a man, an unpleasant, cynical man if his current mode of expression was representative.

"Pick it up, you fucker you. I know you're there. Don't jerk me off."

Though Doug included amongst his acquaintances nobody who could have spoken in this style except in jest, he felt an inexplicable obligation to reveal his presence at the other end of the line.

"I'm afraid," he said into the instrument, "you have the wrong number. That is —"

He was interrupted brutally before reaching the first digit.

"No," said the voice, "*you* got the wrong phone, sonny boy. Now put it down and get me Chaz."

Offended by the man's tone, Doug hung up. Hell with it, why give civility when it wasn't returned. He put the phone back into the box. In another instant the machine was accepting another call. After listening to his own recorded voice announce the number and ask for a message, he again heard the voice of the previous caller. This time it was even uglier.

"You do that to me again, dicklicker, and I'll make you scream for mercy. Now you go find him. You tell him Jack Perlmutter says okay. You do that and maybe I won't hurt you." Perlmutter, assuming it was he and not some spokesman for him, rang off abruptly.

Though Doug had every reason to be furious, he was mostly frightened. To speak so to a man whom he did not know, Perlmutter obviously possessed considerable power. Else how could he so easily assume that Doug would not prove dangerous if provoked? Unless of course the man was a nut case of the sort it was routine to encounter in the city. There are persons who if denied what they believe is their right of way will leap from their car, draw a pistol, and shoot down the other driver. One read in the papers that on public transport a passenger will knife another who trips on his foot, and Doug had had personal experience of cabdrivers who verbally abuse their passengers and threaten to do worse if any complaint is sounded. How is it that the target of the aggressor never happens to be one of the other violent people at large? Is it never dangerous for the threatener, on whose approach the intended victim might draw his own gun and get off the first shot? Not only would such reversal of roles seem to violate a basic law of human intercourse, but the Perlmutters of the world have an unerring sense of when to strike. Doug was no coward, but he had been taken utterly offguard.

He went into his bedroom and lay down. Had Chuck been spying on him? Only now did it occur to him to wonder whether Chuck might be Perlmutter's "Chaz." Or rather, only now did he summon up the courage to entertain that possibility: underneath it all, he had never been in doubt.

Lydia's family had the biggest pool in town, and there were always relatives in the water who would teach a younger child to swim. Bobby's story of being purposely almost drowned by a malicious larger cousin could be matched by nothing in the history of Lydia's childhood.

The Graveses' pool was of normal size, and therefore if only one more person shared it with her, she felt crowded: this was true even if the other person happened to be Bobby, who however — and unexpectedly, given his proficiency at the other summer sports — seldom entered the pool, and when he did so, swam none too well. As to the nearby ocean, no one from the Graves family went into or on it, and when Lydia once asked about this abstention, Bobby failed to give a real answer, mumbled something about currents and shrugged lugubriously, and hoping as she did to overcome the influence of her mother, who on any pretext would querulously question her father to the point at which he lost his temper, Lydia did not pursue the matter, though it seemed unusual that people would spend their summers surrounded by an element into which they would not dip their toes.

By now the day had become warmer and more humid than it looked when one faced the inland greenery. There were individual air-conditioners in the rooms, but it went against Lydia's grain to resort to unnatural cooling at oceanside. However, when she plunged into the pool she found the water sickeningly warm as soup. This could not have been the effect of mere sunlight, which owing to the nearby trees fell directly on only about half of the surface.

God's sake, was the pool heater on? She climbed up and out on the chromium ladder at the deep end and walked drippingly to the little structure that contained the filtering mechanism and the heater, here of utilitarian design and screened by bushes, not the miniature Swiss chalet her father had had specially designed and conspicuously situated.

Indeed, the thermostat was set at 92 degrees, and why, when the older Graveses never swam there, and Bobby's style was to paddle briefly at the shallow end, then climb up to sit on the rim, long shins in the water, to watch her racing dive and three fast laps, each in another style: breast, butterfly, crawl. That she might have been Olympic material had been routinely pointed out by relatives and friends, and nowadays her husband as well, but the truth was that in this day and age only obsessive-compulsives could compete for any kind of prize: people not simply willing but fanatically eager to incinerate the self to fuel a career. Ha, Lydia would say, I've got too much sense for that. By now of course she was a decade too old for a sport in which you were prime at twelve.

She brought the thermostat down to 60; in this season, despite the cool nights, the water by noon was always naturally warmer than that. But her swim had been put out of the question this afternoon. It would take hours for the temperature of the water to fall to an acceptable level — unless the ocean were considered. Why this seemed a daring, almost forbidden thought had altogether and exclusively to do with the moral atmosphere of the Graves house. Millions of human beings swam in the ocean that surrounded the islands comprising the earth, some even in places where sharks and barracuda patrolled the shore or where pollution was a scandal, or where terrorists might swoop in on rubber rafts and slaughter everybody on the sand. None of these hazards was to be feared in her in-laws' waters.

Lydia thereupon decided to go down and swim in the sea. The most direct route was through the house, but attired as she was, justifiably so in the open air, she felt indecent when under a roof. Why then she had failed to wear a robe from room to pool could not be explained except as defiance of her own prudery. In any event she displayed less than had Chuck when wantonly asleep. Lydia was not overfleshed at any point; there were even times when she considered herself flat-chested. She was hardly spilling out of the bathing suit.

The beach, when she finally reached it, was floored with stones, not sand: no surprise, but what she had not been prepared for was the difference between walking here with and without shoes. Her route to the water was uncomfortable, and the ocean on her entry was so cold as to numb the lower extremities as it rose to cover them, and when nevertheless she bravely launched her body in the horizontal attitude, the frigidity of the destructive element all but paralyzed her organs of respiration. But in an instant that concern was as nothing to the awful knowledge that she was immediately the captive of a violent undercurrent that could not have been anticipated from the appearance of the modest surf.

She was being swept away, and nothing helped that she had learned from near-Olympic feats in quiet pools. She had no technique, no self-command, and chokingly full of water, too soon (or perhaps, in another view, for it was all terror and pain, too late) she had no existence.

. . . Even in the dream she was quite aware of the impossibility of puking while you were being kissed, yet that was what was happening. Next she lay prone on an unyielding bed of gravel. A creature larger than herself clung to her back, perhaps trying in some monstrous fashion to copulate with her. It was ugly and absurd. She wept.

"*Lydia!*" a stern, almost military voice cried down. It was the person, a man, who had earlier been kissing her, not for erotic purposes but to claim her for life; not trying to penetrate her sexually, but rather performing the emergency maneuvers by which she might be revived.

He turned her over and stared down. He was still straddling her thighs. "Are you okay?" He was Chuck Burgoyne.

She gestured feebly. He pulled her to a sitting position. Her head was almost unbearably heavy. Her air passages felt raw.

He grimaced. "I got more than I bargained for from the kiss of life. I then used the old but still effective hands-on technique. You hadn't been under long." He stood up, then bent, offering both hands. "Let's do some walking. Yes, right now! Else you'll feel worse."

He did almost all the work in erecting her to her feet. She had little will for the effort and less strength.

He supported her, but demanded, "Come on, *walk!*"

She was offended by the tone, but in the next instant remembered it was he who had saved her life and so acquired a certain authority over it. She wept softly, humiliated by the memory of the powerlessness into which she had fallen with the first grasp of the undertow.

He misinterpreted the tears. "You're all right now!"

She smelled the vomit on herself, and cried more bitterly.

He walked her to and fro. He was right: she felt somewhat better. He was wrong: she felt much worse.

"I'm a good swimmer," she said resentfully. "I could have —" She struggled for self-possession. She thanked him for saving her life.

"Lucky I spotted you when I did," said he. "I guessed you might not know of the undercurrent. I grabbed the jacket and came running down." Until this moment, in her desperate solipsism she had overlooked the bright yellow life jacket he wore. "*They* keep out of the ocean," he said with an edge of contempt. "Are you strong enough to climb the steps?"

They were near the stairway of log-halves. "I guess so." She looked up at the house. "Do you think anyone up there saw any of this?"

"I assume they'd be out now if they had," Chuck said.

She turned to him. "Could you do me one more favor? This is asking quite a lot, but could you possibly not mention that I went swimming down here?" The request was outrageous of her, she knew, disqualifying him as it did of all recognition of his heroism.

Yet he agreed immediately, and what was perhaps more remarkable did not ask her to explain. She was suddenly aware of their affinity: this was embarrassing, given her previous repugnance for the man.

"Im really grateful, Chuck," said she, and put her hand on his. He was still supporting her at the waist without emotional significance; he could have been a professional nurse.

Audrey now saw them from the house, but she had witnessed nothing of the earlier events and therefore was not aware of the saving of Lydia's life. To her there seemed no question that her daughter-in-law and the houseguest were embracing, and blatantly, there on the beach where they might be seen by anybody. Appalling as the incident was, Audrey was gratified to have been given, without the expenditure of effort on her part, evidence that confirmed the suspicion she had been entertaining since Bobby had first brought the girl home, viz., that Lydia was an insolent little tart.

Now the problem was how to deal with the matter. She could not remember the last time she had spoken with Bobby on any really personal issue: perhaps she had never done so in the course of his life. With no precedents whatever, how then could she bluntly inform him that his bride and his best friend were lovers? Nor could she find it possible to forgive Chuck Burgoyne. She had assumed his taste in women would be as superior as everything else about him. Surely he could have had his choice: then why this one? For the degrading reason that she happened to be the nearest? If so, he was no better than Doug. And now Audrey felt justified in admitting the possibility that Doug too might have had his moment with Lydia. He was more slippery a customer than of old. Her surveillance being what it was in this house, she could have sworn that for once there had been no congress between her husband and a girl brought home by his son.

Not that all the young ladies could, in justice, be blamed: most had resisted, some complaining to Bobby, and one was sufficiently outraged as to apply to Audrey. But irrational though it might be, Audrey could never forgive any of them, least of all the girl who complained to her. She simply detested anyone her husband found attractive, and had the ill fortune to be married to a man who when it came to women could be called both insatiable and omnivorous.

Her sole confidante, Molly Finley, was still abroad, thus could not be invited to come up from the city to help with the problem. Molly was the only friend of Audrey's never to have been the target of Doug's advances, being candidly homosexual. Her friendship with Audrey was conspicuously nonerotic, to the degree that Molly eschewed all physical contact, even to the shaking of hands. If one accidentally collided with her, she could be felt to recoil. Yet morally she was the most comfortable of intimates: she was the unique friend whom nature had disqualified as a competitor.

But Molly, an art dealer, was on the other side of the world, in quest of new work to sell in her gallery. Audrey was unlikely to purchase any of it, given Molly's penchant for crazy, provocative mixed-material pieces, fur-and-copper, say, or ceramic-and-newsprint, which set Audrey's teeth on edge. For her part, Molly no doubt despised Audrey's predilection for geometric arrangements in the primary colors, on the one hand, and primitive daubs of barns and daisies on the other, if indeed she ever looked at a wall of Audrey's, which in fact she had never been caught doing.

After many summers on the island, Audrey had yet to meet a woman she liked, and she would sooner have shared the current scandal with one of the Finches than with anyone of her summer acquaintance. That Marge Meers would cackle in triumph went without saying, and Jane DeHaven had an old score to settle because of Doug.

Audrey suddenly realized that she was thinking exclusively of her own embarrassment and not poor Bobby's humiliation. To be cuckolded so soon must be especially devastating to a man. Was it therefore more humane to do what one could to keep him in the state of blissful ignorance? He seemed genuinely fond of Lydia, but fortunately he displayed no hint of passion for her, whereas Audrey had been really gaga for Doug and therefore was all but destroyed at the first evidence of his infidelity. She had actually put the razor blade to her wrist and was restrained only by aesthetic considerations, therefore overdosed on pills instead, gulping so many as to upset her stomach, and she threw up before coming anywhere near death. Nobody learned of this episode. She hadn't even had to call a doctor.

The screen slid back, and Lydia and Chuck, still embracing, boldly entered the wide doorway. Audrey flinched, having no idea of how to deal with such provocation.

"I was dumb," Lydia cried. "I almost drowned. Chuck saved my life."

"Good gosh," said Audrey, feeling spiritually naked after having been so decisively disabused. She smiled brilliantly at the houseguest. "Our hero!"

For a moment Chuck seemed modestly to hang his sleek

head. Then he made a burlesque wink and said, with an assumed accent, but too light a one to be identified linguistically, "Wade till you get duh bill!" He released Lydia. "She should get some rest after that ordeal," he said to Audrey, and to his patient: "You go lie down. Do you need help?"

"I can walk all right," said she. She lowered her head and carefully left the room, watching where she stepped, as if on a pathway of intermittent stones.

Audrey was now alone with Chuck, and for an instant she was too frantic to find a topic of conversation. Then, "I gave in to my baser instincts a while ago and tried to call one of my so-called friends on the island. But the phone doesn't work."

Chuck had those unusual blue eyes that are quite as warm as brown. "I'll take a look at it."

"Golly," she said with delight, "don't tell me you can do that too? Chef, lifesaver, telephone techni——"

He narrowed those remarkable blue eyes. "Are you making fun of me?"

She was horrified by the possibility he might not be joking. "Oh, please —" And caught her breath, for Chuck had extended his right hand to cup her left breast. She felt more fear than desire, expecting as she did that his purpose was to hurt and not to caress her: in the next moment he would begin to squeeze, and there was nothing she could do about it.

But he defied her flight forward and did nothing else: she got neither fondling nor pain.

"Don't you worry," said he. "Everything's in order."

His hand was suddenly snapped away as if by spring.

§ 4 §

Doug had done nothing whatever to deserve the tone in which Perlmutter addressed him. The unprovoked attack, the display of bluster: the classic tactics of the bully, in this case all of it behind the impermeable electronic curtain. Perlmutter could well be a little down-at-heels clerk, who in a pre-telephone age would have been but another Cratchit.

Doug was not obliged to suffer threats from anybody but the women with whom he went illicitly to bed and, sometimes, their husbands. He would be prepared, next time Perlmutter phoned, and he would do what he could to insure that the man did call back: Doug had no intention of giving a message to "Chaz."

Scarcely had he made that resolution when he betrayed it. Someone was rapping sharply on the door of the study. He went out and opened the door. It was Chuck Burgoyne.

"Say, Chuck," Doug said plaintively, "there was a phone call for you, from a guy who for no reason at all was really insulting. He —"

"Look here, Doug," Chuck said, grimacing, "Lydia almost drowned in the ocean just now. Luckily I was there to pull her out. You should make sure your guests know about that undertow: you should post signs on the steps to the beach."

"Lydia?" Doug asked, as if he had difficulty in identifying her immediately. "Lydia? Is she all right? Anything I can do? Should we call a doctor or something? That won't be easy on a Sunday, I can tell you. The people up here are not moved by compassion. They close the hospital on the weekends so the staff can go fishing, for God's sake." This was of course an exaggeration, but once when the child Bobby had fallen on slippery shore rocks and broken his arm, the volunteer ambulance, a Finch at the wheel, took forever to collect the boy and take him to the island hospital, where the lone attendant had to summon a doctor from his home, halfway around the bay. When the physician arrived he said he had been smoking mackerel, and smelled of it.

"I'm sorry you were bothered by that call," said Chuck. "No doubt it was a wrong number. People can be nasty as they want when they remain anonymous."

Doug felt a quick affection for the houseguest, as he always did for those whose theories echoed his own. "You know, I was just thinking the same thing myself? It doesn't take much courage for a man to —"

"The coward wouldn't give his name?"

Doug frowned. "Actually, he did. . . . Jack Perlmutter."

After a moment Chuck said, "I imagine there's been some mistake."

"I'm sure I got the name right."

"No doubt," said Chuck. "But I know Jack Perlmutter. He's a decent man, Doug. Under no condition would he speak abusively. He's known for his geniality." Chuck slapped him on the shouldercap. "But why are we just standing here? It's easy enough to get to the bottom of this." He went to the desk as if he owned it, opened the oak box, and removed the handpiece of the telephone. He brandished it at Doug and grinned. Without an obvious search of memory he quickly punched a series of buttons.

"Hi, Jack. . . . That's right." Chuck explained why he had called. "One moment —" He took the phone from his face and handed it to Doug.

Doug was reluctant, but finally he accepted the gift and made a lugubrious hello into it.

He was greeted by a voice that *could* have been that of the earlier abusive Perlmutter: there was no way of telling for certain. Whatever, it was downright submissive in tone.

"Mr. Graves? I'm sorry to hear you got a call from somebody who was nasty, and who gave himself my name. I guess it's not an uncommon one, though. I just want to say it certainly wasn't me, but if you'd like, I'll apologize for anything rotten done since the world began by anybody named Perlmutter. How's that?"

"I probably just didn't hear accurately," Doug said. He saw no reason why he should be grateful to this man for making a silly joke of the incident. He returned the telephone to Chuck.

The houseguest produced a clicking sound with his tongue, then said a brisk good-bye. This behavior would fit the two-Perlmutter theory: the caller had wanted with some urgency to talk to "Chaz," but Chuck's remarks at this end of the wire now had not suggested the reception of any message.

Chuck returned the phone to its box, and for the first time in his relations with the houseguest, Doug struck a negative note.

"No offense, old fellow, but that telephone is supposed to be private. There are extensions of the main house line in just about every room."

"Oh," said Chuck, "that number's been out of order. Hadn't you heard?"

Doug stepped to the desk and touched the oak box. "Then I'd better call the company. But don't expect anybody to come out on Sunday."

"Oh," said Chuck, looking him in the eye, "I've already taken care of it."

Doug moved the wooden box an inch or so from where it sat. When he looked up, Chuck was still staring at him.

"I trust you're not worrying about the Connie Cunningham matter? I thought I had set your mind at ease."

Doug said, "Now that you mention it, I guess I *was* a little concerned." He coughed in embarrassment. "This will sound crazy to you, I know, but when you said you'd take care of it, you meant you'd just talk to her . . . ?"

Chuck made an expansive gesture. "I've got a friend who specializes in affairs of the heart."

"He's a psychiatrist?"

"A professional. Don't worry."

"All right," said Doug, displaying more relief than he really felt. "Connie's a nice person. I didn't want to hurt her, but you know these things come to a natural end. The excitement obviously can't be sustained forever, and of course that's the idea."

Chuck continued to smile. "You and Audrey have it all worked out."

"That didn't happen overnight. Also, there's the financial aspect. We couldn't ever really have afforded to split up. We own everything in common." Doug raised his eyebrows. "And then she's as good a wife as any, really."

He frowned. "This is new to me, this sharing of my private life with a male friend. I don't ordinarily have the least urge to do so."

"I assure you I don't care to take your confession," Chuck said, not smiling. "I'm just curious. Why do you have to fall in love on such an occasion? Because you do, don't you? Why can't you just hire women as you need them? Don't tell me it wouldn't be cheaper in both money and emotion."

The man was diabolically prescient: how could he know this? Doug now did, contrary to what he had just said, feel a need to impart most private information. "The damnedest thing: I can't perform any more unless I'm in love with the woman, or think I am, anyhow. That hasn't always been the case."

Chuck winked at him. "I think it has something to do with the quality of the stuff you get: it's not that attractive unless you delude yourself somehow. I could introduce you to some special people who could get it up on a corpse."

Doug recoiled in spirit. Since the matter of Connie had emerged, Chuck had revealed a side of himself the existence of which could not have been suspected in the affable, efficacious young man he had been hitherto, with his cooking and all.

He thanked Chuck nonetheless, and said he would think about the offer. He was not exactly afraid of him, but saw no need to offend.

"Okay," said Chuck, "I'll do what's necessary. Oh —" He gestured. "This is always an awkward business, but it has to be dealt with. I'll need some . . ." He extended his hand, making prominent the thumb and forefinger, rubbing them together.

Doug must have looked quizzical, for Chuck soon elucidated, though for some reason in archaic terms: "Mazuma, moolah, spondulicks . . ."

Was the man a pimp? Whatever, he was still a guest in one's house. Doug found himself, as if in a dream, going back to the bedroom closet and taking his wallet from the appropriate jacket. When he turned back, Chuck was standing in the doorway, but readily stepped aside to permit him access to the study.

"I've only got a hundred or two," Doug said. "I don't carry much on me these days: too hazardous." What an irony then that he would in effect be shaken down in his own home!

Chuck smirked. "Get yourself one of these." He lifted a foot, and placing the shoe against the edge of the desk, raised the left leg of his chinos. God Almighty, a small holster, the brown butt of a revolver protruding from it, was strapped at his ankle!

Doug now could admit to himself that Chuck did indeed frighten him. To the houseguest, however, he gave his best smile and asked, "Is that real?"

Chuck said genially, "Might not stop a charging rhino, but it's amazing what damage such a little slug will do to human tissue."

Doug was lightheaded as he looked into the compartment of his wallet that should have contained folding money. It was empty now, though it had held a number of bills as recently as when he stopped at a newsstand in the airport to buy afternoon papers to read on the flight up.

"I'm sorry," said he. "I was sure I had some cash. I can't understand —" He broke off at this point, believing without a doubt that the money had been taken by Chuck, who had earlier proved to have had easy access to these rooms. But Chuck carried a deadly weapon. Always leery of guns, Doug had never even tried skeet shooting, another of the sports offered by the club, which had its own range.

Chuck seemed to be humming tunelessly. Doug actually was about to offer to see what kind of money Audrey had in her possession when Chuck said, "I guess it will be okay if you agree to cover whatever expenses are entailed."

"Oh," said Doug, relieved, "that's simple enough." However, as yet he had no sense of what particularly was meant: call girls, back in the city? But at the moment he was here. "We'll work something out."

Chuck was smiling at him. "Let me have a check. That will protect us both. You can always stop payment." He laughed aloud.

Doug joined him in the laughter, but said, "But how are *you* protected, if I can stop payment?"

"Oh," Chuck said, "I trust my fellow man." Now he roared with laughter. "That's why I carry a piece!"

Doug's checkbook was in the other inside breast pocket of the same jacket that had held the wallet. If Chuck had made free with all else in these rooms, he surely was aware of the precise balance in the account. But it was all too likely that he had simply taken the checkbook and was making the current suggestion only as sadistic sport. Within a moment or two Doug had decided that Chuck was not a mere rogue but rather a dangerous criminal, capable of anything. Leave it to Bobby to introduce such a person into the house! The strategy was clear: the man must be placated till he got what he came to these rooms for. What had been his full purpose in coming to the house was not to be thought of at this moment.

One must assuredly not panic, but rather proceed

towards proximate goals. Having decided on his style, Doug became more stable than heretofore. He had a second trip to the bedroom closet and was pleasantly surprised to find the checkbook where it was supposed to be and, given the numerical agreement between checks and stubs, intact. This was Doug's private account, in which at the moment the balance was lower than usual, for he had finally sent a peevish tailor a largish sum to discharge some of his obligation to him and also had given something to one of his favorite restaurants to forestall the reminders which in recent months had got ever nearer to outright rudeness (he was nowadays careful to act before the situation deteriorated to the point at which the proprietor of Allons, Enfants! had threatened to embarrass him before a guest).

Again Chuck had accompanied him to the bedroom.

"What amount would be needed?" Doug asked, withdrawing the slender gold pen from the elastic loop that held it inside the lizardskin checkbook holder.

Chuck had not lost any of his smile. "That's impossible to say at this point. There are always unforeseen eventualities in a game of this kind. Suddenly someone will pop out of a rat hole and must be shoved back in, and that can be expensive."

Doug had not the slightest idea of what the houseguest was talking about, but he thought it politic to pretend he was in the picture lest he reveal his utter helplessness.

"Obviously you know the ropes. Uh . . . how about five hundred?"

"Excuse me?"

Doug grinned vulnerably. "I had to start somewhere."

"I thought I just said I couldn't name a precise figure," said Chuck. He lifted his hands slowly and let them fall, as if in exasperation. "Look, Doug, am I boring you? I'm honestly trying to help, you know."

"I do know," Doug said in haste. "I want to cooperate, Chuck, believe me. It's just that I don't quite —"

"Sign one of these checks for me," Chuck said in a stern voice. "It's only money, and you've got plenty."

But Doug had found courage now. This was a sensitive subject. "Now, don't go saying that kind of thing! I don't have much at all, really. People think that because of the name — but it's not true, I assure you. My father squandered most of what he got. It's the others in the family who have all of it."

Chuck pretended to yawn. "That's what they all say. Just sign the check. Don't fill in any of the rest at this time. We wouldn't want it traced."

Doug was still worried that he should be thought rich. Thus he had sufficient nerve to note somewhat testily, "You can't exactly keep a check secret if you expect to cash it."

Chuck said regretfully, "I thought we had come to an agreement, Doug. I hope you're not making fun of me."

Doug hastened to say, "Oh no. Certainly not! I was just pointing out —"

"Let me handle everything, please," Chuck said in a voice that seemed to Doug to be only superficially genial. "After all, this is my operation."

Doug raised his hands. "Of course." He did not want to be shot. He signed a blank check but was clever enough to alter his signature. Ordinarily he scrawled his name; now he took pains to write clearly, and produced a version that looked as inauthentic as if done by an untalented forger.

However, no sooner had he handed it to Chuck than it occurred to him that the houseguest could and probably would compare it with one of his genuine signatures, an example of which was easy to find, and then the fat would meet the fire.

But to his relieved surprise, Chuck failed to glance at the face of the check: simply, quickly folded it in half and thrust it into one of the back pockets of his chinos, and said, "That's that, then."

Now that Doug felt he had evaded current danger, he was able again to wonder just what "that" consisted of, but he was afraid to ask. Nor did it matter, for Chuck was leaving the study now.

Doug waited awhile, then peeped into the hallway to see whether Chuck had actually left. He found it hard to believe that the man would pull something like this and then walk away, leaving him with a working telephone, but the passage was empty.

He took the telephone from the oak box. The emergency number that was the standard summons for the police elsewhere in the country had no efficacy on the island. He dialed 0 and was answered by a man's voice.

"Have I reached the telephone operator? Connect me with the police."

"Is this an emergency?" the voice asked with a heavily dubious intonation. "I'm supposed to take your word for it, is that it?"

"Goddammit," cried Doug. "Connect me with your supervisor."

"All *right*," the operator groaned. "I'm just going to do that, fella. I'm going to call your bluff!" And after the briefest of moments a woman's voice was heard.

"Are you having difficulty in placing your call?"

"I certainly am! I'm trying to reach the police."

"Are you aware," asked the supervisor, "that you must

specify *which* police you want? There's Milledgeville and there's Swanson; there's Crockett, Duntown, and there's Saint James, and there's the state force, and if you're in an unincorporated area of the county, you should call the sheriff."

"Please," Doug begged. "No more of this. Just get me the island police."

"*Island?*" the woman asked incredulously.

After another exchange Doug discovered that he and the telephone service represented by this supervisor were at least a thousand miles apart. He must have misdialed somehow. . . . Unless this was a hoax in the service of which the wires of his phone had been tampered with by Chuck Burgoyne. The voice of the supposedly female supervisor *could* have been a man's in falsetto. It was not out of the question that the parts of both operator and supervisor were played by the man who had called himself Perlmutter. Or they might be three different people, all fellow conspirators with Chuck. But what could be their motive? The blank check was of limited worth: the current balance in the account did not reach two thousand dollars. Not to mention the phony signature he had used, nor his intention on the following morning to call his bank in the city and stop payment. That is, if he could find a working telephone by then — but if he could get a phone to function, he would first of all *get the police.*

He lifted the instrument at hand, intending to dial more carefully this time. But now no tone could be heard. This line too was dead.

Lydia had told Bobby that she almost drowned, but he was always a bit confused when awakened suddenly from a nap. Usually she found this another of his endearing ways,

but never before had she nearly lost her life. A thirtyish
cousin had been killed in a car crash; and two of her
grandparents had died, but at a substantial age each. She
had had no reason to see existence as being especially
fragile. Right now it seemed an inexplicable wonder to her
that, with the hazards available, anything stayed alive for
long. That she knew this state of mind could, with the
physical chills, be identified as shock helped not at all: the
application of reason was a mockery here; instinct was all.

She spoke sharply to her husband. "Did you hear me?"

Bobby sat up and rubbed his tousled, now dingy blond
head. "Oh, hey," said he. "I was going to the club but the
car quit before I got to the end of —"

Lydia shouted, "Are you awake? I just almost drowned.
Look at me." Occupied with the one emotion, she was
innocent of vanity. She was wet, and dirty with vomit.

"Oh," Bobby said, rising from his seat on the bed's edge.
"That's bad."

Lydia was weeping again. Bobby did not act on her
implicit idea that she should be embraced, vomit and all.

"Chuck!" she cried. "He saved my life. I was helpless!
Oh, God, I thought I was a strong swimmer."

Bobby smiled. "Is that right? Good old Chuck." He was
keeping his distance from her. "You get a cramp?"

This was not that absurd a question, but in the current
circumstances it infuriated Lydia. She showed her teeth.

"I was in the fucking *ocean!*"

Bobby made his eyes round. "You shouldn't ever go in
out there. Didn't I mention the undertow? That's no
swimming beach, Lyd."

She found it impossible to speak with him. She trudged
to the bathroom and showered without closing the glass
door and while still wearing her bathing suit. The linings of

her nose and throat, stung first by saltwater and then lacerated by acidulous digestive juices, hurt when she breathed and swallowed. Her mother would have had a remedy; her mother-in-law was hardly the person to go to when wounded. She detested her in-laws, this house, and the island; and for the first time in her life she feared the water, into which she swore never to put herself again, not even a pool. As to Chuck Burgoyne, however, he was beyond the reach of any doubt. She revered him. What greater triumph could a human being achieve than saving the life of another? She hated Bobby for not being there at her moment of need.

She shuffled through the standing water on the bathroom floor and went out into the bedroom. Bobby was before the window, staring at the ocean. His tallness repelled her now, as did the apparent lack of hair on his limbs in a certain light, so lightly colored was it. She had once found this attractive. The men to whom she was related by blood were all black-furred, on shoulder blades as well as chest. She wished she could recuperate at home, amongst them.

She hurled aside a sliding door and took out one of the thick woolen blankets stacked on the shelves of that part of the closet. She cocooned herself in it, without having toweled off the water from the shower.

Bobby turned, wrinkling his nose. "You've still got your suit on."

"Go fuck yourself."

This was so uncharacteristic an utterance, in either idiom or emotion, that he ignored it, perhaps genuinely did not hear it.

Lydia lowered herself onto the bed, but despite the warm embrace of the moist blanket she began to shiver again.

Bobby at last reacted appropriately. "Brandy," said he,

snapping his fingers. "You could use a drink." He left the room. Some time later he was back, producing a clinking sound and saying, "Lyd . . . ?"

She reluctantly opened her eyes.

"Take some of this," said Bobby.

Hand emerging from the cocoon, she took the tumbler, and thought better of him until she swallowed the fiery liquid and ravaged her sore throat. . . . But the slow aftereffect was finally anesthetic. Everything was transitional; no feeling long had a home.

Bobby stood alongside the bed, gazing down at her. "Maybe you ought to be looked at, at the hospital. The wagon should be in running condition. Want me to take you?" His voice had weakened by the time he reached the question.

Lydia took a second drink from the glass she had retained. Her throat felt all right.

"I'll be okay," she said. "Thanks."

He was still holding the brandy bottle. "For what? Chuck deserves all the thanks. Just lucky he was there. I don't think I'm that strong a swimmer."

Suddenly Lydia felt a personal need to build him up: it was not for his sake. "Oh, sure you could have done it," said she. "It's just a very strong current. It's not some force that can only be overcome by superhuman means. I could have held my own if I had just been prepared for it, but I was taken by surprise. I'm not effective on the spur of the moment. I have to know what's coming."

"You're like that in school, but you *are* always prepared. That's what's so great about you, Lyd: you can handle yourself. This is just a fluke. Don't get depressed by it."

Bobby was now being more morally responsive than she had ever known him to be. She had always been the one who gave him confidence, sexually, academically, and even socially. At first it was astonishing to find that Bobby Graves had difficulty in talking with people, but it was true.

Thinking of him in this way, Lydia began to feel the familiar stirring of a desire for Bobby: obviously she was recovering. But when she asked him to lie down with her, and began to unfurl the blanket, Bobby retreated.

"Better get all the rest you can," said he. "The whole system can be affected by an experience like that."

Again she despised him, but this time was strong enough to remain silent as he left the room.

Bobby was simply revolted by such things as vomit and snot, which to him were more repulsive than the wastes excreted by bladder and intestines, perhaps because the central organs were designed for that negative purpose, whereas the nose and mouth had nobler functions. But he was also repelled by the very idea of menstrual fluid. Until he had moved in with Lydia, in her little off-campus apartment the year before, he had never been aware of how much of a repulsive nature is characteristic of female life. He had never since birth been that close with his mother.

So seeing Lydia covered with puke and mucus had surely killed, at least temporarily, all physical taste that he might have had for her, and the truth was that her appetite had always been keener than his own, though he could perform well enough if asked. That was the trick, and in his varied experience with women only Lydia had consistently divined it: he was proficient only on demand. When, with prior partners, he had taken the initiative, all desire was gone by the time he entered bed. Lydia had introduced him into a new state of being in which every responsibility was hers: to attain success all he had to do was be present.

Going along the hall in the direction of the central part of the house, Bobby met his father, who was coming his way.

For once his parent greeted him with what seemed genuine interest, even clutched at his elbow.

"Let's find a private place," his father said, in an undertone though no one else was nearby. He led Bobby through a glass-walled conservatory full of mostly long-fronded, probably tropical greenery, but there were colorful blossoms too: this was a hobby of his mother's, who had a lot of potted plants specially brought up from the city every spring and taken back in the fall. The atmosphere was moist, unpleasantly heavy as was, for altogether different reasons, that of his father's quarters, in which one could never elude the peculiar scent of a soap or lotion used by his male progenitor for at least a decade. He was pleased now when they went out the door at the far end. The ocean was below and beyond. How foolish Lydia had been to ignore the warnings about swimming there.

"Listen, Bobby," said his father, peering about as if in apprehension, "ordinarily I wouldn't consider it my place to criticize your friends or your wife's." He swiveled his head again. Bobby had never seen him when he was not perfectly barbered and shaven. "But how do you happen to know Chuck?"

"Chuck?" Bobby asked. "Chuck? I met him here."

"On the island. But where? The club? Someone's house?"

"Yeah," Bobby said, smiling. "*Your* house, this house. He's your friend, isn't he? Or Mother's?"

His father frowned. "I'm not joking, Bobby. I'm afraid he's a dangerous man."

"Huh?"

His father moved closer to him. "Are you aware he carries a gun?"

Indeed, Bobby had not believed his father was jesting till now. He grinned. "A real hood, huh?"

"Please take me seriously," said his father, being dramatically grim.

However, still suspecting that he might be the victim of a hoax, Bobby said, "Okay, Dad: no, I don't know he carries a gun, but it sounds unlikely. I'd have to see it."

His father glared at him. "*I'm* telling you he does. I *saw* it. Furthermore, he used it to get money out of me."

Bobby waited a moment, and then he groaned and started to say, "Oh, *come* on," but had got only to the first syllable when his father slapped him in the face.

"Goddammit," cried his father. "This is an emergency! This guy threatened me with a gun in my own home! Who is he, some gangster associated with Lydia's family?"

Bobby now understood that his parent was genuinely exercised. He could not remember previously having seen him in this state, but something was obviously wrong with him. He would have to be placated.

"I'll look into it. Would you like that?"

"He threatened me," said his father, "and he claimed that he had just saved *her* life. Or anyway that's what he boasted of doing."

"He did that all right," said Bobby. "She ignored what I told her about the undertow and jumped into the ocean. She would have drowned except luckily Chuck was there. He must be *some* swimmer."

"He's a thug, is what he is!"

Bobby hastened to say, "Why don't I look into the matter and get back to you?" His face at last began to sting where he had been struck, else he would not have believed it had happened: to be slapped by one's father when one was twenty-three years of age, newly graduated from college, and recently married was incredible. Bobby did not resent this so much as he wondered at it: what could cause a man to behave with so little self-discipline? He was aware that paranoia is never a thing-in-itself but rather a symptom. Was his father at last impotent? But was not impotence itself symptomatic of something still beyond? In human affairs perhaps there was never an end to any phenomenon, unless of course one was religious: everything pointed to still another signpost pointing elsewhere. After taking a number of courses in psychology, Bobby was not at all certain he had learned anything that would give him moral support when dealing with other human beings.

For example, what in the world could he now say to Chuck? "Look, I promised to ask you about this. I know it sounds crazy, but my father now goes around saying you carry a gun. And what's more, he claims you actually robbed him at gunpoint in this house."

Obviously he would have to approach the subject more delicately than this. Chuck had saved Lydia's life, and Bobby had yet to thank him for that. But having done so, could he then pursue his father's matter without an implied repudiation of the gratitude he had only just expressed, and without poisoning his friendship with Chuck?

His father continued to stare indignantly at him. "All right," Bobby said, "I told you I would look into it. I'm sure there's some explanation." He thought of one on the instant. "Maybe he's a law-enforcement officer."

"He's a cop and he extorts money from me? Did I tell you that *both* phone lines are out of order, suddenly?"

"I'm going to talk to him," said Bobby.

"I should think you'd learn a little about the background of someone you invite here."

"But I didn't invite him."

His father looked away contemptuously. "I think you ought to take a stand somewhere, Bobby. It's high time you developed some integrity. Okay, so you never expected this. Nobody's saying the sole responsibility is yours. But to try to weasel out of the matter altogether is another thing."

"Dad," Bobby said levelly, "I know it will require the most strenuous effort you have ever made, but *try* to listen to what I am saying. Chuck is not my guest. That is to say, I never invited him to come here. I couldn't have. I saw him for the first time in this house, what was it?, a week ago. That's Point One. Point Two is I haven't any explanation for what you tell me. All I can say is I've never known any houseguest who has worked out as well as Chuck. Not only is he always in a good mood, but he's made himself useful in countless ways, including now what I would call the ultimate, saving Lyd's life."

"Bobby," said his father, after having glanced back at the house, "I suppose it hasn't occurred to you that the only testimony as to this alleged lifesaving has been Chuck's own and, I gather, Lydia's."

Bobby felt the oncoming of an emotion he could not immediately identify. "That's right," said he. "Who else's do we need?"

"Why," said his father, "where's the corroboration?"

Bobby now believed the emotion was suppressed rage. "This is not some abstract legal thing," said he. "It's life and death, for God's sake."

His father wore what might have been a thin smile; if so, there was no true amusement in it. "I'm thinking of something a little less lofty, if you'll permit me." He showed two fingers in tight parallel. "I wonder if Lydia and Chuck don't seem unusually close. I don't like to say this, Bobby, but I wonder if he might be putting it to her."

"Oh, shit!" Bobby cried, now giving vent to his rage. "That's really nasty of you. There was no call for that remark, none at all. Go back to your whores, you bastard. Let us alone!"

Nothing like this had ever happened before. He had never been close enough to his father to quarrel with him. Thus not even during Bobby's teenhood had they been antagonists — not that Bobby had been an unruly adolescent: a little drinking, a few pills, was all.

His father was silent for a moment now, then said, "I ask *you,* anyway, to give me respect when under this roof."

It appeared to be more of an appeal than a request, but Bobby stayed indignant. Since first learning of his father's infidelities, many years before, he had felt his own manhood was impugned. That the same person now called him cuckold was unbearable. He went to look for Chuck, who remained someone to look up to.

§ 5 §

It was Audrey's practice each summer to bring to the island — or rather, have sent by road and then ferry, while she traveled by air — cartons of outmoded clothing to give to the locals. The distribution of these garments was handled by the housekeeper, Mrs. Finch, and no doubt went mostly to her own female relatives, for though the Finches managed such business as there was on the island, they gave no indication in their visible way of life that they earned large profits. They drove shabby vehicles, lived over or behind their places of business, such as the grocery and the gas station, or in mobile homes with front yards full of firewood for sale and fishing shacks at waterside on the unfashionable stretch of the shore. So presumably various hearts were gladdened, for these frocks and suits and sweaters bore the best labels (whether or not the recipients could appreciate the names) and showed scarce sign of wear. But as Mrs. Finch accepted no gift with more than a curt nod and never reported back with a word of gratitude from anyone to whom she had forwarded it, Audrey had to take it on faith that her generosity did not go for naught. Surely it was preferable to do this than to deal with one of those charitable

organizations in the city that were always being investiga-
ted for something to do with either corrupt finances or
perverted sex.

In an odd emotional state owing to the cupping of her
breast by Chuck Burgoyne — in retrospect she could not
believe it happened in quite the way it seemed at the time
— she went to her rooms to see whether she might
augment the collection of Finch-bound garments with
several other items from the extensive summer wardrobe
with which she stocked her closets: this included a selec-
tion of evening gowns, though for at least ten years there
had been no island occasion for which such a garment
would have been appropriate costume; and equestrian
attire, jodhpurs, even a riding mac for rainy days, though
no one she knew kept horses locally in this era. She had
ridden well as a girl and was reasonably good at archery.
But at golf she was hopeless, never really learned to serve
at tennis, swam poorly. Her breasts had been well shaped
and in fact remained so, largely as a result of fanatical
determination. She believed her eyes were too small and
pale of iris, but her skin had always been a great strength.
At quite an early age her thighs had thickened, obviously a
matter of genes, for no diet or exercise subsequently
affected them, and she had since never been seen in shorts
or bathing dress.

The closet complex included a vertical stack of built-in
drawers, a number of which, cedar-lined, were filled with
sweaters to be worn on chilly island evenings, which were
not unknown during the season, but even Audrey in a
reflective mood had to admit they were not so frequent as
to require more than a dozen sweaters in just two styles,
V-necked and cardigan, and only three colors, white,
beige, and navy, but she must have owned twenty-odd, all

knitted of cashmere, with the exception of a few routine woolen examples of her own purchase. All of the former had been presents from Doug on the giftgiving holidays, in addition to which he often presented her with a brooch made in the form of a miniature animal with eyes of diamond chips or another gem. Within three years he was capable of repeating himself, and thus she owned two identical little rabbits and also a matching pair of ruby-eyed frogs. On discreetly (though not accidentally) finding that Doug owed his favorite jeweler, the same who had served his family for generations, for too many such gifts, Audrey quietly paid the bill insofar as it pertained to what she had received, naturally letting ride the charges for what he had presented to a succession of his bitches, items which she was amazed, and pleased, to note were usually less valuable than those he gave her.

It had occurred to her that it might be nice to turn over to Mrs. Finch some of her excess of similar sweaters. The housekeeper was far too rawboned to fit into any of them, but presumably there were those who would do amongst the female kin to whom the other garments had gone, over the years. The difference was that the cashmere sweaters were not outmoded in style, hitherto the criterion for disposal. Thus the giving of them would be authentically generous, a true instance of charity in the classic sense of the word. Audrey had finally arrived at an age for performing an act that was uncompromisingly virtuous.

But the moment had come too late. Of the former collection of sweaters, as the all but empty drawers now informed her, only the humble woolen examples were still in her possession. Like moths, who after all are merely practicing their métier, the thief or thieves could discriminate amongst yarns. The obvious culprits would have been the cleaning team, who had been to the house on Friday and would come again on Monday morning, were it not that Audrey had gone through the sweater drawers on Saturday morning, searching through the lookalikes for the particular cardigan into the pocket of which, back in town, she had tucked the latest letter from her traveling friend Molly, that which contained Molly's schedule for the following month, more than a fortnight of which had now passed.

And as of that time all the drawers were filled. Thus the cleaning women were exonerated even before being tried. Which left Mrs. Finch, who of course had for many years had access to all summertime possessions of the family and guests and had never been known to steal any articles of clothing. Why would she start now and in such a conspicuous manner, taking at once the entire cashmere collection?

There could be no evading the fact that the possibilities had been immediately reduced to her daughter-in-law. She knew nothing of Lydia — in any event, nothing that had been confirmed. Bobby had married this girl in some county clerk's office in rural parts, not far from the university from which they had both only just graduated. Audrey had met Lydia for the first time when the newlyweds arrived on the island a week before, only hours before the coming of Chuck Burgoyne, after which she had been distracted from reflecting on a situation in which she found a touch of squalor, and all the more so when she heard, for the first time, that Bobby had been living with the young woman for most of the last year of college — yet had never mentioned her in his occasional telephone calls, which were always and solely concerned with begging more money from home. Neither Audrey nor Doug had gone to the commencement ceremony, but then no invitation had been received.

As to Lydia's bloodline, it could scarcely be less prepossessing, the family business, however profitable, being private refuse collection, and indeed the less said of her the better, a principle devoutly honored by both Audrey and Doug, but if the girl proved to be a kleptomaniac, what could one do? Then again, better her foible be kept within the family than revealed to the outside world. What if she were apprehended in a shop? One of Audrey's cousins had had a messy divorce that got into the papers years before, but that had been a glamorous embarrassment, what with the references to figures with meaningful names to journalism: statesmen, financiers, and the like, her cousin's reputed promiscuity having been an issue. And some relative of Doug's had once got into some trouble with the Securities and Exchange Commission. But no one in any familial association with Audrey had ever been charged with ignoble common theft.

Tact was called for here. Lydia had left the house and grounds only to go once, with Bobby, to visit the club. That had been three or four days back, before the sweaters were missing. Therefore they must now be no farther away than her room. Could she be that brazen — or demented? But it took a special sensibility to perform such a theft at all — from an in-law and one's hostess, when furthermore you were the only person under the same roof who could fit into the garments in question.

But perhaps it was intended to be conspicuous, as a provocation of some sort. Who could say what were the motives of other people, especially those of not only another generation but also another class? It might even be a kind of malicious joke, designed to elicit a hysterical response from herself; then, once she had lost self-command, the sweaters would be returned secretly and revealed with much derisive laughter. Of course, this was to make an inordinate flight forward of the kind against which she had been sternly warned by her doctor, who insisted that only a little self-discipline was needed to withstand the impulses of a masochism that was by no means of natural origin but demonstrably acquired.

She was well aware that she encouraged others, especially men, to take advantage of her basic generosity. For example, in her affair with Max Hopworth (which unlike any of Doug's was characterized by true love on the part of both participants, though to be sure Max's had not proved long-lived), it had always been she who had to defer to what at the time he presented as his obligations (wife's birthday, rituals pertaining to his kids, etc.) but what in retrospect she strongly suspected were merely his own wishes. Yet even when she discovered that she was only one of the two women with whom he regularly consorted extramaritally, she could manage no more than a weak protest which was soon replaced by a gasp of great feeling as he put his hand between her thighs. Many years had gone by between Max's doing that for the last time (Bobby had been a small child, and Dr. Hopworth was his pediatrician) and Chuck's recent touch of her clothed breast, with nothing (but a few drinks) in the interim, yet Audrey had never thought of herself as being forever beyond the reach of passion.

But, as she was totally dependent on Chuck to make the next move, which might not come soon, what with, God damn him, Doug's decision for once to stay beyond the weekend, she had time enough to investigate the matter of the missing knitwear. Her first job was to gain access to their room while the young people were occupied elsewhere. Bobby must be encouraged to remove Lydia from the house, perhaps take her on a tour of the grounds, most of which of course consisted of dense woods, but there was the antique gazebo amidst the grove — where one of Bobby's teenaged girlfriends had charged that she had been sexually importuned by his father and then ardently molested, all but raped. True, Doug was capable of that, but the little bitch did habitually mince about in abbreviated clothing and obviously found Bobby wanting.

That had happened during the period in which Audrey had definitely decided Bobby was homosexual, and in fact nothing much since had occurred to change her mind until he now turned up with too vulgar a wife for an invert to marry: they invariably chose long-lipped, horsey-looking women with contralto voices.

Just as she was ready to leave to look for Bobby, her husband came into the room, as usual without knocking though he demanded that courtesy be shown by visitors to his own quarters and in fact usually made it a necessity by having thrown the lock.

He acted as if he were pursued; he peered about, then quickly turned the key in the door to the hallway.

"Come over here, Audrey." He drew her to a far corner between the vanity and the bed that had been left unmade, for it was Mrs. Finch's day off. "We are in trouble."

Despite his hunted manner, she refused to take him seriously, and disparaged his assertion without making any effort to find sense in it: only by this means had she ever been able to hold her own with him, if such it could be called.

"I'm sure you're mistaken."

As always he paid no mind to her reaction, but went on

as if she had assented. "He carries a gun, by God. Oh, it's real all right, and I have no doubt he'll use it if he has to."

"Doug," Audrey said, stepping away, "are you *on* something?"

"Both phones are out," said he. "Look here." He went to the nearer of the two little ivory cabinets that flanked the head of her bed, and lifted the pale blue telephone that was there. He listened at the earpiece for an instant, then brandished the instrument before replacing it. "Then there's a confederate named Perlmutter. It occurred to me that he might even be hiding somewhere in this house — unless the guy merely changed his voice. I suspect Chuck knows something about phone systems. I'm sure I dialed Operator correctly. How could anyone make a mistake dialing *0*? Yet a woman came on who claimed to be Information way out West in some godforsaken place." His breathing was labored.

Audrey went farther from him. "I haven't any idea what you are talking about. Have you been drinking?"

"*Chuck Burgoyne,*" Doug said, with the emphasis given that which inspires unusual emotion.

For Audrey too the name inspired feeling. "Yes," said she, "ask Chuck about the phones. Maybe he can fix them before the repairman gets here."

Doug at last attended to her. "Haven't you been listening?" he asked in rage. "It's Chuck I've been talking about. He's a criminal!"

Audrey now advanced on him and laughed in his face. Doug slapped her across the left cheek, and she recoiled against the vanity.

Slowly returning to the upright position, she used an idiom that was unique for her. "You motherfucker." She groped at the top of the dressing table and came up with a tiny cuticle scissors. "I'll cut your balls off if you touch me again."

But her husband was once again in the state in which he seemed unable to see or hear her responses. "He's just a little runt," said he, "but what chance would I have against a gun? I'm no coward, but neither am I suicidal."

"Get out of here, you cocksucker," Audrey cried. "And don't ever come back." All the same, she had a terrible sense of powerlessness: never in her life had she voiced such language and thus now suspected it lacked the passionate conviction with which it was delivered by those to whom the gutter was home. In any event she always cowered when she heard it directed to others of their own kind by base types in the city, people with tattoos, shirts with the arms severed at the shoulders, caps bearing indecipherable devices, pushing wheeled contrivances or operating heavy machinery.

Doug continued to remain deaf to her speech. Could she be only *imagining* she spoke aloud? Of course she had for some years been given to abusing him tacitly in these terms, which strangely enough had seemed much stronger in the unspoken medium.

"But maybe, just maybe," Doug was saying, "if his attention could be diverted for a moment, he could be successfully jumped. I don't know. I've kept myself in good shape, but he's at least twenty-five years younger." He glared at her. "God Almighty, Audrey, must I be asked to perform a miracle?"

So the obscenities had not been of service. Audrey therefore returned to her old style, though she was still holding the cuticle scissors. "You're overwrought," said she. "That woman has got you running in circles. You don't have the self-possession of years ago when you chased jailbait. You may be over the hill, Doug: you don't seem to know when it's over."

Her husband was obliviously squinting past her. "You know, Aud, *you* could distract him. You have a motherly effect on him, Audrey! I've noticed that. He likes to impress you. That's what the cooking is all about." He stared at the ceiling, as if exasperated at heaven. "What a pretty pass, when a man has to ask his wife for help in this kind of matter and can't expect any from his son, who is a gutless wonder."

Audrey wondered whether to try to defend Bobby. The trouble here was that she basically agreed with Doug's assessment of their son. And Doug had just ignored her worst, which accurately reflected her genuine emotions. Furthermore, she still did not believe Doug's charges against Chuck. But that he was authentically exercised seemed obvious.

"All right," she said for motives of practicality, and sighed. "Okay, I'll take it up with him if that will calm you down. There's nothing at all wrong with Chuck. He happens to be the nicest houseguest we've ever had. He's sweet and kind and, and . . ." She really did not want to praise him to someone whom she despised: it was the worst of taste. She at last found the nerve to look at herself in the dressing-table mirror, and was amazed not to be able to discern the mark of Doug's blow, which she still could feel — or had that too been only imaginary?

Doug now astonished her by saying, with apparent gratitude, "That's all I ask."

"Just don't do anything desperate," Audrey said. "There's a reasonable explanation for all of this, I'm sure. It's an optical fantasy or something. You'll see." There was something here that might be puzzling but it could hardly be sinister. The fact was that Doug, despite his bluster, was a coward. Small wonder where Bobby got his own character. Were Audrey to take any of this seriously, she might well hope that Chuck would use his so-called gun to shoot her husband.

Bobby's search for Chuck was quickly successful. As he came in from the greenhouse after the outrageous encounter with his father, he saw the houseguest on the point of entering the sitting room off the deck, and he followed him.

Without turning to see who was behind, Chuck said, "Sit down. I want to talk to you."

They chose facing chairs. Chuck spoke in a lowered voice. "Bobby, I'm sorry to say that I have been made to feel unwelcome here, and I'm leaving."

"Aw," Bobby groaned. "It's gone that far? Listen, *he's* the one that will be leaving any minute now. He always flies back on Sunday evenings. Stay till next Friday, anyway. He won't be back till then. *Everybody* wants you to stay." Bobby had been right to refuse to take seriously Lydia's lack of enthusiasm for the houseguest: the next thing Chuck had done was save her life!

Chuck was shaking his head. "I'm afraid that would miss the point. There's a matter of pride, you know, of honor." He crossed his legs. The cuff of his trousers rode up, exposing the gun in the ankle holster.

Bobby's reaction to this phenomenon was as it would have been to Chuck's sudden exposing of his genitals apropos of nothing. Blood suffused his face. It took all his strength not to permit his eyes to descend again, and the gun-bearing leg, supported by the other knee, was within the lower margin of his proper field of vision unless he stared above the houseguest's sleek scalp.

Bobby did what he could to steady his voice, but he was none too successful. "I wanted to, uh, say how grateful I am — we all are, even Dad had to admit that —" His voice cracked here, and he tried to clear his palate. Finally he shouted, in physical and moral desperation, "You saved Lydia's life, for God's sake!"

Chuck nodded silently.

"Well," said Bobby, "there you are. We can't tell you how grateful we are, we all are. . . ." He had successfully brought his voice under control, but now it rose again to a shout. "*It never happened before:* a guest saving anyone's life!" That his father had been right, that Chuck carried a gun did not necessarily mean that he did so with criminal intent, but the problem was how to ask him about it without being offensive and inhospitable.

And Chuck was not helping. He continued to nod in silence.

"With my father you have to consider the source. He's jealous. Everything manly has to be done by him. He couldn't forgive you for saving the life of a young female, furthermore his daughter-in-law. He sees that as reflecting adversely on *him.*"

Chuck leaned forward with an arched eyebrow and spoke at last. "What are you saying, Bobby? That he and Lydia —?"

Funny, Bobby had quarreled with his father in response to a suggestion that Lydia and Chuck might be sexual partners. "Oh, no," he said hastily. "Nothing like that."

"Then he's changed his ways?"

How could Chuck have known? Bobby had never mentioned his father's nasty habits to anyone but . . . Lydia. He shook his head violently. "No," he repeated. "That's not true."

"What's not true?" Chuck asked. "That he never made advances to the girls you brought here in the past, some of them underaged? Or that he simply hasn't got around to putting the make on your wife?"

Bobby hated the turn the conversation had taken, because it required him to defend his father. "Really, Chuck," he said, "I think you've got the wrong impression, with all respect. Dad might not be perfect, but —"

"There's a lot of deceit in this house," Chuck said. "That's what strikes me as a guest: how much you all lie to one another. Unless you're all simply that insensitive and unobservant."

He might very well be correct, but Bobby felt awfully squeamish about considering such a theory with a stranger, which apparently was not an unfair designation for Chuck, whom it had been established that neither his father, Lydia, nor he had known prior to Chuck's self-institution as houseguest . . . unless of course Lydia was lying.

Bobby found the courage to ask, "Are you an old friend of my mother's?"

"Q.E.D.," said Chuck with an air of triumph. "Now, what is that, mere insensitivity?"

Bobby was embarrassed. "Well," he said finally, "the important thing is we all want you to stay. Don't pay any attention to my father. He goes off half-cocked."

"I haven't had any trouble with Doug. Far from it! He's been a perfect host." Chuck frowned. "If you must know, Bobby, it's Lydia. She seldom misses an occasion to make it clear she dislikes me."

Bobby felt enormous relief. He cried out in false exasperation, "And you just saved her life!"

"I'm afraid that hasn't made much difference," said Chuck. "She has some kind of basic aversion, I guess. Perhaps it's a visceral thing."

"Oh, that isn't true at all! All she can talk about now is what a hero you were."

Chuck said sadly, "I'm afraid she hasn't told me."

It was not right for Lydia to withhold her gratitude from the very man who most should hear it. A new facet of her character was here being revealed. When with Bobby, she talked only of Chuck's feat. She was using this thing as an instrument of power. Bobby usually submitted to her wishes, but he could not put up with this situation, which placed him in a sensitive situation with Chuck, and Chuck, for whatever reason, carried a gun.

Bobby therefore decided to pass the buck to his wife. "Say," he told the houseguest now, "you go and knock on her door. She's just napping. Go and tell her you're leaving, and you just see what she says."

"I don't know," said Chuck. "Isn't that somewhat degrading?"

"I don't think so. She really ought to do the right thing, and I'll say this: it isn't like Lydia to neglect something like that."

"Oh," asked Chuck, "you thought I was referring to myself?"

The question was too cryptic for Bobby, who shrugged and said, "Please do it, Chuck, and please don't leave. We need you." The houseguest had long since crossed his legs the other way, but the cuff at his armed ankle had caught on the butt of the pistol and had not descended. Bobby had been peripherally looking at the weapon throughout the conversation, but he still lacked the nerve to ask about it.

Chuck slowly smiled at him. "You may be right. Still . . ."

"Oh, don't worry about waking her up. Look, but for you she wouldn't be safely napping in a dry bed."

"Maybe you should lead the way."

"Oh, no," said Bobby. "This is something between you and her. It would be bad taste for me to intervene." Furthermore, he had missed completing his own nap, from which he had been harshly awakened by Lydia with the news of her near-drowning, and the encounter with his father had exhausted him further. If left alone he could easily snooze while slumped in the wicker chair in the far corner of the room, away from the deck.

"It's your idea then," said Chuck. "You have only yourself to blame."

His father had turned out to be right about the house-guest's carrying a gun, but was it likely that a criminal would be so emotionally vulnerable as Chuck had proved? Leaving a house because his feelings were hurt? Wouldn't a criminal simply shoot the offending person? Not that Bobby did not pay the revolver the respect it deserved. It was just that he saw no reason to panic. This was an appropriate era in which to possess an effective means of self-protection. The so-called martial arts were useless against a vicious assailant. The college karate champ, on a visit to the city, was all but killed when attacked, on a crowded midtown street, by a crazed man wielding a souvenir dagger.

Whatever the ambiguities with respect to Chuck, he had done a certifiable job of lifesaving — or, at any rate, according to Lydia, and what motive would she have had to lie?

"You'll see," Bobby told the departing Chuck. "She thinks the world of you."

*   *   *

Lydia was experiencing that kind of sleep that is profound yet does not delude the sleeper into believing for a moment that it is routine consciousness: the bogeyman cannot appear, and one does not suffer from a sense of one's unpunished criminality or a monstrous passion for a near blood-relative. It is the sleep that, with luck, sometimes follows the worst phase of an illness, signifying a definite turn towards recovery. That she now enjoyed it rather than a nightmare suggested the basic soundness of her being, body and spirit. In her sleep she began to develop a conviction that she was invulnerable. A Chuck would inevitably appear to pluck her back from the brink of catastrophe. Hers was a charmed life.

Therefore when Bobby changed his mind and came back and got into bed with her, she determined not to wake up more than just enough to receive him, for with thorough consciousness would come the reasonable recognition that she was as mortal as ever, if not, given the near-drowning, more so. But her slow opening of legs was not quick enough to meet his unprecedented impatience. He spread them violently and with little preamble thrust himself into the closest of all connections, even hurting her a little, though she never could be called tardy in response, and she approved of this new brutality, at the outset anyway, as an appropriate sequel to her brush with dying.

Weary, she easily relinquished the self-command ordinarily at stake here: at the moment it was more sensible to serve than to lead. Only a determination not to wake up made it possible for her to admit to no amazement at Bobby's transformation into a savage lover, but then everything in existence was all at once unprecedented since her death and miraculous rebirth. Her husband furthermore was now proving inexhaustible, he who formerly had come and gone so briskly, and even in her somnolence she was undergoing a series of intensities, each nearer the edge of paroxysm than the last, and had each not been accompanied by more distracting pain of a nonerotic nature, she might have expired of pleasure . . . but the fact remained that while he made "love," he was mutilating the skin of her back and buttocks with bladelike fingernails and then, without disengaging at the pelvis, managed to writhe into a position in which his teeth were embedded in a sizable piece of her breast.

Fortunately, his formerly elongated body had lately dwindled to be hardly more than hers, and with a great heave that used more strength than she ordinarily commanded, she dislodged him and rolled out from under, over the edge of the bed, hit the floor, and was up instantly and in a rage.

But he was not Bobby. He was Chuck Burgoyne.

Lydia was aware that she had license to faint at this moment: it was not fair that all these things could happen at once, if ever, to a person like her, who always tried to do the right thing. But she was also aware that on awakening again she would never be able to find more than a few fragments of her former self.

Chuck was spread-eagled on the tangled bedclothes, which included the damp towel in which she had earlier come from the shower. He too was visibly damp at the groin, with matted hairs, and some of this wetness was surely of her own secretion, her property, to be dispensed only of her own volition. He was therefore a housebreaker.

He grinned and spoke genially. "You must have liked it: you came three or four times." He reached for her at the lower thigh and was rapidly ascending as she jumped away.

She went even farther from the bedside, but made no move towards her clothing or even to cover herself, modesty being beside the point now. "I could kill you for this," she said. Her breast was stinging where he had bitten her, but that was the least of it.

At last he began to suspect that her reaction did not honor him. He jeered. "Kill me? I just saved *your* life. That means you're *mine,* I've got a right to you. Just think about it, and you'll have to agree."

"No, I don't!" she cried. "I don't *have* to do anything."

The statement made him smile. "Come on, we've got something, you and me. We're not like *them.*"

Lydia was breathing as rapidly as if she were still performing the act of copulation. "I'm not like you," she said. "Don't ever think that."

"Hell," said Chuck, stretching, yawning, "you don't know me. But that can be easily corrected. Meanwhile, just get back over here. Don't worry about that prize husband of yours: he's occupied. He won't walk in on us — not that I'd care much if he did."

In truth she had not yet given Bobby a thought, but now, guiltily, she cried, "You haven't hurt him?"

He guffawed. "What would you care? You're out to take him for all he's got. You haven't fooled me for a minute."

"Where is he? Have you done something to him?"

Chuck compressed his lips, then opened them to say archly, "You've got to come over here to find out."

Lydia was beginning to feel her nakedness in a moral way. She backed towards the built-in dresser drawer that held her underwear. Somehow she believed her least vulnerable side was that which gave clearest access to her sex organs, perhaps because he had already used them. She bent slightly at the knee, and with a hand behind her, opened the drawer. Funny how vanity could not be forgotten altogether no matter the extremity: by touch alone she tried to find one of her more attractive pairs of pants. Obviously this was not for the purpose of inciting his ardor, but rather an honoring of her mother's principle that the victim of an accident need never feel shame when wearing clean underwear. For what had happened here was a terrible accident, of which she had clearly been victim and not perpetrator, but then why did she suffer from such guilt? How could she, in a state of pristine ignorance, have failed to respond to him? Oh, retroactively it was easy enough to recognize the many differences in touch and rhythm and warmth and texture and on and on, including smell, Bobby being virtually odorless while Chuck had in recent memory used shaving lotion or cologne and soon exuded the natural musky scent of sex. But in the heat of the encounter details were as nothing; ripeness was all.

Damn, she could find nothing identifiable with the groping hand behind her back. She turned and seized any old pair and climbed into them. She whirled around, now in the white hip-huggers but still bare-breasted, and shouted at him, "All right, you saved my life. You have a right to my gratitude, but not to my person! I don't care what your theory is!"

"I hope," said Chuck, "you're not going to claim you didn't enjoy it." At least he was finally limp by now, and consequently not quite as arrogant, and he had lost his grin. His hair had stayed perfectly combed. Lydia's own was undoubtedly a mess: soaked in the sea and then the shower, roughly rumpled by towel, then slept on, then whatever happened to it during the act. She could not yet bear to look at herself in a mirror.

She stared at Chuck. "You raped me, you bastard. I was sleeping!" Which though not exactly true in particular, did support the general incontestable point, namely, that one's body was one's own, and lawful access to it by another could be gained only by permit, real or genuinely implied. Nowadays not even marriage provided unconditional license to one spouse to use the other without the latter's agreement. "I never did *one thing* to suggest I wanted your sexual attentions. Not *one thing!* God damn you."

There was an awful feeling in the crotch of her underpants. For an instant she believed she had, humiliatingly, urinated in the emotion of the moment, but suddenly understood that it was instead the emerging of the semen that had been injected into her, under false pretenses, by the man on her bed, and she was on no contraceptive medication; Bobby nowadays used condoms, his idea: the constriction helped keep him firm. . . . God, she was full of the stuff, her pants were soaked, and one only microscopic spermatazöon could do the job of procreation. What if she became pregnant by reason of this scum's scum?

She rushed into the bathroom, tore off the pants, used the toilet, then quickly douched, but the complexities of the process of generation were such that none of this provided any insurance whatever. At last she stared at herself in the mirror. She looked exactly like somebody who had been drowned, brought to life, and raped.

Chuck entered while she was so engaged, marched to the toilet bowl, and grossly, with a powerfully pressured torrent, began to empty his bladder. Had she possessed a weapon, the time to get him would have been now, as he spread-legged himself before the toilet bowl. But if the weapon had a keen edge, what a mess there would be! A bludgeon might be aesthetically preferable, but would she have had the strength to deliver a lethal blow? That he would get away with this vile deed, however, was insupportable. It went without saying that her father and brothers would be eager to avenge her, but this was precisely the kind of shame that she would do anything to keep secret from those of her own blood, for irrespective of the necessity for revenge, no male of her family would *really* believe her account, given the peculiar circumstances. To begin with, her father had always thought her too tarty ever since the onset of her pubescence. First she had been indecently premature in wearing a brassiere and makeup; then when, after a few years, she gave up the former altogether and the latter in part and shortened her hair, she "looked like a boy," and that was perhaps even more immoral. Taking up with Bobby Graves was the ultimate example of character failure: the Graveses would have been unpleasantly astonished to know how poorly they measured on the gauges of religion, culture, and even social status when the criterion was "our own kind." "You know what *they* would call *that*," Lydia had blurted in sheer exasperation. "Gangsters!" At which her mother said her mouth should be washed out with soap, and her father had not subsequently spoken to her though had sent an outlandishly large check on hearing she had married the guy. They had yet to meet Bobby. On this visit she was meeting his parents for the first time. And within a week she had been raped by another guest under the same roof.

She silently left Chuck where he was and went out to the bedroom and quickly covered herself with beltless jeans and an oversized man's blue workshirt. While this was under way she heard the sibilance of the shower. His effrontery was, alas, impressive. Obviously he had no concern about Bobby's return. Chuck's contempt for her husband could not but have its effect on Lydia, who blamed Bobby now for not having been at hand — while worrying that he might return and catch her within a private enclosure with a naked man. Somewhere here too was a concern for his emotional well-being. Physically he was at least a match for Chuck, who unclothed was even shorter and slighter of build than when dressed, as opposed to the way it was with her brother Tony, who pumped iron but looked deceptively slender in a dark suit. On the other hand, Chuck was psychically a thug. She must get out of this room and find her husband, forestalling a confrontation until the ground had been well prepared.

But the person she found first — he was just coming into the main sitting room from the deck — was her father-in-law. For the first time he appeared not quite well groomed, though no detail supported this impression: it was one of mood.

They spoke at the same time. Doug could not distinguish her words. What he said was, "Have you seen Bobby?"

Obviously she had not heard the question, for she broke off and then resumed, with her own version of what he had said to her. "I'm looking for my husband." She had been briefly attractive when seen in the swimsuit, but now she was back to being even less fetching than usual: hair damp and disordered, her face blanched, eyes reddened. If she was a confederate of Chuck's, she had none of his style.

"I just asked you the same," Doug said, with a chilly

elevation of his chin. There was no longer any reason for courtesy if she was a participant in a conspiracy to take power in his home. She might be the weakest link, easily overwhelmed unless she too was carrying a concealed weapon, but before jumping her he would remain cautious until he could define the precise nature of her role.

As she stared at him now her eyes began to fill with tears. Of course it could be a hoax — he had had more than one mistress for whom weeping was but another manipulative device — but his daughter-in-law suddenly seemed genuinely forlorn.

Nevertheless, he stayed his distance, asking warily, "Why are you crying?"

She hung her head and spoke as if to her modest bosom. "Oh, God, how can I . . ."

"I heard about your problem with the undertow. Bobby really should have made it clear that swimming there is ill-advised."

"Chuck," Lydia began chokingly, as if she could hardly rid her throat of the name. "He —"

Doug was icy now. "Oh, yes," he said, "your friend. He supposedly saved you, didn't he? Well, you're partners after all, aren't you?" She certainly looked vulnerable at this moment. Surely he could deliver a disabling blow before she could draw the gun she carried in the waistband of the jeans, under that oversized shirt.

Lydia raised her face and asked, "*My* friend? He's my *friend?*" Her tears had stopped flowing.

Doug could make no sense of the shifting emphasis. "Well," said he, "he's hardly mine. Furthermore, he pulled a gun on me. Can you imagine that? A guest in my house? Threatens me with a gun?" This incident had continued to burgeon in memory: Doug had by now convinced himself that Chuck had thrust the muzzle at him and cocked the trigger. "How's that for a Sunday at the shore?" he asked. "You can get your head blown off *for no reason,* by a houseguest *you don't even know.*"

Lydia was frowning. "Then whose friend is he?"

"He isn't yours?"

His daughter-in-law glared at him. "He just raped me."

Doug accepted this startling announcement with exterior aplomb, though within he was agitated morally and erotically. "Would you like to lie down?" he asked. "I'm afraid we can't call the police: he's done something to the phones. I don't have any weapons. Maybe I can get out to the cars before he spots me, and make a break for help."

"He's put at least one of them out of commission," Lydia said. "That's why Bobby couldn't get to the club. I'll bet the other one won't run, either. How did he get here himself? Where's his car?"

"I suppose he got a ride," said Doug, thinking of this matter for the first time. "He has a confederate, you know."

"On the property somewhere?"

"I don't know, but we're in an extreme situation." She had begun to weep softly again. He had to do something by way of comfort: she was young and female and a relative. He touched Lydia at last: he took her cold hand. "We'll get him, dear. We'll get him."

Lydia's fingers stirred within his grasp. "I didn't see his gun."

"Carries it in an ankle holster," said Doug, releasing her, not wishing to convey the wrong idea. He had actually started to feel protective, an emotion unique for him.

"Damn!" she said. "Then it must have been someplace in the pile of his clothes on the floor. If only I had known!"

"Would you have shot him?"

"Sure!"

Doug was impressed by the girl's spirit. "All right," he said. "Good for you." He was not himself the kind of man who could take a woman against her will. The thought was repugnant to him: he could scarcely desire a female who had to be forced to accept him, which would be the nullification of all that he sought when resorting to the opposite sex.

"By now, though," Lydia went on, "he'll be finished with his shower and be just about dressed. We should take cover somewhere."

Doug led her out of the room. "We better not go to my part of the house: he's back there all the time. I've got it: the utility room: we can talk in private there." This was the site of the oil furnace (whose heat was available if required, the house being equipped for all seasons though routinely used for only one), the water heater, and washer-dryer; it lay behind the kitchen and except for vents for the appliances had no communication with the outer world. A cul-de-sac in which one could be trapped as well as hidden.

They entered this place and closed the door. A naked bulb of low wattage jutted from the wall; it was kept permanently lighted, for reasons of safety.

"Now," said Doug to her dimly illuminated and thus even paler visage, "you're not going to be crazy about this plan, but in view of the existing situation I think it would work. But you'd have to go to bed with him again — that is, get him to undress and take off his gun, and keep him distracted just long enough for me to come in and get the pistol." She was grimacing. "I'm sorry," he said quickly. "Forget it. Bad idea. We'll think of something else." He was continually being astonished by this new delicacy of his.

"No," said she. "No, it's a fine plan. But *I'll* get the gun. You don't have to come in."

He shrugged. "You're so modest, even in such an emergency? I assure you —"

"No," said Lydia. "I don't want you to risk your life. This is *my* problem."

He was injured by her selfishness. "Didn't I say he robbed me at gunpoint?"

She had expressive eyes; they understood him. "All right, we'll be partners, but I still don't want you to take such a risk. Let me grab the gun, though. Then I'll yell for you."

Now that he had learned of the eloquence of her eyes, he examined them for a moment. "You don't want to just capture him and turn him over to the police. You want to shoot him, don't you?"

"I don't know what I want, except to make the first move against him. I hate the way he made me feel."

"Did he really save your life?"

"I can't deny that. But I can't live it down, either, till I pay him back. It's all of a piece: the lifesaving and the rape. One can't be separated from the other. I have to even the score."

She might be seen as demented to a degree, yet Doug felt she made a certain sense. He and she had affinity in their common concern for honor.

§ 6 §

Strange things were happening, such as the disappearance of her cashmere sweaters, which she had not mentioned to Doug lest that too be blamed on their houseguest, but Audrey knew that if Chuck were involved in any of these occurrences there was a rational explanation for such involvement.

She was aware that her position with respect to Chuck had deteriorated somewhat: until now she had refused to put him anywhere in the picture of negative events. But on reflection she could say that while Doug was a skilled evader of the truth, he had never been a blatant liar unless his sex life was the subject at hand. It would therefore be utterly out of character for him to cut from the whole cloth such a tale as that in which Chuck robbed him of money at gunpoint.

Perhaps Chuck did possess a firearm or something that resembled one and coincidentally Doug had espied this real or fake weapon while the houseguest was asking him for a loan. For it was not out of the question that Chuck might find himself financially embarrassed at the moment, in need of pin- or mad-money, say, and would find it necessary to apply to the father of his best friend. As everybody close to their son would know, Bobby was always out of pocket, irrespective of how much had lately been given him, and was himself always and exclusively a debtor.

Perhaps Chuck had been acting in Bobby's behalf. Bobby was quite capable of putting a friend in such an uncomfortable position, and from what she had observed of Chuck, it would be in character for *him* to undertake such a selfless mission.

She had seen nothing in Chuck that was untoward with the exception of that instant in which he had suddenly, irrationally, clutched her left breast. But in retrospect she could now identify that incident as being a product of pure fancy: which was to say, it had not happened on the plane of that which we know as everyday reality but was rather an emotional projection of some sort. Having made that identification, and without a doctor's help, she could go now without uneasiness to find the charming houseguest.

The door to his room was ajar when she reached it. Therefore she did not knock but opened it farther while asking, "Chuck?" Receiving no answer, she stepped in and repeated the name. But no one answered. Both bedroom and the bath were as neat as though they had yet to be used, on this Sunday afternoon, two days since the latest tour of the cleaning staff, nor had Mrs. Finch been on the premises since 4 P.M. Friday. In like circumstances, at least before his marriage (since which his mother had scrupulously avoided visiting his quarters), Bobby's room would have been an unspeakable sty, and when the help were not at hand Audrey herself rarely even pulled up the bedclothes on arising. Actually, Doug was somewhat more self-reliant in these matters, having been sent at least one summer as a child to a camp that imposed quasi-military discipline on its charges, and certain residual effects persisted: when making a bed he could even, if he chose, give the sheets an army tuck.

But there had been no precedent for Chuck's spit-and-polish. It was routine for Mrs. Finch to complain about the slovenliness of guests, but now it occurred to Audrey that the housekeeper had not made a single reference to Chuck, and small wonder, given the condition of this room even on a weekend.

As the current resident was not on the premises at the moment, Audrey had no legitimate reason to remain, except to wonder at the unusual orderliness. Was it likely that so neat a man could be ethically irregular? She decided just to peep into the closet: there were those who hid confusion behind closed doors.

A single garment hung on the horizontal rod: a simple tan jacket of the sort worn at golf. Apparently Chuck at all times wore the remaining entirety of the outer wardrobe he had brought with him, and it was of such an unobtrusive nature that one did not easily notice it never changed. Also there was the considerable distraction of his personality. . . . Was his intimate apparel in comparably short supply? She opened the nearest of the drawers that, as in every other room, were sunk into the wall, the architect having had a distaste for pieces of movable furniture that served principally as receptacles, and Audrey had gone along with all of his ideas, being as enchanted with him as it was possible to be in the case of a man who was demonstrably without a sexual taste for women.

The first drawer opened by her was empty save for a lone paper clip, which slid forward with the motion to clatter against the front panel. The second, nearer the floor, held a number of cashmere sweaters. For a moment she assumed that, like her, Chuck had owned a collection of such garments, but unlike her had retained possession of his own. Which is no more than to say that her first impulse was as always to give the houseguest the benefit of any possible doubt. Not even the labels were accepted as conclusive proof of theft — but there could be no arguing with the size of the sweaters.

While she squatted at the ordeal of investigation, Chuck came in from the hallway. She knew it was he without turning, and for an instant she flinched, expecting to be throttled from behind.

Having been allowed to survive, she spoke to the open drawer. "I'm sorry. It's unforgivable of me."

He advanced to a position beside her and gave her his hand. He pulled her to her feet.

"Here," he said, "take a look at this." He went to the closet and slid open the door on the right: his lone jacket hung at the far left end of the rod. On the floor of the closet, in the rear right-hand corner, sat a sizable cardboard carton. Chuck thrust in his head and shoulders and drew the container out into the room, folding down the flared flaps of its top to make visible a mailing label.

Audrey submissively placed her hands on her knees and bent to examine the legend on the label. Fortunately it had been hand-printed in large capitals and was legible in the absence of her eyeglasses.

FATHER DICK O'TOOLE
CHRISTIAN MISSION
SANTA LUCIA
REPUBLICA DE PONGO

"You have so much," Chuck said softly, behind and above her. "And they have so little."

But this was not a note that Audrey found easily persuasive. She turned and said, frowning quizzically, "But that sounds like the tropics."

"It gets frigid every night in the mountains where the peasants have been driven by the big landowners."

"Presumably they come down every day to work on the plantations?"

"Exactly," said Chuck, with a leer that seemed to hover on the edge of nastiness. He pushed the carton back into the closet and hurled the door to the closed position.

Audrey sighed. "I don't really care. I hate those sweaters. I hate everything Doug gives me, because I hate him."

Chuck kicked shut the drawer full of cashmere. "What does that mean?" he asked. "That you want me to do something about it?"

Audrey sighed again. "Only if you'd like to." She realized that this could seem pitiful if misinterpreted, but was at a loss as to how to direct his reaction.

He looked away, though probably not in delicacy. "There are expenses."

After a moment or two, Audrey came back decisively from her dream. "Oh, no," she said. "I don't want him killed. Oh, God."

Chuck shrugged. "You'd better make up your mind."

"Well, I certainly did not suggest *that*." She stepped towards him. "Please be patient with me, Chuck. I think I have a certain sense of things, but of a pretty naïve kind, I suppose, by your standards. You're younger than I, but you've undoubtedly seen more of the sort of life —"

He winced. "Stop driveling!"

The command was much harsher, and more fearsome, than the slap in the face she had been given by her husband, and her response now was not anger but rather self-pity.

"Take the sweaters," she said tearfully. "And I've got a lot of other stuff I don't need, which the poor people down there can undoubtedly use. Take anything — anything in the house. Just don't be nasty to me. I can't stand that."

His smile was like that of a young boy. "I don't need your permission. You have nothing to bargain with."

Audrey was frightened, but she was also strangely thrilled by Chuck's sudden display of what must finally be his true colors. "Then it *is* true? You do carry a gun?"

"Right here." He put his hand to his groin. "Just do as you're told. That shouldn't be a strain on you: it's your normal way of life."

"Are you going to kill me?"

He laughed heartily. "Why would I want to do that?"

"We won't obstruct you," Audrey said. "We're not used to this sort of thing. . . . Do you mind my asking? Are you a friend of Lydia's?"

Chuck jovially raised and lowered his eyebrows. "Only since a little while ago. But I had her number the first time I laid eyes on her. She's not your kind."

"No," said Audrey, "she's not."

"The rest of you are useless. At least she's a good fuck."

Audrey remembered that this was all a dream. Therefore it did not really matter what she heard, or what she said in response.

"Chuck . . . I thought perhaps you and I had — well, a certain sympathy, affinity . . ."

He let her drift for a while, then said, "*You?* An old lady like you?"

She did not ask permission to leave his presence. She went from the room, passed through the breezeway, and was back in the main house. The door of Bobby's room was open, offering a view of the rumpled bed. The image had obscene and disorderly connotations for Audrey, whereas it seemed natural that Chuck and Lydia should connect sexually. She had only profited by her expedition to the room of the houseguest: her theory that those two had conspired against the Graves family had been decisively confirmed.

That called for a drink, which could be taken openly, boldly, in all conspicuous self-righteousness. She steered for the little bar-pantry just off the dining room. In ransacking her room Chuck must have discovered the half-gallon jug of vodka, which Mrs. Finch discreetly and regularly replenished. Then he wasn't as cruel as he might have been: he could have called her a drunk. She was not all that old. She came off better than she could have hoped. Injustice is always easier to bear than punishment for the failing of which one is guilty.

Bobby woke up when his shoulder was shaken. It was his mother, who looked uncomfortably animated.

"Hi," he said slowly, and closed his eyes again. "Is dinner ready?"

"Bobby, please."

He reluctantly opened one eye.

"I can't find either your father or your wife."

"Lyd just went to the room." He looked at his wristwatch. "My God, have I slept that long? Well, an hour or so back she went to take a nap. You remember she almost drowned."

His mother peered in turn at each of the doorways. She lowered her voice. "How long have you known Chuck?"

Bobby scowled in exasperation. "Dad keeps asking me

that! He refuses to believe me when I say I never saw the guy before meeting him here."

"Then his connection is with Lydia. That's been my feeling all along."

Bobby adjusted his long body to sit up on his buttocks rather than his sacroiliac. "This is getting to be quite the joke," said he. "Lyd didn't know him, either!" He remembered something. "Dad's got it in for Chuck for some reason. We had an argument about that and Dad slapped me. Imagine that: at my age."

"Chuck is not a good man, Bobby. He's been stealing things from this house."

"Oh, come on, Mother, not you too! All at once you both have gotten so *weird*. There are a hundred good reasons why Chuck would carry a gun. After all, he hasn't exactly shot anybody around here, has he?" Except when fooling with her plants, his mother always seemed to wear a dress, not even a blouse and a skirt. Bobby was noticing that consciously for the first time. She also always gave the appearance of being well balanced, even now. He therefore could not believe anything was out of order, even if it was she who said it was.

"I don't know why a person would carry a gun if he had no intention of using it."

Bobby stood up and looked down at her. "Self-protection, Mother. Now if you'll excuse me, I've got to answer the call of nature."

"Where *is* Lydia?" His mother blocked the route to the little lavatory in the central hallway, the one used by cocktail and dinner guests.

"I told you. In my room."

"She's not there. And I can't find your father, either."

"Where is Chuck?"

"*He's* in his room. We must find your father, Bobby. He was right about Chuck, as it happens. I hate to admit it, but he was right."

Bobby had a grievous need to pee, but he overcame it for the moment. "Now, listen," he said with uncharacteristic energy. "Just stop this crazy business right now, before it gets seriously out of hand. Chuck was just in here a while ago telling me he was going to leave because he thought Lydia didn't like him. Can you beat that? After saving her life? He's a sensitive man: oversensitive, in fact. I don't care if he carries a gun or not: he wears his feelings on his sleeve. That's what's so nutty about you and Dad calling him a criminal."

His mother stared at him for a moment, and then she said gently, "You just go to the toilet, Bobby. And if meanwhile you run into Chuck, try not to anger him. If he's stealing something, *let* him, for goodness' sake."

In the lavatory Bobby peed out of the left leg of his shorts, without having to open his fly, as he had done as a little boy: it was less trouble.

Lydia and her father-in-law were sitting at the kitchen table. Before leaving the utility room they had come to a preliminary agreement on the plan to deal with Chuck Burgoyne: she would lure him into an intimate situation and, when he was thereby thrown off his guard, would seize the pistol, then call for the nearby Doug to rush in and take over. That was the agreement, but Lydia had no intention of honoring the final clause before punishing the houseguest for humiliating her as he had. She wanted to see his reaction when she thrust the gun barrel between his legs and cocked the trigger.

She said now, "We agree that Bobby is not to know a thing about this until Chuck is taken prisoner."

"And the same for Audrey," said Doug. "Those people

aren't cut out for emergencies. They have to be shielded when the going gets rough. Furthermore, they both think Chuck is wonderful. Now, that can help us to keep him in a state of false security. Whereas even if they agreed with us, neither could ever be a convincing actor."

"I know what you mean about Bobby," Lydia said. "And it's not a criticism. I admire such openness and honesty." But a spurious note was creeping into this, and she desisted. Also she remembered that Bobby had often told her of his suspicion that contempt was very likely the deepest emotion his father felt for him.

Doug was on the point of speaking, perhaps to say something that would reflect on this very matter, when Audrey came in from the dining room. She glanced at Lydia in what would seem distaste, and said to Doug, "May I have a word with you?"

He raised his left hand and splayed it. "Feel free."

She made some facial gestures. "Please."

"Can't it wait?"

"No, it can't," Audrey said with force. "Something must be done about Chuck." She turned to Lydia and snarled, "I know he saved your life." Turning back to her husband, she added, "But he's bad news for the rest of us."

Doug was squinting at her. "What are you trying to pull now, Audrey? When I tried to tell you much the same, you defended the bastard. Fact is, you convinced me. I find him a capital fellow, salt of the earth."

He pronounced these words so convincingly as momentarily to shock Lydia, who was not prepared for irony at this instant. She hastened to make common cause with her mother-in-law.

"You're right! He's scum."

Now Audrey was the one to be astonished. "You?" she asked rudely.

Doug broke in. "If I thought you could be trusted, it might be a different story."

Lydia suddenly felt a unique urge of sororal feeling for Audrey and spoke in her interest. "Of course we can trust her! She's found something out, don't you see? And we need all the help we can get."

Doug wore a faint grimace. He could be suspected of wanting to exclude Audrey at least a while longer, whatever the emergency, and he also very likely resented Lydia's gesture towards his wife, assuming his own influence might henceforth be outweighed by femininity.

In a dramatically lowered voice he asked, "Should we be shouting, with him at large somewhere?" This was an exaggeration; there had been no cries. But his point was not without merit: it was an awfully public place, where, plans formulated, they had come so that, if found by Chuck, they would not be suspected of conspiring against him. Lydia had intended to prepare tea, but could not find the makings.

She was now aware that Audrey had been staring at her awhile. Finally her mother-in-law asked, "Can I believe what you are telling me?"

With all that Lydia had undergone this day, she could not endure persistent rudeness. "Please don't address me in that tone. I was Chuck's first target." Contrary to the common theory, it had been much easier for her to specify her experience to a man than to tell it now to a member of her own sex, at least this example.

When Audrey looked to Doug for clarification, he said only, "For God's sake, Audrey, this is no time to be dubious. The girl's been put through the wringer."

Audrey turned back to Lydia. "Then you too have been missing articles of clothing?"

"For Christ's sake, Aud," said Doug.

To him Lydia said, "It's okay now." She addressed her mother-in-law. "I could kill him."

Audrey recoiled slightly. "It's only a few sweaters. I really don't —"

"Shut up, Audrey," said Doug. "I thought I heard —"

The screen door was suddenly thrust open, and Chuck entered from outside. This was at the end of the kitchen, nowhere near the table, but it was not out of the question that he had heard some or even all of their conversation.

"Well, well," he said with a good imitation of heartiness, "are we all back here already? After just eating that big breakfast? I came in to wash my hands. I'm afraid I have only bad news where *both* cars are concerned. I can't get either one of them started now."

Even in her hatred of him Lydia had to recognize how careful he had been to acquire an air of authenticity: the hands he held up for display were covered with grease.

Doug responded with a fake bluffness of his own. "You oughtn't have bothered, old man! We're none of us going anywhere."

Chuck vigorously wiped his hands on a length of paper towel he tore from the mounted roll on brackets under a cabinet. "Still," he said, "it's reassuring to have available transport. It's pretty remote out here without it. That's the negative aspect of privacy."

Lydia realized that they had better deal with Chuck without delay: she interpreted this speech as an implication that he intended to savage them all. Call her fear preposterous, but such things did happen from time to time in isolated houses. Mass murder was lately in vogue and Chuck Burgoyne when seen in this context was the typical perpetrator: a loner, but eminently respectable, genteel, handsome, charming. It was just a pity that she and Doug had worked out no plan by which they might together jump him as he washed his hands at the sink, a totally unprotected back towards them, gun way down inside his socks — if to be sure he was even carrying it now. Only Doug had seen this weapon.

She tried now to catch her father-in-law's eye, but he was utterly occupied with Chuck and seemed at the moment interested only in foolishly topping him verbally.

"But then," Doug was saying, "that's pretty true of all of life, isn't it, Chuck? You give up one thing to get another. Speaking for myself, I'd give up security any day for privacy."

Chuck dried his hands with another paper towel. He stared at Doug. "Security? Nothing criminal ever happens around here, does it? Isn't that the idea in coming here? To get away from all that?"

Doug stared back. "It's what I always thought."

Lydia was getting nervous. She had not expected that Doug would act as though moving towards a showdown with their adversary. She popped out of her chair. "I could use some exercise."

"Haven't you had enough for one day?" Chuck asked, with gentle derision. "Not swimming again, I trust."

She could not help responding defiantly. "I'm not afraid to go in the water again!"

"I'd be worried if I took you seriously," said Chuck, with apparent irony. He was a master of the disarming effect.

This was the ideal moment to institute their plan. "Well,

then," she said, "at least I can take a walk. How about it, Chuck? Want to come along?" She tried to leer.

"What a good idea!" said Audrey, pushing back her own chair. "I could use a constitutional at this point. It's been a sedentary Sunday."

This was where Doug should have come into the picture to obstruct his wife, but he acted as though he and Lydia had never had their colloquy. "Oh, the devil with that," said he. "Let's play bridge instead." He too rose.

Lydia changed her mind when she saw that Chuck was now at a physical disadvantage. He was not much taller than either woman, and of course Doug loomed over him.

Their instant was brief. The houseguest drew a large chef's knife from one of the slots of the hardwood block on the counter.

He said, with a snicker-snack movement of the long triangulated blade, "I've got to make dinner, if we expect to eat here, and obviously we do if the cars won't run."

Doug backed dramatically away, though he had not been formally threatened. "Sure," he said with a placating outthrust hand. "Don't worry about us. We'll keep occupied."

Audrey suddenly made the neighing sound of what was probably supposed to be a laugh. "But Lydia doesn't play bridge — unless she's just been pretending."

"That's right," Lydia assured her. "Someone at college once was teaching me to play hearts, but I'm afraid I have forgotten all I learned." No doubt because she despised cards and in fact most other games: she couldn't really understand why time should be in need of that sort of killing.

"We'll go find Bobby," said Doug. "Surely we can find something to play as a foursome."

Doug was proving to be useless. Lydia saw she would have to make her own move. "I can't boil water," she told Chuck. "This might be a time when I could take a few cooking lessons."

The houseguest smiled at her. "As it happens the moment is not opportune. I've got some delicate tasks to perform."

But she had claimed the initiative, and moved quickly to exploit it. "Oh, I'll just stand over there, out of the way, and watch. You'll never even know I'm present." She had no doubt that he would reject her plea, which was eminently reasonable, and thereby weaken his position morally, for what honorable objection could be made to so modest a request?

But in fact he shrugged and said, "Have it your own way."

Doug and Audrey were leaving the kitchen. Lydia tried to think of something she could say, if not to detain them, then at least to reaffirm the solidarity of the threesome against Chuck, but her parents-in-law failed even to glance at her as they made an exit. Could this be treachery? Were they double agents who had now delivered her to the enemy?

"In fact," Chuck was saying, "you *can* help. Get those lobsters from the fridge."

"There are lobsters in there?" If so, they had come from nowhere, certainly were not in place when she had got the makings of the grilled-cheese sandwich she prepared for breakfast. Yet nobody had left the premises.

"Look in the crispers," Chuck said, gesturing with the enormous knife.

She opened the refrigerator and went where he directed her. The enameled bin on the lower left held two dark-green crustaceans. They appeared comatose but not dead despite their removal from the water many hours earlier: there was a slight movement of feelers and, if one watched long enough, an even slighter indication of claw that suggested the creatures were still sentient. Lobster eyes told nothing, ever. These beasts were closer to insects than to fish, irrespective of habitat.

At home, lobsters like steaks were men's work. Lydia had not been able to watch the boiling alive — and even worse was done by her maternal uncle Vincent, who favored grilling them over charcoal.

But she could not show the white feather to Chuck. She snatched up one of the lobsters, a finger on either side of the hard smooth shell, and carried it to the counter. The creature's spark of life was thereby fanned. She felt the considerable power it could manifest by merely curling its tail. The two claws vigorously severed lengths of air.

"Look there," Chuck said, laughing. "The pegs have fallen out. They can take off a finger with one snip, you know."

She had not noticed till now that the little wooden or plastic claw-restraints were missing. When eating the cooked version she had always thought briefly how unfair it was to deny a creature its only means of defense, but as with so many other moral stances this one required modification when put to a test. Undoubtedly Chuck was right about the power of such weapons. For a moment she was leery about putting the thing down: how quickly could it turn? But at last she did so, backing away too briskly, surely destroying much of the impression she had sought to give of self-reliance.

Chuck moved the lobster to a chopping block and with three decisive strokes of the big chef's knife cut the animal into four parts, each of which proceeded to assert an independent existence of its own, with much more power than had been displayed before the loss of general integrity. The tail writhed with such force that had he not seized it, it might have plunged to the floor and in inchworm fashion walked out of the kitchen. The claws continued to snap lethally.

"Hey," Chuck said, grinning at her as he asked the disingenuous question, "how can this ever be?" To the lobster: "Why don't you lay down and die, old son?" He asked Lydia to fetch him the other one.

"For God's sake."

"Oh," said he in a mocking little voice, one hand on a hip, "does Missy think it's cwoo-el? Worse than boiling alive? Which takes a minute and a half to do the trick, for your information. To experience that for yourself, stick in your pinky for ninety seconds. Next time you eat a ham sandwich, reflect that the pig you're chewing had his throat cut while his buddies watched and waited for their turn." He used the knife like a wand. "Are you ever honest about anything? You can't even admit to yourself that I brought you to a climax at least three times. . . . Now, get me that other lobster!"

She could endure this no longer and fled from the kitchen, her strategy in ruins.

Doug and Audrey had only just reached his room when Lydia appeared. Doug's regard for her had been highest when they had conspired alone near the hot-water heater. At that time he had been impressed by her ferocity towards Chuck. But in action she had proved disappointing, and now here she was, in distraught retreat and for a silly reason.

"Oh," said he when they had heard her complaint, "there's nothing sinister in that. From the sound of it, he's probably making Lobster *americaine*. That's just galvanic action, you know. They're dead soon as the spinal cord is cut, however it might look."

Lydia sat down on the straightbacked chair near the desk and met her falling face with rising hands. She spoke through her fingers.

"I'm not getting far."

"We've just got started!" Doug noted, with false energy. "I never thought it would be easy. He's pretty well entrenched by now. We shouldn't have let that happen, but it did." He shook a finger at Audrey, who was about to speak. "Oh, I admit I am as responsible as anyone else. He seemed harmless enough in the beginning."

"Harmless!" Audrey cried. "You thought he was wonderful."

"Now that makes sense," said Doug. "We've got this criminal to contend with, and you attack *me*."

"My point is simply —"

Lydia screamed here. "Stop, stop!"

Doug nodded. "She's right. What we need now is not vindictiveness, but some constructive thinking. Here's my idea: I don't know a lot about cars, but I suppose I could recognize it if he sabotaged them in a simple way, like taking off the distributor cap. I've seen that done in a movie. I'm willing to have a try after dark."

Audrey was hostile even to such serious planning when it was done by him. "Wouldn't that be nice?" she asked. "You drive off and look for help. What do you think

Chuck will be doing to us while you're gone? Because he'll certainly hear the car."

Doug remained amiable, surprising himself. "I see what you're getting at: you mean those left behind will be hostages. But there's an answer to that. We'll all get ready to go. I'll slip out first and see what's wrong, and if it's easily rectified, I'll do it. Then the rest of you run out, and off we go. I've just thought of a refinement: even if he has some means to get the remaining car going, I'll deflate all four of its tires."

His wife was still grimacing bitterly towards her shoes, but Lydia said, "I prefer the first plan. I just haven't yet had time to apply it. I'll have to wait till after dinner now. But it's the best bet."

"It's the most likely to get you hurt or killed," Doug said. "I'm sorry I seemed to agree, earlier on. It's not a good plan, Lydia. It's too dangerous."

Lydia gave him a look in which he thought he could recognize a certain nonerotic tenderness, something not all that familiar to him even as a young boy with a widowed mother who had been in fashion in her era.

"I know what I'm doing, Doug. I'm not afraid of him."

Now he was disappointed again: she was too arrogant, which could never be a strength. She had too grandiose a sense of her sexual attraction, and that was pathetically ironic, for to Chuck she must now be seen as used merchandise. Lydia was that most vulnerable of females: she who believed she could dominate a man by means of sex.

"Well, *I'm* afraid of him," he said, "because I'm unarmed. I've always hated guns, and I've seen a lot of them. My father owned a virtual armory. He hunted big game and belonged to clubs with private firing ranges and trapshooting. And one day he took one of his finest pistols, puts its muzzle into his mouth, and blew his brains out."

"Oh, my," said Lydia.

"I didn't want to make you feel worse," Doug said. "You didn't know him." He cleared his throat. "What I wanted to say was, I have always detested guns for obvious reasons, but I wish I had one now, unloaded of course; I couldn't shoot a man. I'd just use it to disarm Chuck. Once he lost his advantage, he would be nothing. He's just a skinny little squirt. He's got a few years on me, but I could take him with one hand." This was no empty boast: Doug had boxed intercollegiately as a light heavyweight and in his city office had a silver cup to prove it. He was that rare sort who in middle age weighed five-ten pounds less than his youthful fighting weight. His left jab had been deadly of old; there was no reason to think Chuck would not buckle and drop when it hit him. If not, then the following right uppercut would lift the little skunk out of his shoes. But it was folly to think of such matters as long as the houseguest was armed and he was not.

At this point Bobby entered, using the loping stride his father hated to see in a man who was no longer a teenager.

"Oh," said Bobby, "*here* you all are. Where's Chuck?"

Doug had neither locked nor even closed the door, for he did not want Chuck to arrive without warning, as had happened at the outside entrance to the kitchen, and he had counted on being able to hear the man's footsteps in the long uncarpeted hallway. But here was Bobby, having come silently on tennis shoes. Doug went to look up the hall. It was empty. He closed the door and turned the key.

If Chuck did appear and found himself locked out, retaliation could be expected. Therefore dispatch was essential.

He spoke sternly to his daughter-in-law. "Lydia, kindly tell Bobby how serious the situation is. He won't listen to me."

Grimacing, she complied. "Bobby, Chuck is no good. . . . He's evil, he's —"

Audrey broke in. "Suffice it to say he's not the man we took him for. He swipes things. He takes advantage of our hospitality. . . ."

Bobby smiled without mirth. "You're all three in it now? He's a great guy. I just don't understand why you all want to knock him. And you, of all people, Lyd!"

"Lydia," Doug said, "it isn't my place to tell your husband what must now be told. You'll have to. Go back to the bedroom."

Bobby followed his wife; she closed the door behind them.

"Do we really need this overdramatizing?" Audrey asked. "All that's required is that you simply go to the boy and lay down the law. I thought that's what Lydia was supposed to be doing in the kitchen."

"Don't you yet know that Chuck raped her?"

Audrey bit her lip. She seemed angry. "I wonder if we can believe that."

"Who would make up such a story? Isn't rape the kind of thing women tend to conceal?"

His wife shook her head. Her jaw was stubbornly prominent. "Not when it might give them prestige."

"Something's wrong with you, Audrey." And he knew what it was: she was cold sober.

The bedroom door opened and Bobby emerged. He wore a foolish grin. Looking at neither of his parents, he walked methodically to the door, unlocked and opened it, and left.

After a moment Lydia came out. She spoke to her father-in-law.

"He doesn't believe me," said she. "Can you believe that?"

§ 7 §

The more the rest of the family attacked Chuck Burgoyne, the more sympathetic Bobby found himself to the houseguest. Perhaps Chuck *had* helped himself to certain items that were, speaking legalistically, someone else's property, but if Mother had discovered a towel or two in his luggage, or even an ashtray, the primary question should be as to why she had snooped through the room! Surely it was a shocking breach of hospitality. Given his father's own moral situation, Chuck's was veritably monklike, and a few petty misdemeanors were unlikely to stain it.

Which left the outlandish charges made by Lydia. So far as Bobby was concerned, the whole business came down to this: if Chuck was guilty of raping the woman he had only just saved from drowning, then all of reality as it had been known to date had, with one event, been turned around to be precisely the reverse. Bobby disliked thinking further on this matter, for there could be no evading the possibility that his wife was suffering from a disorder of the mind, so ludicrously incredible had her story been. Were she simply being malicious (and if so, what could be her motive?), she would hardly have neglected to bring into the narrative the pistol, the existence of which was acknowledged. How could rape be accomplished without at least the threat of force? Yet until this moment Lydia had been the most rational person with whom Bobby had ever had personal association. He had now to recognize the possibility that madness might strike anyone without warning and especially in the aftershock of a brush with death. It was to be hoped that this would prove temporary and soon everything would be back to normal, at least with his wife. As to his parents, their aversion to Chuck was to be explained otherwise — and by someone other than him. Meanwhile, amends must be made to the unoffending houseguest, and there was no one left but him to make them.

When he reached the kitchen, Chuck was frying something in a big skillet.

"Making one of your gourmet concoctions?"

Chuck probed the contents of the pan with a long wooden spoon and ignored the question. He could get into a trance when he was preparing food. Bobby envied someone with such concentration and direction.

"Chuck," he said, taking a seat at the kitchen table and addressing the back of the houseguest, who wore his usual clothing while cooking and not the pretentious long apron that males in the movies donned when at the stove or grill, and so deft was he, he apparently never got splashed. "Chuck, I realize now I was at fault in sending you to see Lydia at a time when she had not yet recovered emotionally from the experience in the water. Maybe waking up suddenly like that, she made some kind of confusion of you with the experience of drowning, and you got the blame. Pretty obviously, she was not herself. I've known her for quite a time. We were roommates at least a year before we got married."

Chuck said, over the sound coming from the skillet and without turning, "She's one sweet piece of ass."

Bobby heard this clearly, but he told himself that Chuck had actually, under the noise of the bubbling pan, commended Lydia for her sweetness and "class," and that was worthy of note, for as she had confessed to Bobby, what she had worried about before meeting his parents was whether they were prepared to accept someone of her class into their family. Bobby assured her that nobody in this day and age took that sort of thing seriously. Now, in addition to having saved her life, Chuck was certifying her social position.

"Mighty decent of you to say that —" Bobby hesitated. "Actually she has a very high opinion of you. Just give her a day or so to recover, and you'll see, she'll once again be her old sunny self."

"I want you to move her stuff from your room to mine," Chuck said, stirring the pot. "You get that job nicely done, and I might even give you a bite to eat."

Bobby heard these words as one hears a foreign-language conversation in which one could define the meanings of the individual words but cannot make sense of their roles in the syntax at hand. Therefore he had to fake a response.

"Great! I'm looking forward to dinner. You know, we're all impressed by your culinary prowess. It's certainly improved life around here on the weekends: it's no longer terror time on Mrs. Finch's days off. Best we used to do was eat the leftovers from the Saturday dinners made by the caterer, who's also a Finch incidentally and in fact is one of the cleaning crew that comes Mondays and Fridays.

They must be the ugliest women in this part of the world, which is saying something!" Bobby chuckled and shuffled sidewise towards the door. "Well, I'll get out of your way. I understand gourmet chefs can't stand having people breathing over their shoulder . . ."

Chuck turned partially yet kept his dripping wooden spoon over the pan. He said, "You're virtually an idiot, aren't you? In a poorer family you'd be kept at home and given a little yardwork to do, trimming the edges, raking leaves, et cetera. They wouldn't let you marry and pass on your inferior genes."

Bobby kept smiling, trying to pretend he was not going insane. First, Lydia's statements, now this from Chuck. He had heard of a disease, formerly exotic but nowadays not all that rare, in which the sufferer, always a person hitherto polite to the point of docility, suddenly begins to shout vileness in public places. In his case, he had begun to hear it. And it was getting worse.

He now had the terrible delusion that Chuck had said, "I'm telling you I fucked your wife! What are you doing about it? *Thanking* me?"

Bobby put his hand to his head. "I'm sorry, Chuck. I'm not feeling well. I'm a little dizzy at the moment. I've got to go and lie down. Don't worry: I'm sure I'm okay. I'll be fine by dinner." But Bobby was being politely hypocritical; he really had no faith that he could recover in time, yet it would have been inconsiderate to tell that to the guest in the house, who was obviously enjoying himself at the stove.

"I'll put yours in a doggie bowl," Chuck said merrily. "And make you eat it on all fours."

Bobby believed he was being called on here to laugh, and he did so, if not as heartily as he would have liked, for he felt very faint. He regretted he could not live up to expectations; he was in no condition for hijinks.

"There's always been something wrong with him," Doug was saying.

"Yes," said Audrey. "*You.*"

Lydia kept shaking her head. "I know the truth has always made Bobby uncomfortable," said she. "But that was in little matters. I never expected anything like this."

Audrey cast her a sidelong glance of hatred. "Where may I ask is this thing supposed to have taken place?"

"*Thing?*" asked Doug. "Are you too trying to deny it?"

Lydia continued to be touched by her father-in-law's loyalty to her cause. She would not have expected it, but she had now to rely on it.

Audrey bitterly shrugged or perhaps even shuddered. "It just seems to me that —"

"I was asking for it?" said Lydia. "I thought that was what *men* were supposed to say."

"I don't care who's supposed to do or say what. Things seem to be falling apart in this house, which until recently went along serenely summer after summer."

This was spoken in a manner that could only be called venomous. It was clear whom she blamed for the loss of serenity: not Chuck Burgoyne.

Though resentful, Lydia however understood that so long as the quartet of defenders was distracted by divisive, intestine matters, their cause had no hope of triumphing. This one man would continue to be successful in his campaign to bring them down. Therefore she spoke firmly to her mother-in-law.

"I really love Bobby. You might not understand why, but eventually I hope you'll at least give me the benefit of the doubt. But at the moment we've got a bigger problem than whether I am a suitable member of your family. Maybe I'm not. But right now we've got to deal with the evil man who has taken power here."

Audrey sighed, almost plaintively. On the instant she was more melancholy than angry. "I'm not feeling very well."

Doug went into the bedroom and shortly returned with a silver flask. He unscrewed the cap before delivering the container to his wife.

Her gratitude looked genuine. She tilted face and flask and joined them for a longer moment than expected. On no greater evidence than this episode, which comprised Doug's actions and expression, Lydia identified Audrey as an alcoholic. The information was useful: in an emergency, ignorance of one's comrades is perhaps worse than the destructive traits found amongst them, the worst of which were only human. And so was Chuck. He was mortal as well.

Since at this moment Audrey was licensed to drink openly, she was delighted to taste cognac in the flask. Vodka had to be used for its property of odorlessness, but it was an awfully boring drink day in and out. No one could criticize her for drinking at this juncture, with the house in such peril. . . . Now that the worst of the pressures on her had been relieved, she could at least entertain the thought that Lydia might be more of a friend than an enemy, though she still considered the "rape" as surely exaggerated. Perhaps he had kissed Lydia against her will and done some fondling, but to take a woman carnally without her permission was the work of a street criminal, not a civilized man like Chuck, who was rude and cruel and unscrupulous but hardly a felon. Distinctions must be maintained.

In the next moment came a kind of scratching at the door, and unthinkingly Audrey unlocked and opened it, too late reflecting that it might have been Chuck, though of course if he were armed, he could not long have been kept out.

But it proved to be Bobby, who came in as if limping, though she could not identify which of his limbs was damaged so as to produce that effect.

Bobby spoke to his wife. "I'm sorry, Lyd. I'm sorrier than I can say." Lydia tried to embrace him, but he fended her off. "No, I don't need comforting. I've got to do something. I haven't figured out what, but I've got to."

His father spoke. "I gather you've seen the light."

"Not really until I was halfway back here!" Bobby cried. "Can you believe it? He was humiliating me, and I still thought it was some good-natured joke. I never had an experience like that before. He posed as our *friend!*" Bobby looked pleadingly at his father. "Can't you trust *anybody* these days?"

Audrey was moved by her son's appeal. "He doesn't belong here, that's obvious. He doesn't put *us* in a bad light." Nobody was watching her, so she took another taste of the flask.

"He's in there, making one of his fancy meals," Bobby said. "Now would be the ideal time to jump him, while he's distracted, with his back to the door."

"And wielding that big knife?" asked Doug. "He has the reflexes of a cat, I've noticed. I doubt he could be snuck up on, and if he spun around blade first it could be lethal."

"Rope," said Bobby. "Years ago, in camp, I learned how to lasso things, like a cowboy. If we can find some rope around here . . ."

"But if you miss," said his father, "we'll be in hotter soup than we are now. The essential thing as I see it at this point is to let Chuck assume we're continuing to passively accept his outrages, that we wouldn't dare try to resist. And then when we strike, do it devastatingly, without mercy and with as little risk to ourselves as is humanly possible."

Lydia wore an expression of dubiety. "How much experience does any of us have in dealing with a man like Chuck?"

"And what of the horrible Mr. Tedesco? Could he be lurking somewhere in the vicinity?" Audrey told them of the telephone call. "He sounded no better than a common thug." She was still not quite ready to see Chuck as being as bad as the others characterized him, but she could easily condemn this supposed confederate of his.

"And there's another pal, named Perlmutter," said Doug, "but I somehow don't think these people are in the neighborhood. I would say they're members of his gang in the city, though they might well be on call. When we strike, we must immobilize him quickly and unconditionally. He can't be permitted to send a signal of any kind from this house."

Bobby was exercised. His mother had never seen that side of him, if indeed it had existed before now. "I don't think I can pretend to submit to him!" he said savagely. "It's too soon after I've really *been* doing his bidding. What a goddamn fool I was."

"We can all say the same," Lydia told him.

It seemed a piece of insolence to Audrey that the statement should be so inclusive, but she did sense that the girl's purpose was to give some consolation to Bobby, who was not growing calmer. His mother could do no less than join in.

"We were caught at a disadvantage by our sense of hospitality. A guest has always been sacrosanct under our roof. The mistake, if such it could really be called, was in not finding out more about the man when he first appeared, but we each assumed the other knew him well or he would not have been here in the first place."

"But," said Doug, "do you think for a moment that we'd have been able to find any reliable information about him from himself? In fact, I think that if we had tried we'd have only brought this current situation about sooner."

"But we wouldn't have been so vulnerable during the week, when Mrs. Finch is here every day and the cleaning women come twice." Audrey spoke with indignation, which Doug always and in general had coming even though in this instance he bore no more guilt than anyone else. "He wouldn't have found it so simple then to keep us prisoners."

Lydia gestured. "How we got into this predicament can be examined after we get out of it."

"*If* we do," Audrey said dolefully. Her spirits, so briefly raised by the alcohol, were already falling. It was no secret to her that such was the necessary progress of drinking: the end was ever below the lowest beginning. This reflection normally would have intensified her thirst, but for once she resisted the first impulse, for her daughter-in-law had moved close to her and now took her hand and spoke with seeming sincerity as well as probable conviction.

"We *will*. He's just one man. There are four of us."

Bobby said desperately, "I'm willing to rush him. I don't care about the personal consequences. I've got a score to settle. If he's occupied with getting me, he won't be able to stop the rest of you."

It could have been predicted that Doug would not like

this idea, which made Bobby the obvious hero, even possibly the martyr. He strode about, saying, "No, no, no."

Lydia continued to hold Audrey's hand. "What we don't want is recklessness," said she. "Remember the general who told his troops he didn't want any of them to die for their country? 'The idea is to get the *other* poor sons-of-bitches to die for *their* country.' This should be a communal effort."

But Bobby could not accept an arrangement in which he believed he might be denied personal revenge.

"I'm going to kill him," he said. He addressed Lydia particularly. "I can't accept what he did to me."

She dropped Audrey's hand at last. Now she was angry. "No! No, you're not going to get away with this. He did it to *me,* not you. All he did to you was tell about it."

"That's worse!" cried Bobby. "Because at first I didn't believe it even then. Then he treated me like a dog, and I thanked him. . . ." It seemed as if he might weep at any moment.

Audrey was aware that a man's amour propre was something fixed, whereas a woman's could prove more responsive to changing conditions. But for the first time she was on Lydia's side.

"Bobby," she said to her lone offspring, "everybody is aware of what you've been through, but now is not the time to be selfish. For a while there, Lydia was standing alone —"

"Speak for yourself," Doug said. "*I* was his first victim."

At this point the telephone rang inside its box. The others participated in a symbolic rush towards it, but Doug was closest, and it anyway was his property.

Through the receiver Doug recognized the voice of the man who had called himself Perlmutter, and disregarding what he considered the false placation of the man's most recent remarks (in which, prompted by Chuck, Perlmutter had in effect apologized), he was taken by surprise by the caller's amiable words.

"Doug? Jack. So how's it going, fella? I'm glad it's you and not You-Know-Who — or is he nearby? Can you talk freely? Just say yes or no."

"He's in the kitchen."

"Okay, then," said Perlmutter. "Let me take this opportunity to give you a friendly warning — or can he pick up another extension and listen in?"

"This is my private line."

"In which case I'll speak openly. Just keep your eye on that boy. Don't turn your back on him for a second."

"Mr. Perlmutter, look, I don't want to be rude, but —"

"Please — *Jack*."

But Doug had as yet seen no reason to fraternize. "I don't want to be rude," he doggedly repeated, "but why would you give me, a stranger, such a warning against someone who's apparently a friend of yours?"

"Aha," Perlmutter barked. "Not an unreasonable question. One, he's not my friend: we happened to find ourselves now and again in the same place at the same time, and had the choice of either trying to cooperate or going for each other's throat. Two, I'm trying to make up for that nasty call you got earlier today from someone who used my name. Anyone could do that, of course, and there's not much I can do to stop them. But even though it's irrational, I still feel as if I have a peculiar responsibility to do what I can to atone."

"You're a charlatan, Perlmutter."

"C'mon, now, Dougie, you can't mean that."

"Oh, but I do," said Doug. "You're either a member of Chuck's gang, a co-conspirator in other words, or Chuck himself with an assumed voice. In either case, let me give *you* a warning: you'll be dealt with."

Perlmutter emitted a kind of wail. "What did I do to deserve this vicious attack? You need all the friends you can get. You should learn to be more elastic. So not everybody can live up to your own high moral standards — should he then be discarded?" If one had not known better, one might have been taken in by this protest that was also a plea. Perlmutter concluded, "Everybody's got a little good in him." He paused. "Except your houseguest."

For an instant Doug was tempted to pursue this issue, but as quickly decided against it. First, he really did not wish to get involved in a medieval kind of inquiry into the strife between virtue and vice. And then he was more certain than ever that Perlmutter was a fraud.

"No," said he. "I don't need and I don't want your help." He hung up.

The other members of the family remained silent. Doug sat down in the desk-chair, which Audrey had been using but vacated on his hanging up the telephone. He had been struck by a feeling of intense despair, and had all he could do to suppress an impulse to say, even to scream: *We haven't a chance. We'll none of us get out of this alive.*

"And that Mr. Tedesco I spoke with," said Audrey. "Who can these terrible people be?"

This provoked Doug to rally. He raised his chin. "We shouldn't magnify the power of our enemies and let them be successful in their efforts to scare us. Because that's all, at least at the moment, that Perlmutter and Tedesco have done: just speak on the phone. It seems to me that if they were on the premises somewhere or at a public telephone nearby, we'd have seen them by now. Why should they conceal themselves?"

"Perhaps because it's more terrifying that way," said Lydia. "But I agree with you, all the same." She turned to her husband. "What do you think, Bobby?"

He seemed annoyed at the question and shook his head. "The target is Chuck. I don't want to think about anything else." He lifted his reddened eyes to his father. "You could distract him while I jump him. I'm not afraid. I know I could do it."

"Any hand-to-hand will be done by me," said Doug. "I was the college boxer, after all. And I have stayed in good shape. All it would take is keeping him from his weapons. He's nothing otherwise." He saw from the corner of his eye that his wife had unobtrusively placed the flask at the far end of the desk, having no doubt emptied it. For years she had been always under the influence but was almost never seen to be drunk in the slurred-speech, staggering sense. He believed he was one of the few people in the world who were in possession of this truth about Audrey: to believe it you had to have known what she was like before she drank to excess.

"The telephone works again," she now said quietly. "Let's call the island police and be done with it."

Doug lifted the instrument, listened at it for the briefest instant, and waved it at her before hanging up. "I was prepared for that: he's got it rigged for incoming calls only." He brought his fists together. "All right, let's go get him!"

"Without a real plan?" Lydia asked.

"We've got a plan!" cried Doug. "The rest of you distract him. As soon as that knife is out of his hand for a second, I'll floor him. As soon as he goes down, I'll get the gun from his ankle. Then we're home free."

"I want a crack at him," said Bobby. "I'm not just going to stand there."

"I still like *my* plan," Lydia said stubbornly. "He'd be most helpless then."

Doug remembered that Bobby had not been present when his wife talked of luring Chuck into a bedroom, and it could be assumed that he would hardly concur. Indeed, just hearing of it might drive him over the edge.

"We'll try it my way, right now. We've got to make some progress on this matter."

With no more discussion they started for the kitchen, Doug first, then Bobby and Lydia, with Audrey bringing up the rear.

When Lydia tried to take Bobby's hand he snatched it away. Obviously he did not want to be diverted from his concentration on revenge. She herself had been in a similar state before he became a believer. But now that he had joined the cause so fervently, it had, to a degree, been taken from her — unless, looking for positives, one should see it rather as a liberation. Whichever, her former rage had become something more reasonable. All she wanted now was the subduing and not the destruction of Chuck. She was even beginning, against her will, to consider excuses for his taking her in the act of love. He had genuinely desired her; it was hard to detest him merely for that. Nor had he taken her with force. Misrepresentation was not savagery. False pretenses, while deplorable, were not necessarily felonious. And it should not be forgotten that he *had,* immediately before the event in question, saved her life. Did she not have an obligation to return the favor if Bobby was serious about killing him?

That her husband was intending to commit the supreme act of violence would have been a preposterous thought only a quarter hour earlier, and perhaps even now she was foolish to entertain it: she had never known anyone with so tender a spirit as Bobby's. But he was not given to bluster. More than once she had read that persons who speak often of suicide generally end up committing it. Could the same be true of those who spoke so easily of murder? After all, she and Bobby expected to enter law school. Whatever was done should not be such as to jeopardize their careers.

Her father-in-law was first to enter the kitchen. The doorway was sufficiently wide to admit Lydia and Bobby simultaneously. The table was laid. Chuck stood before the stove, on which at least one vessel was still cooking with visible vapors.

"You must be mind readers," he said pleasantly. "I was just about to call you to dinner. We'll eat in here this evening, if you don't mind. It makes things simpler for me."

Lydia was struck by the word "evening," which proved to be just: she was shocked to identify the waning of light outside the windows. Notwithstanding their predicament, time was playing its habitual role.

Her fears about Bobby turned out to be needless. At the sight of Chuck, the tension had appeared to leave him. In fact he looked almost comatose.

Audrey spoke in a crooning note. "May I help carry something?"

"No," said Chuck. "Sit down, all of you." He gestured not with a knife now but with the big bland paddle-blade of a wooden spoon. He was weaponless. Why didn't the Graves men attack him?

Instead, both Doug and Bobby slunk to the table, which was round and therefore could not inspire considerations as to head and foot and the relative power-values of the places between. Both men took chairs on the far side, given Chuck's situation at the stove. Audrey sat down on the curve near the refrigerator. Lydia remain standing awhile, but having lost all of her allies, she finally abandoned that posture, sitting down, willy-nilly, nearest Chuck. .

The houseguest cheerily took a big pot from the stovetop and went around the table, serving rice to everybody with the wooden spoon. It would have been a subordinate's role to play waiter in the dining room; in the kitchen he who dispensed food was master of those who received it. Lydia could see that her husband and his parents were obviously cowed by this maneuver in their own house.

Having returned the rice pot to the stove, Chuck next claimed another vessel from atop a burner, but this time he served only the plate that was to be his own and that which sat before Lydia. So this was what became of those fragmented lobsters that had been quick though dead! Now their parts had been given a home within a thick sauce in which pieces of tomato were evident.

Doug leaned forward across his rice and said, "I think I was right. *Homard americaine?*"

Chuck nodded. "You used to eat that with Gloria Denton. And then for dessert you'd eat her."

Doug paled and retracted himself.

Lydia waited a moment and then when nobody else had made a sound, she said to Chuck, "We're not going to sit here and take this, you son-of-a-bitch."

The houseguest looked genuinely puzzled. "What's your complaint?" he asked, returning to the stove. "*You're* getting lobster."

Lydia pushed away from the table and leaped up. Doug

apparently interpreted this movement to mean that she was about to attack Chuck singlehanded, and he rose as well. Though Chuck's back was momentarily turned, he could reverse himself much more quickly than her father-in-law could come around the table, and his weapon was a steaming potful of vegetables.

He thrust it in Doug's direction and said, "Sit down."

Having no taste for being scalded, Doug did as told, his morale in disarray. He turned to Audrey and said, almost whimpering, "It isn't true, you know."

"What difference does it make now?" Audrey asked stoically. She picked up a fork and began to trace figures in her plateful of white grains.

"Get going on your rice," Chuck ordered the Graveses. "It's more than many people have to eat this night."

Lydia was still standing. "Oh," said she. "You're a defender of the interests of the deprived?"

With a slotted spoon Chuck was serving a green vegetable to her plate. "Sit down and eat," he said. "When I think of what you could do in bed on an empty stomach, after almost drowning, you must be a marvel when well fed."

Humiliated by this observation, she obeyed him. She was aware that he would use the same moral weapon on her when she tried to resist, and there was no getting away from the fact that it was devilishly effective, more so than would have been a gun or knife, for such crude armament could change hands at any time and so alter the structure of power, but that she had enthusiastically made love with a stranger in her bed would remain true forever, even if she finally expunged the man himself.

At the first sight of Chuck on entering the kitchen, Bobby had instantly returned to reality from the unrestrained fantasies of rage. The houseguest was not going to be overwhelmed by simple frontal assault. He had too many resources, not even counting the gun at his ankle. All manner of edged implements were at hand as well as metal vessels with boiling contents. He was at his most formidable in the kitchen. Therefore, as loathsome as Bobby found it, groveling for a while longer was obviously the only tactic that made sense.

He dug into his plain rice. After all, it *was* food and not the filth that Chuck might very well have made him swallow. But it was awfully dry.

Chuck at the moment was pouring wine for himself. Next he put some in Lydia's glass. Bobby swallowed dolefully, hoping his parched throat would make a sound. Chuck would hardly be moved by such an appeal to compassion, but Lydia could not decently fail to respond.

It seemed, however, that she was unaware of his presence. He began to develop a case against his wife: she could not evade all responsibility for exciting Chuck's lust. And what of his father's blustering insistence on leading the attack on the houseguest? The man of action! The college boxer! The notorious lecher had proved, as might have been expected, to have no courage at all. Whereas Bobby was merely pretending to be a coward while waiting for the moment to strike. That was the difference between them, and it was profound. Underneath it all, Bobby was the man, and their only hope of salvation.

"Bobby," said his mother, as if all were normal, "Bobby, may I have the salt and pepper?"

Reluctant to act without permission and so bring Chuck's wrath down upon him before he was in a position to act decisively, Bobby looked at the houseguest.

Chuck grimaced and said, "That won't be necessary."

Bobby shrugged at his mother and went back to eating his own tasteless rice and watching for a visible weakness in Chuck's defenses.

"I wasn't criticizing the food," his mother obsequiously told Chuck. "It's just a nervous habit."

But the attention of the houseguest was on Lydia. "You aren't eating."

"I'm not hungry."

"You're hurting my feelings," Chuck said. "If you reject my food I at least deserve a reason."

Lydia wore a ghastly sort of grin. "You're really a prize," said she. "You weren't even invited to come here, as it turns out. You aren't *anybody's* friend! And yet you take over as if you own the place and the rest of us are outsiders. And then you want to be congratulated!"

Chuck grinned too, though in his case with apparent self-satisfaction. "I'll say this: it was like knocking overripe fruit off a tree. It is *too* easy. I wish I could get a challenge out of somebody, but they're such worms. Let me demonstrate." He stepped to the counter and found the big chef's knife. He went around the table to a point midway between Doug and Bobby.

"Gentlemen," said he, extending the knife across his left forearm, point reversed, handle forward, steadying it with his right hand at the center of the blade. "Help yourself to a sword."

Bobby had no intention of participating in this stunt, which was surely a trick. He raised his hands in backing-off pantomine.

His father said indignantly, "I'm not some dirty scum from the gutter! I don't fight with knives."

"You don't *fight*," said Chuck. He looked at Lydia. "Q.E.D."

"But you don't dare make me the same offer," Lydia said.

"Hell no. You'd cut me in a minute. I know that. We *are* the scum of the gutter, you and I." He guffawed. "That's why *we're* eating the lobster!" He raised his hands against her protest. "All right, so you think you're a lady. I mean *underneath it all.*"

Bobby hated Chuck, but he still thought him brilliant: there was something to be said for this theory. Bobby himself had been attracted to Lydia by what he had always seen as her charter membership in a commonality to which he could never quite belong and with which the best he could manage was an accommodation always to his disadvantage.

As the houseguest was passing her, Bobby's mother suddenly shoved her chair back against him. Taken by surprise, Chuck temporarily lost his balance, and in recovering it he dropped the knife to the tile floor. It slid to her feet, and she picked it up.

Though he had only just refused the knife when it was offered to him, Bobby believed that the moment for action had now arrived, for Chuck could not have included contingency plans for this misadventure. He sprang up and started around the table.

8

Doug too seized this opportunity to charge the houseguest, leaping from his chair just as Bobby was coming around him, and they were first entangled in each other and next were carried by momentum into Audrey, whose grip on the chef's knife was tenuous. Reclaiming his equilibrium, Chuck deftly stepped in and did not so much take the knife from her as relieve her of its weight.

If Chuck had lost any emotional balance, he had regained it so quickly as not to suggest even a momentary loss. He placed the knife on the lip of the sink and, with a positive lilt in his voice, saying, "Let's eat this dinner," sat down at his place.

Lydia was disgusted with the Graveses for so botching their best and perhaps only advantage, but she was also fair enough to admit that she herself had not even tried though she had been as close to the action as Doug and much closer than Bobby.

But Chuck was unarmed now, seated and eating with keen appetite, and yet neither male Graves made a move towards him. Perhaps the three of them were playing fixed roles in a ritual of virility that she was not supposed to understand, let alone interfere in: an example of the master-slave arrangement that some said was fundamental to the homosexual experience. In any event, it was insultingly obvious that no one expected anything of her: she had been morally excluded. She suddenly became aware of the longing gaze that Audrey was directing towards her wineglass, and would have offered it to her mother-in-law had Chuck not been sitting between them — but in so thinking she was being as pusillanimous as her men.

She made a violent effort to regain self-respect. "All right, Chuck," she said, "we *are* the same kind, you and I, birds of a feather. We've had to fight all our lives just to hang on, whereas these people have had it all handed to them. Why should we show them any mercy?"

But while she was aware that the Graveses had been thrown into a state of shock by this speech, Chuck was not impressed by it. He continued eating in silence for a while; then he raised a fork and stabbed the air between them.

"Where's your judgment?" he asked. "Did you really think I'd be taken in by a simulated change of heart — coming as it does just after the utter collapse of the only opportunity they have had, or will ever have? You've just given up on them, have decided to throw in with me for purely negative reasons. But don't you think I'm smart enough to know you'd just be waiting for me to show the slightest weakness?" He lowered the fork. "By now you'll have to do better than that. It's gone on too long. You could have joined up at the outset. Now you'll have to prove yourself to gain admittance."

So she had thoroughly compromised herself with all parties while having the highest motives. It was necessary to act decisively now or be lost forever.

She seized the wine bottle by its neck and swung it at Chuck's head as hard as she could. His flinch did not begin until the bottle was too close to avoid. The impact was soundless and more awful thereby: a man could be killed with no more noise than that? As he was in the (for some reason) extremely slow process of slumping in the chair, his body having (nonsensically) gone rigid before his head had (improbably) fallen to the left shoulder, in the direction from which he had been struck — she had never before sapped a human being — while watching all of this she yet was careful to return the wine bottle, contents intact, to an upright situation on the table.

For a long moment no Graves made any response whatever. Had an observer, or a camera, been looking only at *them* during this episode, no emotion would have been seen to register on any countenance. Or so it seemed to Lydia, who of course had been mostly watching Chuck.

Finally Doug asked, "Was it necessary to go that far?"

"With the phone off," said Audrey, "we can't call an ambulance. And the cars aren't in running condition."

"And who's responsible for that?" Lydia screamed. But underneath it all she was already frightened by her own sympathetic feelings for the fellow man that had been downed, even though when up he had been an enemy.

Bobby was the only one to rise. He came to stand over Chuck.

"A goner," said he, showing his teeth in an emotion that was hard to identify with certainty but might have been a grin of terror.

"What," asked Doug, remaining in his chair, "became of our idea to take him prisoner?"

Audrey was performing a series of shrugs. "We've got

Band-Aids and cotton, I suppose, but what first aid can mend a broken skull?"

Lydia was being seriously threatened with panic now. She held it at bay by attacking her in-laws.

"Cowards! You talk violently but do nothing, and then when someone else finally acts, you condemn her. You're worthless. Go to hell!"

But she was immediately taken aback by Doug's reversal. "She's got a point," he said. He left his chair and walked in the direction of Chuck. He stopped when he reached Audrey and put a hand on her shoulder. "We're all involved, willy-nilly, under the circumstances. In for a penny, in for a pound. We'll have to dispose of the body."

Bobby seemed relieved to have a task to discuss. "He's just a little runt," he said. "He won't be hard to carry, and we'll only have to do it as far as the edge of the bluff, where he can be rolled off. Then we'll go down and push him into the water. The undertow will take over from there."

Lydia was supersensitive to this reference. "Oh, no!"

Audrey's face was in her hands. She began to make a distant moaning sound but took it no further as she offered a suggestion of her own, one that might be called poetic. "There's a little grove of paper birch just off the lane . . ."

Bobby produced a *chok-chok* noise with tongue and teeth. "We'd better get going while there's still some light outside." He slid his hands into Chuck's armpits and heaved. The inert body did not move. Bobby grunted, adjusted the angle of his hands and shoulder, and braced his legs in another way. "He's heavier than I thought." He tried again and more strenuously, his face coloring and neck tendons in evidence, but had no success. He straightened himself.

"I can't believe this. I can't budge him. Dad?"

It was unclear whether this was an appeal for help or a rhetorical question. Doug showed no hesitation in taking it for the latter, and came no closer. "It may turn out to be necessary to get a board of some kind, or a big thick branch, to serve as a lever." His brows came together over his nose, as if he were thinking of even more sophisticated measures by which to move the body.

Lydia went to the sink and vomited for the second time that day. But she had eaten nothing since the first session and therefore was not relieved of any burden while her throat was once again made sore. What an outrage that it was possible for a person of her character to become a murderess merely by trying to protect her existing interests — that is, with no hope of illicit gain or any other criminal motive.

Bobby said, "We might just leave him in the chair and slide it out the — no, we'd have to lift it when we got outside, wouldn't we?" He sighed heavily. "What a pain in the neck! If anybody told me I'd be doing this on Sunday evening . . . !"

"If a ghoulish joke was needed," said Doug, "I might say that big knife's handy for making a large package into many small ones." He did not accompany this with a laugh, but Bobby chuckled hollowly while backing away from the body as if avoiding temptation.

Lydia returned. "Look," she said, "I'm sorry. I didn't know what else to do. I'll take full responsibility if trouble comes from this. None of you were implicated. I'll make that clear." She stared at each of them in turn. "I saw the chance and took it. I guess I'll regret that the rest of my life."

Bobby said, "Okay, Lyd, but we've got a problem here that goes beyond ego."

Doug looked at his son with apparent respect. "Bob's right. Any connection with this will stain us if it gets known outside this house. We *must* dispose of the body so that it can never be found. Now, that might sound like a simple, straightforward job, considering that we're surrounded on three sides by dense woods and are facing an ocean, but I haven't as yet heard of a method of burial that is one hundred percent secure against discovery. We'll have to settle therefore on the least likely to fail quickly. Now, the undertow is attractive insofar as it will take all labor out of our hands once we get the body into the water — no grave need be dug." He smiled. "But that same current that taketh away is quite capable of bringing back what it took. It will require hard physical labor. A grave must not only be deep but every grain of extra earth should be taken away from the site and pine needles and other normal forest-floor debris placed carefully over the area, but not so obviously as to call special attention to it. This will need some artistry. Audrey can advise us on the landscaping." He smiled encouragingly in her direction, but his wife was seemingly preoccupied, eyes fixed on the plateful of rice before her.

Bobby was shaking his head. "It seems that no sooner does someone hide a body in a woods than kids suddenly start playing ball nearby and soon enough one of them hits the ball into the trees, where it inevitably rolls up to the very toe of the corpse."

"You haven't listened to a word I said," his father observed, more in melancholy disappointment than in anger. "In the first place, there's no meadow or clearing where ball could be played until you're on the other side of the island. Then did I not say a deep grave? There'd be no exposed toe for a ball to roll up to."

"Animals," said Bobby, "wild or domestic, have keen noses which can smell a decomposing body through tons of earth."

"So big rocks are rolled into the grave," said Doug, in a tone that suggested his patience was thinning at last.

Audrey raised her placid face. "Fire," said she.

"Oh," said Doug, "that's the worst, absolutely the worst idea of all."

"It's the best." She was serenely stubborn. "Don't you see? It takes care of everything at once."

"Now, just let me explain why it's *not* good. The furnace here only burns oil: there's no provision in it for burning anything other than fuel oil, no place to *put* anything else. And I trust not even you would suggest one of the fireplaces. What does that leave, a forest fire?" He had not looked at Lydia for a while, but he did so now, showing his derisive smirk.

"You're not getting the point," Lydia told him. "Audrey means burn down the entire house, leaving Chuck's body inside. Don't you, Audrey?" Her mother-in-law did not appear grateful for the elucidation of her plan: perhaps she had wanted to withhold it temporarily, provoking more exasperation. As it was she ignored Lydia and stared silently at her husband.

"Are you serious?" Doug asked, dividing his glances between Lydia and Audrey, so that the former anyway could not decide who was being addressed.

Audrey finally spoke. "Mrs. Finch, the cleaning gang, Tedesco, and Perlmutter knew that Chuck was staying here — to name only those we can be sure about. There may be others. The most certain way to call unwelcome attention to us would be to have him disappear completely."

"But to burn down our house!" Doug cried. "That would make big news here and certainly get back to the city among our friends and relatives. And if a *body* were found in the ashes, it would certainly be picked up by the city media: Sunday's a traditionally thin news day in world events. My family is not unknown in this part of the world. Nor is your own, for that matter."

Bobby said, "We'd have to identify Chuck, and who might not hear about it when it hit the news? We'd be targets for *his* friends and family, if any."

"I was just getting to that," his father noted jealously. "Can you imagine the lawsuits? Or worse, the possible pathologic individuals who might seek revenge for its own sake?"

"It's clear, then, that there is no answer to your problem. Fortunately for you, the problem does not exist."

These words were spoken by Chuck, for he was not dead. As he briskly straightened up in the chair, it seemed unlikely that he had even been hurt.

Lydia's relief was almost immediately replaced by cha-grin. The bottle had made so little noise in striking him because it had hardly struck him. The episode had been the kind of movie-illusion used by stuntmen in on-screen fights. From the viewer's angle the punches find their targets, whereas really they only just miss. She was therefore not a murderess or even a true assailant. On the other hand, she was back with ineffectuality, and Chuck was in a stronger situation than ever to demand com-pliance from his captives.

To the credit of all of those on the Graves side, no one even feinted in the direction of pretending that the ruthless-sounding speculations as to how to dispose of the corpse had not been serious. Both Doug and Bobby silently and promptly returned to their seats. It was Audrey who spoke.

"We were only doing what we had to. You can't blame us for that."

"You're wrong," said Chuck. "I'm your guest. I can blame you for everything. That's the beauty of being in my position, you see. And by 'everything,' I mean either failures or successes, as unlikely as it would be that you'd have any of the latter. You people give a new meaning to the word 'inept.' For example, why didn't it occur to someone to take my pulse?"

Lydia said, almost involuntarily, "I guess we were too eager to believe we had gotten rid of you!"

The houseguest lowered his eyes briefly. When he brought them up, anyone seeing him for the first time would surely have believed him a man of guileless virtue. "You'll say anything to me, won't you? I'm supposed to have no feelings that can be hurt. Only *you* are sensitive, isn't that it? You don't eat my food, you insult me to my face, but why not? I'm not a member of your select little crowd. I'm not good enough for your courtesy. My room isn't even in the main house, but rather out there in that godforsaken garage." His face displayed what for all the world looked like genuine bitter indignation. "Let me ask you: who was your darky before I showed up?"

This outrageous speech seemed to have no effect whatever on her in-laws, but Lydia was provoked by it. "You're actually pretending to be *our* victim?"

Chuck shrugged. "Did *I* just hit any of *you* in the head with lethal intent? Then sit here at the dinner table, the meal going cold, and callously discuss how to get rid of the body?"

"I didn't try to kill you," Lydia protested. "My God, I

never before hit anyone with a bottle. I did it without thinking, because I was desperate. It was really not even personal." She was beginning to despise herself for this pleading, but she could not stop. "It was just to get out of an impossible situation."

Chuck raised his brow. "I suppose it never even occurred to you simply to ask me to leave? Wouldn't that be worth trying before you resorted to murder? You're more depraved than I thought. Human life means so little?" He shook his head, took up knife and fork, and began to eat. But hardly had he tasted the first mouthful when he spat the food back onto his plate. "It's cold now," he said petulantly. "See what you've done? You people aren't civilized."

Audrey seemed peculiarly stung by this comment. "Oh," said she, "but *you* are? *You?* You shouldn't even be here. You weren't invited, and nobody knows you. We would be well within our rights to ask you to leave. I agree that murder may not be the right answer, but you have certainly tried our patience."

The houseguest pushed away from the table. "Isn't that nice?" he asked. "Try to kill me and then excuse yourselves with sophistic reasons. I haven't laid a hostile hand on anyone in this house. You people really stink." He abruptly stood up. "Now clean up this kitchen! You've got fifteen minutes. That's more than enough time for the four of you." He strode out the passage to the dining room. His soft-soled shoes made little sound, and one could not be sure whether he had continued on or had stopped and was lurking within earshot.

Lydia therefore put her finger against her lips in the hush-hush signal, but Bobby perversely chose to disregard it and speak in a louder voice than normal.

"Wow," said he. "How hopeless can we get!"

Doug scowled at his son. "None of that defeatist talk. We've had a few setbacks, that's true, but nothing more. This thing is far from being in the final innings." He looked at Lydia. "Better leave the strong-arm stuff to me in the future."

"It's just that I had the opportunity," she said, her eye on the doorway through which Chuck had departed.

Doug nodded. "I'm not criticizing you. But whether or not you have the physical strength to pull off a trick like that, you are unlikely to have the psychic fortitude — unless you happen to be awfully unnatural." He grinned quickly so as to dispose of that possibility. "You're no killer."

"But I didn't even want to hurt him!"

"Well, now you're flirting with incredulity," said her father-in-law. "You don't hit someone in the head with a bottle —"

"I wanted him to let us alone! I admit it wasn't well thought out."

"Well, we've got our orders," said Audrey, rising and beginning to clear the table. With a little toss of her well-groomed head, she added, "I'm just relieved I didn't have to eat this terrible dry rice. That's the one good thing that came of this matter."

"Just a moment," Lydia said. "Can you tell me one good reason why we should do as he says?"

"Now don't start that," Bobby said urgently. "We don't want to get in worse trouble than we're already in. From now on we can't afford any more of this impulsive indulgence of our emotions."

In annoyance Lydia addressed the doorway. "Are you taking notes, Chuck?" To Bobby she said sourly, "He's listening to all of this, you know."

But Bobby winced and made violent gestures. Only now did it occur to her that perhaps he had, all this while, been speaking disingenuously, that it had been she who had not understood that what *he* said, at least, was for Chuck's benefit. She nodded vigorously, but the gesture seemed only to irritate him.

"I envy you, Lyd," said he, shaking his chin. "I wish I could share your amusement, but I'm really scared. We keep getting deeper in this trouble, like quicksand, the more we struggle to get out of it. Maybe we should just give up all resistance and accept the situation. Chuck may tend toward the tyrannical, but what can he do if we simply say, 'Okay, you win. From now on we'll do our best to carry out your commands. You're a reasonable man. You have attained your goal. What can we do to help you enjoy the fruits of your victory?' "

Unless this was hypocrisy with the purpose of deceiving the listening houseguest, it was contemptible. In either case Lydia felt she had no option but to assist Audrey in clearing the table. She scraped the contents of her own plate and Chuck's into the pedal can that was revealed by opening the under-sink cabinet door. As she carried the plates towards the dishwasher, she saw through the back-of-counter windows that parallel headlight beams had penetrated the now established darkness of the parking area. Above the clatter being made by the others, no engine sound could be heard, and the silence of this event, and the slow speed with which it was conducted, suggested the sinister rather than the arrival of aid. Were Chuck's confederates now joining him?

To Doug she said, "God! Look here."

Doug arrived at the window just as the door of the vehicle opened and its interior was illuminated. He recognized, from the wide-brimmed hat, Lyman Finch, who though dressing like a sheriff was rather the police chief and indeed, except for a couple of part-timers, the entire force on the island, where crime had never been a major problem.

"The cops are here!" he said. "Our bacon is saved!" He chose to be jocular because now that the danger was at an end it seemed in retrospect to have been negligible. He was almost embarrassed to have played a part in the exaggeration of the possible menaces provided by Chuck Burgoyne. Thus by the time Finch, a large, ponderous figure, had lumbered to the kitchen door, Doug was on the verge of levity.

"Lyman!" he cried, flinging the door open. "What brings you to our humble abode?" He had known the man since they both were boys. Lyman in fact had as a teenager worked for an uncle whom Doug's father hired for some-time landscape work: large chunks of stone were to be relocated on the property, requiring oxlike labor per-formed mostly by the brawny lad, who had since those days put on an additional fifty pounds of belly and jowl.

Finch stayed on the outside step. "Phone trouble?"

Doug sighed. "In fact, yes, we do have. We —"

"Lots of people do, all over the island," said Finch. "They's working on it. You have a emergency, you send up a flare. We'll be right on ya."

"Flare?"

"Get a gun off one of your tubs."

It seemed incredible to Doug that on a small island with only a few other families as prominent as his, Lyman could be unaware that he had never personally used a boat since childhood. He decided momentarily to put aside the matter of flares. "Come on in, Lyman. Have a cup of coffee."

Lyman stubbornly lingered where he was. "Sour stom-ach," said he. "But if you got gin?"

"Please come in," said Doug. "I mentioned coffee because I thought you might be on duty." He realized it sounded like a criticism and would have regretted making it had not Finch's reaction been anything but indignant.

"Oh, I am. But I got a hollow leg. It don't have no effect on me." Having said which the chief lurched into the kitchen and staggered to the table. He seized the back of a free chair and hurled the seat under his bulk, which was further widened by the accessory-belt below the knitted waistband of his jacket, a quilted, high-gloss garment in dark green with no insignia in evidence (so that, as with the unmarked jeep, he could use it in off-duty, civilian hours). The wide-brimmed hat, however, displayed a dead-centered bright chromium badge of office.

"Hyah," he said indiscriminately to Bobby and the women. It was obvious that the man was drunk. Staring at Lydia, he asked, not unkindly, "And who might you be, sister?"

Doug had no option but to play along at least for the moment.

Bobby's face was contorted. "What's going on here? Aren't you going to tell him —"

Doug cut him off. "Come on, we'll find the gin together." He took his son by the elbow and more or less forcibly conveyed him from the room into the butler's pantry in the passage to the dining room. Chuck had last been seen there, but he was gone now.

Bobby broke away and petulantly opened the cabinet above the wet bar. "Here's the damned gin."

"Lower your voice," said Doug. "Look, that fat bastard is already stinking drunk. He'd be no match for Chuck. He's a stupid hayseed even when sober. I think our best hope is to get him even drunker, till he passes out, and then I'll take his gun."

Bobby wore a quizzical scowl. "Are we back to the idea of killing Chuck?"

"No need for that now. We'll have a weapon of our own, and transportation."

"So we'll run?"

"Unless I miss my guess, once Chuck sees that I am armed, and with a working vehicle as well, he'll pull in his horns, maybe even become downright submissive. We'll load him into Lyman's jeep, haul him out some miles down the highway, and leave him there. Oh, of course we'll take his own gun away."

"That's it?" Bobby asked in apparent outrage, gesturing with the gin bottle. "You're not even going to have him arrested?"

"For what? To my knowledge he hasn't committed an identifiable crime." Doug grimaced. "In fact, Lydia assaulted *him*. He could make trouble on that matter, if he wanted to."

Bobby lowered his face. As a child he had had positively golden locks, to maintain which he would by now have had to resort to artificial means, and therefore his head looked somewhat dingy. He had none of the Graves features: the strong nose, firm chin, nut-brown extra-fine hair. "You're taking his side now?"

"Don't be foolish. I'm trying to speak of what's possible. I am after all a member of the legal profession. I am obliged to be rational. I assure you that Chuck has yet to break the law — even in the case of the sweaters your mother asserts he removed from her room. Until he takes them from the premises, he really has not committed theft." He accepted the bottle of gin from his son. "This thing superficially seems simple: an intruder has invaded our domicile and therefore all right is on our side. Not so! It isn't a matter of justice."

Seemingly stunned by this information, Bobby lingered behind as Doug returned to the kitchen, where Lyman's sweaty, red-faced grin was fixed on Lydia.

"— believe it," the chief was saying. "I've lived in the country all my life, and I never before seen that kind of stuff you city folk call fun. By God I don't mind telling you I got real mad when right up there on the big screen out in what used to be a field of rye, where you could see it all up and down the county road, there was this girl taking it up the rear end from a little skinny sumbitch, but he had one on him you wouldn't believe." He simulated the colossal member in reference by extending his right forearm and forming a fist at its end, measuring it with a left hand bladed into the crease of the elbow. "My littlest was in the car at the time, we's coming back late from the mother-in-law's, over Grampton, and she wakes up and looks out and says, 'Oooh, what's that man doing to her heinie?' "

Doug shuddered. "Here's your gin, Lyman."

The chief snatched the bottle away and glared at him. "Wasn't for you city people, they wouldn't try to put a porn drive-in out here, and you know it." His leer quickly toured Lydia's body. "But I ain't got nothing against good clean sex. I like it. I like it a *whole* lot."

This was hardly the time to remind Lyman that a cousin of his, another Finch, owned the drive-in movie, which was patronized almost totally by locals and never summer people.

"Chief," Lydia said, "what's the punishment for rape in this part of the world?"

"That's a theoretical question, Lyman," Doug said quickly. "I'm sure the crime itself is rare on the island."

The chief lifted the bottle and sucked at its mouth: but then he had not been furnished with a glass. When he brought the vessel down he inspected the label. "Is this imported? Or did you take a leak in it before handing it to me?" The question, if a joke, was nevertheless put without evidence of humor or even good feeling.

"Rape?" he said then. "I'll tell you who commits it around here: the womenfolk." He winked at Lydia.

"Well, does that answer your question, Lydia?" Doug had moved into a position back of the chief, so that he could indicate, with violent grimaces, that she should abandon the inquiry.

But she ignored him and continued to address Lyman. "I assure you I am being serious, and I'll thank you to answer me with respect."

Couldn't she see that her tone was the worst to use with a brute like Lyman Finch?

Doug shouted, "Hey, I forgot the ice!" and made as much commotion as he could in going to the refrigerator.

But behind him Lyman said, "You didn't bring me a glass, neither. You figured the likes of me wouldn't drink from a glass, right? We're all shit to you, ain't we?"

Doug turned and said, "No, that isn't the case at all, Lyman. We've been friends for what? Thirty-forty years?" He tried to inject some false warmth into this phrasing, and spoke to Bobby, "Lyman and I knew each other as boys."

"I always wanted to whip his ass," the chief told Lydia. "But they wouldn't let me, not even when he tried to fuck my little sister. She was doin' maid work for them, cleanin' their toilets, and she was only fourteen years of age."

The facts were that at that time Roberta Finch was at least three years older and it was she who had propositioned Doug, successfully, and displayed a good deal more sexual technique than he, seventeen himself and already experienced with "bad" city girls and professional whores, had yet to encounter. When questioned on this, Roberta alluded to home study, as the only sister in a family of boys. It was even likely that her father had had at her, given the appearance of her mother.

"Come on, Lyman," Doug protested, though of course he could not dare to give his real defense. "We were all just kids in those days."

The chief continued to direct his words to Lydia. "What really got Bertie was he offered her fifty cents! Mr. Lottabucks here. A half dollar for her cherry." He swigged more gin from the bottle and banged it down. Suddenly he threw back his head and emitted a bellow of laughter. "Shit, she might of taken it, if it had been seventy-five!"

Audrey had been silent till this moment. Now she rose in her place. "You disgusting, squalid man. Get out of this house."

As if more conflict were needed! Doug began to gesture ineffectually, but could find nothing to say. It was the women who had brought about this latest debacle, damn them.

But a remarkable thing happened in the next moment. The chief removed the campaign hat he had been wearing since he entered the kitchen. He surveyed the tabletop and then slid his chair back so as to accommodate the high-crowned hat on his lap. A dank lock of hair clung to his very pale bald spot.

He glanced sheepishly at Audrey. "I beg your pardon, ma'am. I got a bug yesterday and am on medication." He nodded at the bottle. "This here is all I had to drink I swear. I been running off at the mouth, I know. I'm really sorry."

Doug was relieved but also embarrassed. "Bobby, get some glasses. Why don't we all have a nice drink at this point?" In making this suggestion he was thinking mostly of Audrey: no doubt much of her indignation towards Lyman Finch was due to his having exclusive possession of the bottle.

But Audrey said, "No! This man must leave immediately. We've been imposed on too much today." She was displaying an authority that her husband had never before seen in her.

Saying, "Yes, ma'am," Lyman got to his feet, holding his shield-bearing hat flat against his crotch. "I didn't mean no harm."

But his hostess would not relinquish her advantage. "Sure you did," she said. "You're full of resentment, and you'll take it out on anybody who will put up with it. Go out and give someone a speeding ticket, and let us alone. We're what we are."

"Just a minute," said Lydia, rising to her feet. She was speaking to Audrey. "Don't let him go!" To Lyman she said, "We've got a problem, officer. We're trapped here. It might not look like it, but we're actually prisoners. We need your help. We're being terrorized. . . ."

She was exaggerating outlandishly, and Doug would have jumped in to dampen or deflect the worst of this crazy stuff, which if it became public knowledge through Lyman, who was surely the typical Finch gossip, the Graveses would be derided all over the island and perhaps all the way back to the city. *Did you hear this? How some drifter, a little nobody, just walked in and took charge?*

Doug would surely have acted had Chuck Burgoyne not strolled in at this moment, saying, "Hi, Lyman."

The chief turned and, when he saw who it was, stopped cringing. "Charley! I didn't know you was still here."

"Where else would I be?" asked Chuck, with the warmest of smiles for all. "This place suits me. I'm staying permanently. I hope you're not leaving right now, Lyman. Let's have a drink!"

Lyman put his hat on his head and returned to the table.

Doug asked, incredulously, "You know each other?"

"We're cousins," said Chuck. He made a shooing motion. "And we want some privacy. You all get out of here and go to bed, chop-chop."

Lyman stared at Doug for an instant and then guffawed. "By God, you got 'em trained, Charley." He winked. "That include the little chippie?"

Chuck returned the wink. "What do you think, Lyman?"

Obviously, new plans had to be made now. Even Lydia seemed to agree. At least she did not launch an attack on the cousins, but decorously left the kitchen with the rest of the family.

§ 9 §

"Now what?" asked Bobby. They were back again in his father's quarters, demoralized. "Who could know that the law would be on his side?"

"Not the law, Bobby, just the police chief. There's an important difference that is basic to our form of government." He shook his head. "All the same, it *is* discouraging. I've despised the Finches all my life, but they're local yokels. I would never have thought the likes of Chuck would have a connection with them. At least he's civilized."

Bobby's mother snorted, and his father added, irritably, "You know what I mean: he eats with a knife and fork, et cetera."

Lydia was frowning. Bobby disliked seeing that vertical line appear between her eyebrows. She asked, "These people who run the everyday affairs of the island, they hate you?"

Bobby's mother shrugged. "Well," said she. "You know how it goes."

"No," Lydia said stubbornly. "Don't people like you furnish their livelihood?"

Bobby suddenly got the point, but it seemed that Lydia did not.

"The fact is," said Bobby's father, "we now have to arrange a new strategy. We can't expect much help from the usual agency to which a citizen applies in a crisis."

Bobby's mother said, "I have always respected Mrs. Finch. I can't say I have ever been actually fond of her, as one is sometimes fond of people who work for you, but then why should that always be the case? Common decency would seem to be all that's called for, and she certainly got that from me. I haven't ever lorded it over her, for heaven's sake." She sighed. "I am aware that she's from the same family, but it's not necessary that she be part of this thing."

Bobby said, "Mother's idea of burning the house down begins to make sense."

"Oh, come *on,*" said his father.

"Well, didn't you hear Chuck say he has decided to stay here forever? And we couldn't even get rid of him *before* we knew he was related to the police chief."

"If they *are* all in it together," said his mother, who was essentially talking to herself, "then tomorrow will get worse. Mrs. Finch *plus* the cleaning crew."

Lydia spoke sternly. "Then we have to handle it as soon as possible. How much more that fat cop can drink without falling in his face is in doubt. I think we could take them in the kitchen. Chuck's the more dangerous. Luckily he's seated with his back to the outside door. I'm willing to go out and around the house to that door, and on a prearranged signal I'll burst in and slug him with something, a good solid hit this time, while you, Doug, and Bobby come in through the butler's pantry and take the chief from behind."

Bobby's father asked irritably, "And then what do we *do* with them?" She made a fist. "We have to get *everything* settled before we start *anything,* including every eventuality that could possibly occur, such as what happens if Lyman's not as drunk as we think or even, if so, can still handle himself effectively. He's awfully fat, remember, and that means he can hold more alcohol than most." He made his voice gentle and said to Lydia, "With all respect, do you really have the nerve to hit Chuck hard enough to knock him out?"

For an instant she looked as though she might flare up in anger, but she said slowly, "You're right. Look what happened last time."

The idea came to Bobby from nowhere. "The drapes and blinds and all," said he. "All those cords." He pointed at the window that now was a framed view of the black of night woods. Its venetian blind was in a tight furl, and therefore most of the cord hung free.

"All right," said his father. "We take them by surprise and we tie them up. So far so good. Then what?"

Lydia groaned. "It keeps coming back to the same question, which nobody can answer. And now you can't haul Chuck somewhere out on the highway and abandon him, because what can be done with Lyman?"

"Actually, that idea came from what the rangers do with troublesome bears in the national parks," said Bobby's father. "It probably wouldn't work with human beings, anyway." His eyes widened. "The state police! There's a barracks on the mainland, about a mile from the ferry pier. They'd be free of the Finch connection."

Lydia's face was showing the effects of her ordeal. Bobby's wife had been in the forefront of all the action of the day. She was that kind of person. He was pleased with himself for having found her, though it had actually been the other way around: she had first spoken to him, in the university library, offering her help when he displayed his understandable confusion in filling out the call slip for a certain reference book. He had all too seldom done that sort of thing in three years of college. He was no scholar and never pretended to be. What he was, was a good fellow. He had no malice in him, which meant he was at a terrible disadvantage when dealing with a man like Chuck. His mind simply didn't work that way.

Therefore when he spoke now, it was in the spirit of make-believe. "I just can't see any way to deal with Chuck except to do him in. It keeps coming back to that. Because even if we were able to reach the state police, what could we get them to do? What would we charge Chuck with? We know he's a criminal, but it would be hard to explain to anyone else."

"Carrying a concealed lethal weapon," said his father. "At least. And that's a felony. . . . Of course, if he's Lyman's cousin he probably already has a license to carry a gun on the island, or if he hasn't now, Lyman could easily fix him up with one, make him a deputy. Maybe he's already been deputized. That would account for his arrogance." He stared at his wife. "Do you realize what this is beginning to sound like? That the Finches are making their big move. After all these years! For example, Lyman said the phone service is off all over the island, not just here. Maybe there's a Chuck in everybody's house: we all use the Finches for everything."

Lydia protested to Bobby. "You just can't speak of Chuck now as if dealing with him alone will solve anything. Whether or not your father's right in seeing this as some sort of peasant uprising —"

His father snorted. "Some peasants! They own a lot more than I do. They might be clods, but old Ronnie

Finch, Lyman's uncle, who must be eighty but still does all the local landscaping, pays cash for the heavy machinery he buys. They could buy and sell *me*, that's certain."

"All right," said Lydia, "but my point remains: with Lyman's appearance Chuck has got at least a temporary reprieve from anything really extreme, though I'll admit that anything less probably wouldn't be effective."

"There you are," said Bobby.

His father was still occupied with the Finches' holdings. "Do you realize they own miles of undeveloped shoreline property? It's not for sale either, at least not at the moment. But when the time comes, and the price is right, they'll sell it to the most vulgar entrepreneur. We'll have condominiums and marinas and shopping malls full of overweight teenagers and gaudily dressed people wearing eyeglasses. Supermarkets and soft-drink machines and discount drugstores. Not just Chuck — if only we could exterminate the whole tribe!"

The passion of this speech brought Bobby back to reality for the moment. It was likely that Lydia had relatives, perhaps even immediate, to whom such a commercial vision would have been very attractive. After all, such a complex would produce many tons of rubbish and thus much potential profit for a business like her father's. And had there not been money in private refuse collection, she could not have afforded to attend the university at which Bobby had met her. He was acquiring a new awareness of the interconnectedness of things, so perhaps not all this ongoing episode was deplorable, and then there was the growing, and unprecedented, solidarity within the family. During the last few hours he had spent more time in his father's company than he could remember having done previously in all his life. Furthermore, the man had listened with respect to several of his ideas on how to vanquish their common enemy.

"How about tampering with the brakes or the steering on Lyman's jeep?" he asked now. "You know that big curve just before you get to the village? If he lost control there, especially drunk as he is, it would be quite a fall, and it's all granite boulders below."

Lydia gave him a searching look. "You've got a bloodthirsty side I've never seen before."

His father asked, "Does any of us have enough technical knowledge to do something like that so it would definitely work — and then not be detected later? I doubt it." He assumed a judicious expression. "You see, not only do we have to extricate ourselves from this predicament, but we must do it so that it is brought to an absolute end, with no subsequent repercussions. We must not only keep our noses clean legally, but we must be *extremely* careful not to incur the vengeance of the remaining Finches."

"But," wailed Bobby's mother, "we seem to be suffering from *that* as it is."

"Exactly, and we must not make it worse — and here our work is cut out for us — we must not only rid ourselves of Chuck but dissipate the existing resentment that can be detected in Lyman, which surely must be shared by the other members of the tribe."

Bobby's mother said, "I still insist that Mrs. Finch and I have never exchanged a harsh word."

"That sullen old bitch," said his father. "She's cheated on the household accounts for years."

This was an old theory of his father's, and in the past the occasion for many angry words between his parents, but Bobby now was relieved to hear his mother say, "Maybe you're right. Everything is changing so rapidly."

His father returned the favor and replied inoffensively. "Or maybe it's always been what we only now are recognizing since Chuck has revealed his true colors."

A gunshot was heard at that moment, a sound that had to travel around and through many obstructions, and yet it reached them, as a scream or bellow could not have done if produced in the faraway kitchen.

Lydia's brief expression of alarm was replaced by one of hope. "Could that possibly mean that one of them has shot the other?"

Before she could be answered came the sounds of two volleys of gunfire.

Bobby's mother spoke with her eyes closed. "They're shooting up the house: that's what they are doing."

Bobby could not have anticipated the fear that claimed him at the sound of this distant fire, so different from that heard in movie and TV battles, so flat, literal, undemonstrative. As it continued, it seemed ever so gradually to be coming closer.

With an effort, he rose above what might otherwise have become stark terror, and said, already in motion, "We'd better fortify this place before they get here."

Bobby had taken the initiative. Doug had to grant him that; perhaps he was finally arriving at manhood. Doug followed his son into the bedroom, and together they tore away what was necessary to get to the naked mattress, lifted it off the frame, and carried it to lean vertically against the outer door of the study, where Lydia and Audrey held it in place while the men pushed pieces of heavy furniture against it, the upended sofa and, back of that, Doug's desk, which remained horizontal, offering a surface onto which the bedclothes and sofa cushions were piled.

"Not bad," Doug said when the barrier had been completed, standing back like a general, hands on hips, a posture for which his only training had been in military school so many years before. Of that time his principal memory was of the tormenting of an effeminate boy till he fled the Regiment (calling it "school" could get you ostracized interminably) and went home to Mother. Doug might well have been obliged to be of the company that, carrying out a traditional ritual by which a weakling was shamed, sodomized the lad had not the screaming response to the first attacker alerted the Officer of the Day.

In short, he had had no serious preparation for war, which was clearly what he was faced with now. With an effort of will he avoided dwelling on the fact that the battle had hardly been recognized as such when it was already at the stage of a Thermopylae.

But leave it to Audrey to make the point aloud. "Now our backs are really to the wall," said she, staring disconsolately at the barrier. "But what could we do once the guns started?"

Even Lydia had lost some of her earlier spunk. "Do we just cower in here till they eventually run out of ammunition?"

"I'll be happy to hear suggestions," Doug said reprovingly.

Bobby had a hand to his ear. "They've stopped, haven't they?"

While everybody strained to listen, a voice came from outside the door. Owing to the intervening padding, it was somewhat muffled. "Let me in!" Though slightly distorted, it sounded as though produced by Chuck, but Doug certainly made no answer.

Unnecessarily, Bobby whispered, "It's a trick."

"Doug? It's Chuck. Lyman's out of control. He's gunning for me now!" Chuck was a good actor. His terror would have seemed real enough to someone without experience of him. Doug knew that any response whatever would undoubtedly evoke an impassioned bogus argument and therefore stayed silent.

"It's the alcohol sets him off," Chuck cried. "A chemical reaction. I forgot about that. Maybe I never quite believed it. But now he's turned homicidal. For the love of God, let me in before he finds his way back here!"

Lydia came close to Doug and spoke in an undertone. "*Could* he just be telling the truth?"

"*No,*" Doug whispered with intensity.

She repeated, "*Could* he?"

It annoyed him to have to explain. "I've known Lyman for years. Drunk or sober, he's not dangerous on his own. If he is now, it's because Chuck is manipulating him. Didn't you notice how he pulled in his horns as soon as Audrey denounced him? And he was then already full of alcohol. He's a moron and a coward."

Chuck now shouted, "No, Lyman, don't do it!" A loud shot was heard, followed by more anguished pleading from the houseguest. "Now, that came close enough! Put that pistol down before you do something you'll regret to the end of your life."

Another shot was heard. The gunfire was no longer without reverberation, at such close range and contained within the low-ceilinged hallway. Nothing could have been louder. The mattress-and-furniture barrier looked pitiful now.

There was one last supplication from Chuck, followed by three shots in quick succession. Against his will, Doug listened for the sound of a body striking the uncarpeted floor, but of course heard nothing. Chuck was too arrogant to give the hoax the kind of detail it required.

Bobby said, in a voice of more than normal volume, pain in his pale eyes, "Maybe he was telling —"

Doug cut him off. "Can't you see it's fake? Don't go weak on me now. You've just been doing such a good job. . . ."

Bobby's eyes changed. "Do you mean it?" He seemed to be genuinely moved.

"Yes, I do, son. You ought to know that." Doug suppressed an urge to say, "In case we don't come out of this." Sentimentality could serve only the enemy.

"But what can we do now, Dad?" Bobby asked plaintively.

"Absolutely nothing. I know that's hardest to manage, but you see, *doing something*'s what's got us in so deep with Chuck."

Bobby's nose was wrinkled. "I thought it was just the reverse: that we didn't do enough when he was moving into a position of power, that we could have stopped him in his tracks if we had got him when he was first starting out."

Doug shook his head. "On the contrary! We paid too much attention to him, flattered him too much. He couldn't have got anywhere if he had been ignored."

Bobby made a stubborn nose. "But what about him installing himself as a proper houseguest without an invitation from anybody? Without even *knowing* any of us! The fantastic nerve! But it worked."

"The last chapter hasn't been written yet," Doug said, with a narrowing of eyes. "Who can say what the end will be? Lots of things give the illusion of success at the outset, but that's all it is, an illusion. Oh, I'm not saying we're in what would seem a powerful position, barricaded here and unarmed, with not one but two adversaries frothing at the mouth to get to us, both armed to the teeth. I'm not saying this is the ground on which I'd fight by choice. But they haven't got us, have they? And aren't we in a better situation now than if we were still in the kitchen?"

Bobby nodded but suddenly he seemed to be thinking of something else. In a moment he said, "I've got an idea."

Doug was not pleased to have his principle defied no sooner than it had been enunciated. "I thought I was just saying that we should sit tight, do nothing at all?"

Bobby hypocritically nodded agreement, but proceeded to suggest a course of action. "Now here's how it goes: we pour a puddle of water here, just in front of the door. Then we cut off the cord of the desk lamp, cut if off at the lamp end, leaving the plug end intact. We scrape off the insulation, baring the two wires. We plug one end in the wall socket, and we put the two bare wires into the puddle of water. We take away the barrier and let Chuck in. He steps into the water, and *boom,* he gets the juice."

"If Chuck is wearing rubber-soled shoes," said Doug, "it wouldn't work."

Bobby stretched his lower lip halfway to his nose. "What do you think, Lyd?"

They both turned to her, Doug wryly: every time he began to approve of Bobby, he soon had reason to feel otherwise. Even in an extreme situation, the boy could rarely rise above his fundamental tendency towards fecklessness.

But Lydia was not to be seen. Nor, for that matter, was Audrey. Hearing a sound from the bathroom, Doug and Bobby went together to its open door.

Facing them, knees inside, Lydia sat on the frame of the

high small window in the alcove — that from which Doug had seen her in the afternoon: she was slender enough to do that. Audrey had apparently helped her gain the height and was at the moment holding the little white stool on which she had climbed.

Audrey spoke to Doug in what he heard as a self-righteous tone. "Lydia's going to take the attack to *them*."

With a cursory wave, his daughter-in-law lifted her arms over her head, hands out the window, grasped something above, swung her legs up and out, and dropped from sight. This was done as if by a veteran gymnast, so deftly as to convert any negative feelings that Doug might have had to honest admiration.

He went to the window and looked out, but could not see her. Near the house it was always very dark back there at night, and the segment of the pool area could be distinguished only when the moon was more assertive than it was at the moment.

"She pushed the screen out," Audrey said. "She knew how to do that."

Lydia moved along the wall by touch. She could see nothing, but had no fear of stepping on a loose rake or kicking a lost football. She was not at home; the Graveses hired people who came regularly to tend the grounds, more Finches presumably. Her father on the other hand hired men pretentiously called gardeners (and they did plant special trees and gaudy bushes, all of which usually soon died), but were easily recognized as being the same guys who did freelance masonry, housepainting, and roofing, and on Friday nights played cards with their employer. They were the Santinis, more or less, comprising relatives and friends: another version of the Finches, except that there was not so much, if any, separation between them and their clients. Her brothers were supposed to help with outdoor work, and their habitual failure to do so was the occasion for much clamor and threats of mayhem by her father, yet she could not remember a time when such vengeance was actually wreaked. Whereas as a young female person she had now and again been denied certain privileges when she failed to discharge her kitchen duties to the letter: table-clearing, dish-scraping, loading the dishwasher in a way that would not result in broken glassware. Had she been the daughter of an earlier era, according to her mother, she would have had to assist in the washing of dishes by hand and perhaps clean bathrooms as well. But she was punished worse for using foul language, and worst of all for getting slightly tipsy on apricot brandy at the age of thirteen: the birthday party was canceled at the last minute, and it was left to her to explain to her favorite boy. But when her brother, under one influence or another, totaled the Continental, so great was her parents' relief with his escape from personal injury that he was not even grounded for a day.

Lydia did not nurse a real grudge, but the fact remained that the kitchen was the room for which she had least preference in any house. In the apartment they had shared at college, she and Bobby lived on big bags of apples and takeout from the nearest restaurant, which happened to be Korean.

This house might be amusing when one was indoors, but circumnavigating it in the darkness did not bring affection for the architect. How she longed to be back with the good old banal rectilinear, unnatural though it might be amongst foliage and granite outcroppings. More than once she had to leave a cul-de-sac or backtrack from an impasse, but eventually she blundered upon the rank of lighted casement windows that distinguished the kitchen.

An empty kitchen — which could have been expected if Lyman was truly stalking Chuck through the labyrinthine house. But the deserted table, with its horizontaled, dead-soldier gin bottle, would also make sense if Chuck was playing his possum game in that back hallway long after the police chief had driven off into the night, a much more likely state of affairs given the absence of Lyman's jeep from the parking area, where she next took her investigation.

The two vehicles belonging to the Graveses stood alone once again. Her now established night vision could see that and in fact more: the tires of both station wagon and compact sedan were flat and, as she confirmed by touch, permanently ruined. All eight had been slashed.

Now that was definitely Lyman's work, but was it mere impulsive spite or rather part of Chuck's master plan? For that matter, had the chief made his appearance for the reason he had named or had his arrival too been according to the grand design?

She returned to the house and entered the kitchen via the screen door, to the upper panel of which numerous insects adhered, seeing which she was retroactively aware that she had been bitten by multitudinous mosquitoes while traveling around the outer wall of the house; and with a significant fall of temperature at sunset, characteristic of the shore, the night was cool for her thin shirt. But some natural economy of being had kept these uncomfortable facts from her attention while she was outdoors and admitted them only now when she was safe inside.

She had expected the situation to be much worse: namely, that Lyman would still be on the premises, pistol in hand. If Chuck was once again on his own, what could be done to deal with him that had not already been tested and failed? In a sense the coming of Lyman had opened up new possibilities, which were now nullified by his departure.

While Lydia was dealing with such reflections, Chuck himself sidled furtively into the kitchen. Each was startled by the other.

"Lyman's gone?"

"You're asking me?" she said with disdain. "He's *your* partner."

The houseguest showed her an uneasy smile. "I won't question how you happen to be at large while the rest of them are barricaded in their cowardly fashion back there, but I congratulate you on finally coming to your senses. Now let's get going before he comes back with the whole carload." He was moving towards the screen door.

"What do you mean?"

"He went to fetch the others. Sunday nights, they all drink in the back room of the grocery store. . . . Do I have to get more explicit?"

"I don't care what you get," said Lydia, "except lost. Unfortunately, however, now that you've finally decided to leave, you can't — unless this is another trick."

Chuck winced as though genuinely hurt. "Look, I just risked my life again for your sake. Lyman wanted to go for you. When I stopped him, he pulled his gun on me!"

Lydia stared at him for a moment, then used, uncharacteristically, a scatological term.

"All right," Chuck cried, "call it bullshit, but let's just get out of here before he comes back with that bunch. I'm related to them, but I tell you frankly they're animals when they're full of beer. And they've got nothing to fear: Lyman's the law on this island."

Lydia felt a chill, but she was nevertheless pleased to frustrate Chuck even though she herself would share in his disadvantage. "Didn't you hear me? Nobody can leave now. All the tires have been slashed."

Chuck pursed his lips. "I wouldn't smile if I were you. You're facing a gang-bang, unless I can stop them somehow."

She resisted fright with anger. "It's because of you we're in this mess. And they're *your* people!"

"Maybe I'm being contrite," he said sadly. "Maybe it's no longer just a matter of pulling a malicious joke on those to whom it would be of no permanent consequence."

"Oh, really? I want you to know that I think you're garbage."

"That's too bad," said Chuck. "Because maybe I care for you. Can't you ever put your self-righteousness aside and consider that possibility?" For an instant he had succeeded in getting her attention, but then squandered his chance by adding, "Can't you *ever* be more than the little smart-ass opportunist?"

"You scum," she said. "What are you? A *Finch?*"

She had found the effective term. His face colored. "Just wait till that carload of drunks gets here, kiddo: you'll be begging your Uncle Chuck to save your skin. Some of my country cousins never get a woman year in, year out: they just bugger one another. Imagine what they will do to a little girl like you."

"Stop calling me little!" she cried. "I'm as big as you."

He started towards her. "I'll show you who's big."

The large chef's knife was on the counter: the kitchen police had not got around to it before being interrupted by Lyman's arrival. Lydia now snatched up this formidable blade and pointed it at her enemy.

"Just a minute," said Chuck. "You're no knife-fighter." But he halted his advance.

"Now, just give me that gun you carry." She gestured towards his lower leg.

"Gun?"

"The pistol you carry in the ankle holster."

He jerked his chin in what would seem a silent laugh. He simultaneously pulled up both legs of the trousers: above his low socks only pale skin could be seen on either limb.

This single fact could be devastating. Was the gun altogether a fantasy of Doug's? If so, then Chuck was not dangerous, and indeed not guilty of anything but entering her bed under false pretenses — if even that charge could be sustained. After all, he had not worn a disguise.

Lydia waved the knife at him. "Sit down." He took the chair that had been occupied by Doug at that wretched dinner. "I want to ask you something." But it was not as easy as that. "Look . . . earlier, in the bedroom, uh, did you think I knew who you were?"

Chuck frowned. For the first time she noticed that his mouth looked not quite fully formed: no doubt that accounted for the boyishness of his appearance, but so did the flat hair with its neat parting.

At last he said, "I wish I knew what you were talking about."

"I'm trying to find out some information which might have an effect on this whole business."

He produced a cynical smile. "Yes, it might be nice to know just how it happened that I was transformed from an honored guest into the whipping boy of this household, and why I have been the target of several attacks, mostly by you, on whom I've never laid a hand except in love."

She was angry again. "Oh, is that what you call it?"

He shrugged. "Now I suppose you're going to knife me for saying that? What the hell is wrong with you, woman?"

She would never discover the truth if she continued to be deflected by emotion. "All I want to know," she told him now, "is just what you thought you were doing when you simply opened the door and came in and got in bed with me?"

He smiled as if at an imaginary personage at her side. "God Almighty. I've never been asked a question like that before." He sighed. "What do you think I thought?" He sighed again. "Bobby told me to go back and see you, said you wanted to thank me for saving your life. So when I knocked at the door and you invited me in, and there you were, naked and in bed . . ."

"I *never* invited you to come in," said Lydia, with quiet vehemence. "And I'm even giving you the benefit of the doubt about your so-called knocking: if you did, I didn't hear it. I was asleep."

He extended his forefinger. "Wait a minute." He was grinning in disbelief. "You're not saying you were *sleeping?* That stuff you were saying was mere sleep-talk!"

"What stuff?"

"The dirty stuff." He looked from side to side in apparent exasperation.

She shouted, waving the knife, "I've never talked dirty in my life, in or out of bed."

He sneered. "All right, so while I've got it in you, some *other* girl is bending over with her mouth in my ear, yelling, 'Oh, give it to me, baby!' "

And she had actually been wondering whether he might have had some small argument, however flawed, to justify his actions! He was a hyena, and she might well have attacked him with the big knife, even though he was unarmed, had not Doug, followed by Bobby, rushed in from the butler's pantry. The father seized Chuck and held him to the chair while the son tied him snugly at wrists and ankles with what looked like venetian-blind cord.

"There we are!" said Doug with great satisfaction, as he stood back and inspected the houseguest-in-bondage.

"I didn't say anything of the sort!" Lydia protested, fearing her husband and father-in-law had heard Chuck's most recent and most outlandish lies.

Neither acknowledged the plea. Doug looked at her and said, "Well, that's done."

"Go ahead, Lyd," Bobby urged, ebulliently. "Take your revenge. *He* can't do anything. Carve your initials in his forehead if you want."

Chuck was expressionless. He certainly showed no fear.

Lydia returned the knife to the counter. "I don't want that kind of revenge."

"He did it to you when *you* were helpless!" Bobby cried.

Doug spoke soberly. "I assure you, Lydia, this is no place for civilized scruples. We've been invaded by the barbarians. They don't understand decency, and they take mercy for weakness. Unless we act decisively now that we have the chance, this menace will get worse and worse." Without warning, he turned and violently swatted Chuck across the side of the head. "This little turd, if you'll pardon my language, must be terminated."

Lydia winced. "Oh, please! Is that necessary? By the way, he *isn't* armed."

Doug knelt and in turn roughly raised each of Chuck's trouser cuffs. He rose and slapped the houseguest again, this time across the left cheek. "Where is it, you little shit?"

"Stop that!" Lydia said. "We don't need that."

"But it's so *satisfying*," Doug said, with a grim smile. "Where's the pistol?" Chuck shrugged within his bonds. Doug struck him again.

"Dammit!" Lydia said. "I don't like this."

Doug sneered at her. "Just don't say it brings us down to his level."

"Well, doesn't it?"

"Of course it does," said Bobby. "But that's where we should be. Why expect us to be saints? We're only human." He too slapped the helpless Chuck.

Lydia was nauseated by this behavior. "I don't want you to strike this man again!"

"All right, then," said Doug. "Let's try him, find him guilty, and carry out the death sentence."

"Don't joke like that."

"If you think I'm joking, Lydia, then just watch." Doug sat down and, taking up the empty gin bottle, banged its bottom against the surface of the table. "The jury will here and now assemble." Bobby took a chair across from his father. Chuck was between them. Doug pointed at Lydia. "Take your place."

At that moment Audrey came into the kitchen. "You'll be happy to know I haven't been able to find any breakage anywhere. I don't know what those shots were fired at, but they didn't seem to hit anything of ours." She avoided looking at Chuck. "Where is that horrible police chief?"

"He left when the bottle was empty," said Doug. "That's obvious. He can be disregarded: he's just a hick cop. We've got no reason to fear him or anybody else from these trash. Remove *this* thorn from our side, and our troubles will be over. And we must do it in a way that will cow all the other Finches once and for good."

Lydia was trying to fight off a moral dizziness. For that

reason alone she sat down in the chair indicated by her father-in-law.

"You, too," he said to Audrey, "and be quick about it. This thing has gone on too long as it is." He addressed Chuck. "All right, there you have it, a jury of your peers. You're getting a lot more justice than *you* would give to anyone in your power." He banged the table again with the gin bottle. "The court will come to order. The defendant is charged with criminal trespass, carrying a concealed firearm, grand theft, assault and battery, and rape. I'm entering a plea of *nolo contendere* in your behalf, so you can't say you've been railroaded."

"No!" Lydia said, rising though her head was by no means clear. "He has counsel to represent him. . . . We plead not guilty on all counts."

"Are you demented?" Doug asked. "You're a witness for the prosecution!"

"I won't be a party to a burlesque of justice."

Bobby spoke to his father. "She's showing the strain of her ordeal." To his wife he said, "Calm yourself, Lyd. Take your time, and you will come to understand that there's no other way to deal with this matter. It isn't as if anyone *likes* the job. It simply has to be done."

"I don't agree," she said. "I'll never agree."

"You tell 'em, kid," Chuck said, grinning.

"I wouldn't joke about this if I were you," she told him. "Can't you see they mean it?"

"Sure we do!" Doug said. "We're dead serious, and we're all one in this. Am I right, Audrey?"

His wife performed a slow sad nod.

"Audrey!" Lydia asked. "Do you understand what they're threatening to do?"

Her mother-in-law shrugged, but as if she were physically chilled rather than morally indifferent. "I've always made it my policy never to interfere with Doug when he's convinced about something. There are times when you have to fall in line."

"We're talking about killing a helpless man!"

"Mind you, I don't relish the thought," said Audrey. "But still . . ."

"Lydia." Bobby spoke sternly. "I don't believe you understand that this is just as much my idea as Dad's."

"What's that got to do with it?" Adrenaline was an effective force against vertigo. Lydia had regained her balance. She strode to a position near the refrigerator. "Look, I agree with you that Chuck has acted badly. Undoubtedly he should be made to leave, but —"

"He'll just come back," said Doug. "You know that."

"He's right!" Chuck cackled triumphantly. "That's what I'll do."

Lydia shouted at him. "Will you shut up! Are you trying to put the noose around your neck?"

Chuck laughed. "I can't see the purpose in dissembling at this point. I maintained my mask while it was useful, but whom could I fool now by pretending to be the kind of fellow who tries to do the right thing by the standards of these people?"

"This has nothing to do with standards!" Lydia said, but was immediately aware that she had not said precisely what she meant.

Doug snorted. "Well, I'll give the devil his due on that score: if you can't see a fundamental difference in principles here, then you're really not qualified to render a judgment. Look, this man has *abused our hospitality!* Can there be a greater crime? Think of what that means to the whole matter of civilization."

"On the other side you have my charge," said Chuck. "That these people are worthless parasites. If I were as pompous as this useless human being, I might ask you to think of how that reflects on the culture. You're going to have to make a choice sooner or later, Lydia."

Instead she asked, "What's your own use, Chuck? So far as I can see, you're the most useless person here, and furthermore you're a charlatan."

He finally lost his good humor. "I wasn't born to privilege," he snarled. "Nor did I marry into it. I had to hack my own way up out of the swamp, with damn little help from anybody. I don't mind saying I'm proud of what I made of myself. I could have been just another Lyman."

"Do you really think you're better off?" She found self-righteousness the most contemptible of his traits.

Doug pounded the table with the gin bottle. "I've heard quite enough. The defendant is found guilty on all counts. I therefore sentence him to be put to death by water."

Lydia shrieked, "Stop this! Stop it right now!"

But Doug and Bobby each took one of Chuck's arms and raised him from the chair.

"We'll do it in the pool," Doug said. "It'll be neat and clean, and easily explained as a swimming accident, probably the result of falling in while drunk. The autopsy will support that: he's got alcohol in his system."

"They've worked it all out, Lydia," Chuck said tauntingly. "Going to drown me like a kitten in a bag."

"No," said Bobby. "Like a rat!"

Lydia blocked their route to the screen door. "I warn you," she said, "I'll have to tell the authorities."

"But there *aren't* any," said Doug. "Haven't you figured that out yet?"

Sagging between his captors, Chuck jeered, "Maybe your own days are numbered, Lydia. You'll be next."

"Shut up, you rat!" ordered Bobby, jerking Chuck at the armpit. "You don't know anything about the way decent people act!"

§ 10 §

Despite Bobby's bluster, he was not all that keen on drowning Chuck. Most of his enthusiasm for the project had been feigned, for the purpose of gaining his father's approval. So far as he himself was concerned, while he was not quite ready to let bygones be, he had not been convinced that Chuck's offenses called for a capital response. Then what would be left as punishment for those who committed hideous and irreversible crimes involving mutilation and murder? The concept of civilized behavior would seem to include at least a sense of balance, if not justice in the narrowest of legalistic senses. But he was only too aware of how his father would react if he were so foolish as to bring up such matters.

Not to mention that Lydia, who was rapidly perfecting a style in which she was morally one-up on the rest of the human race, might well, despite her sudden defense of Chuck, at the same time have only contempt for a husband who would not avenge her.

It was pretty obvious to him that Lydia's purpose, whether or not she was even conscious of it, was only to take profits and never suffer a loss. That is, it might well be true that though she had not, at least at first, known that the houseguest was her bed partner, she had nevertheless enjoyed the experience and been outraged by it only when it was over, seeing as her next pleasure Chuck's expected punishment.

Bobby therefore was going along with the crowd as he saw it. He was merely a part of a movement, with diminished personal responsibility. None of this would be happening to a Chuck who had not behaved badly: that truth should never be forgotten. In destroying this usurper they were protecting what was theirs. Chuck should have stayed on his own ground, or if he had none, then put all his effort into acquiring one in a straightforward, manly way and not through guile tried to divest others of theirs. The pity was that had he made honest application, he might not have gone away empty-handed . . . though, in truth, he still might have. They were not an agency for the succoring of the envious. It was practical to recognize Chuck for the vile fellow he was, and be done with it and with him. Certainly they owed him nothing. It must always be remembered that he had come uninvited.

The two of them carried him to poolside, Bobby at the end with the bound ankles and loafer-shod feet. Chuck's shoes appeared only about size 8 at the most, but he was somewhat heavier than he looked, especially at his top half, or else Bobby's father lacked endurance, for twice the latter stopped to rest, yet firmly refused his son's offer to switch ends.

One potential hindrance, however, had vanished. Lydia did not accompany them, and therefore they were spared crocodile tears at what of course she had more than a little hand in bringing about. But Bobby's mother was not merely in attendance: she made herself useful by trotting ahead to find the switch inside the little structure that also contained the filtering and heating apparatus, and thereby to illuminate not only the area surrounding the pool but also the water itself by means of the submerged flood-lamps.

The result, in the otherwise utter black of night, was a startling brightness, so much more flagrant than sunshine but also so starkly cold, and the shadow cast by the complex of two men carrying a third surely had a more gruesome connotation than the same trio in the flesh: in silhouette, Chuck probably looked already dead. Bobby liked this less and less. He wished that either Chuck had never come to the house or that he, himself, and Lydia had stayed away this summer. But the alternative would have been to visit *her* family, at some awful inland lake to which they had been attached since before her father had been successful in business. The worst place to meet new relatives-by-law must surely be at a venue uniquely sentimental to them. Lydia had learned that by now!

Bobby was not a vengeful man. Even at this late date he would have been at least sympathetic to an appeal made by the prisoner, but Chuck continued to show nothing but defiance, either with sardonic comments or an arrogant silence which might be worse, for did it not insultingly imply that this whole business was but a bluff?

His father now slowly lowered the upper half of the houseguest, and Bobby followed suit with the ankles, bringing the heels to rest on the poolside concrete. They were about to drown the man, but characteristically saw to it that he was handled with care until the time came.

"Now, look here, Chuck," said his father. "We hope you're clear as to what we're doing and why."

"It's hardly complex," Chuck said, showing his familiar grin. "You've simply decided not to honor your part of the social contract by which I am your guest. I'm at your mercy: it's your turf, and you outnumber me. If you reject any sense of obligation, it follows that you feel justified in doing anything you want to me, including cold-blooded murder."

Bobby was irritated by the smugness of this summing-up. "Oh, dammit, Chuck, come off it! Nobody was treated better than you were by us until you went too far."

Chuck shook his sleek head. His bound hands were clenched in the area of his solar plexus. "That's what *you* say, but then you have a vested interest in that version."

His father told Bobby, "Don't argue with him. Of course he'll try to play on our sympathy. What else can he do in his situation? Just think of what would happen were you or I in *his* clutches! He's a vicious man, whereas we're decent people who have been pushed too far. Remember that. There *is* a difference."

Chuck sounded a horselaugh.

Bobby's mother, silent till now, came forward and said, "I do think it's not in the best of taste to make him listen to this gloating when he's going to be put to death anyway. It isn't as if he had a chance."

Bobby's father glared at her. "Now don't tell me that after all this, you're back again on *his* side?"

She made a chin. "No, but I hate any kind of bullying. Throw him into the pool and be done with it. That would be the humane thing."

"Thanks, Audrey," said Chuck. "You make me feel a lot better."

She scowled at him. "Are you still being sarcastic? You know, I will tell you that you wouldn't have come to this if you had been able to suppress your cynical streak. You have many gifts, Chuck, but apparently you can't rise above certain negative traits. So don't blame this on anybody else. Until you changed, you were the best guest we ever had. I don't know why that couldn't be enough for you. I don't want to rub it in at this point, but it must be clear to you that ruining us, even if you had been successful, could not have done you any good in the long run. It's people like us, who come in from the outside, who keep this island alive. You see how shortsighted you were? I may be going too far, but I just think that at least the more level-headed Finches will understand why we had to do what we did, perhaps even applaud us in the end."

It occurred to Bobby that his mother had proceeded to do precisely what she had asked his father to refrain from. His father, however, did not make this point aloud. Instead he asked whether Chuck had any last request.

"No," said the houseguest. "There's never been anything you could supply that I would want."

His father nodded judiciously. "You've just demonstrated why I have no compunction about what I'm going to do. You just can't compromise, can you? Let me say" — he sneered at his wife — "and this is not *gloating!* Let me say that in your position I would swallow a *little* of my pride and at least debate the issue, if only to save my skin." Suddenly his face was working with rage. "How *dare* you not give us any argument? Do you think it's somehow morally superior to let us do away with you without making any defense of your position?" He shook his fist at the recumbent prisoner. "Do you think it's easy for us? Do you think we make a habit of killing our guests?"

Chuck's smile broadened. "You mean you *don't?*"

Bobby's father turned away in disgust, but his mother answered literally. "We've never done it before, and so far as I'm concerned, I don't want to do it ever again. This is the worst weekend I can ever remember having spent here, and that includes the one of Hurricane Carmella."

Bobby said, "All right, Chuck, if you insist, I'll come more than halfway. Speaking for myself, anyway, I'd be willing to reevaluate the situation if you apologized." He avoided looking at his father.

"You're a prize," Chuck said. "You actually believe that after everything you've done to me, *I'm* at fault." He looked away, which meant, in the attitude in which he lay, he stared at the black sky above the glare of the flood-lamps. "There's no dealing with you people."

Bobby brooded for a moment, and then he lifted his head and spoke to his father. "Maybe we should call this thing off."

"What's that supposed to mean?"

"Well, it seems cruel to kill somebody who doesn't even understand what he's being punished for."

"Since when do we need the *criminal's* consent? Naturally he's going to pretend that justice was denied him!"

"I just wonder whether Chuck's pretending."

"Who cares?" His father frowned. "Bobby, you're just eventually going to have to acquire some principles of your own. This is as good an opportunity as any."

"But your idea of my convictions is that they be identical with your own."

"Think of this," said his father. "Are Chuck's prefera-ble? Look who's getting drowned." He bent to the house-guest. "Take his feet."

Chuck said, "Don't worry about it, Bobby. You can always maintain it was his idea and not yours. In fact, you even protested against it and were overruled. You're actually a totally innocent bystander."

"You dirty bastard," Bobby snarled. "I'll be happy to get rid of you!" This made him feel considerably better. He grasped the prisoner's ankles and lifted.

He and his father began to swing Chuck between them, counting in concert.

"*One.*"

"Oh, my," gasped his mother, turning her back on them.

"*Two.*" This swing seemed sufficiently violent to have hurled the prisoner halfway across the pool had they let him go, and Bobby could hardly maintain a grasp on the ankles.

On the backswing, the lights went out. Bobby immediately relinquished his grip, and Chuck's legs fell away. But his father obviously had enough momentum established to project the houseguest's body into the water unassisted, for an appropriate splash was heard.

Lydia cried out in the darkness.

Bobby shouted, "Traitor!" For it had been she who turned the lights out: that was clear. The joke was on her, however, for her boyfriend was now in the water, hands and feet tied. . . . How ungodly it must be to die like that, restrained from doing anything to save oneself. The fact was that Chuck had done nothing so loathsome as to deserve such a death.

Bobby went to the edge of the pool, kicked off his shoes, and dived in. As luck would have it, he came down directly on top of Chuck and carried him into the depths. When they came up, Chuck was free of his bonds, and he lost no time in fiercely grappling with what he obviously believed not a savior but rather an assassin whose bloodlust could not be sated.

"Goddammit!" Bobby managed at last to cry. "I'm trying to help you! Stop fighting!"

"Bobby?" asked the other. "You fool, I'm your father!"

The floodlights came on then, underwater and on the poolside standards, his mother having reached the switch. His father was coughing, had probably got a lungful of the strongly chlorinated water. His own eyes were burning. He climbed out, then leaned down and gave his father a hand.

"I thought you were Chuck," he said to his father.

"*You* dropped him to the ground," his father said accusingly. "*I* fell in. And you tied him so loosely he was able to slip right out of his bonds."

The lengths of venetian-blind cord lay at Bobby's feet. Neither the houseguest nor his ally Lydia was to be seen.

Lydia, in hiding behind the filter-house, was amazed to peep out and see that Chuck had somehow made a Houdini-like escape. Her intention had been only to frustrate the Graveses' attempt to drown him after what did not even deserve the name of kangaroo court. She had not wanted to release the man altogether. Now he was once again at large, and surely they were all once more in peril. Seeing that justice was served, yet protecting one's own interests against evildoers was even more complex a matter than it had been represented, and for a moment she was resentful towards those who had so inadequately prepared her for the world. But then remembering that when younger she had naturally resisted all attempts to present reality in other than the most simplistic terms, she now instituted an effort to determine what could reasonably be made of the current mess.

As it was, she did not dare return immediately to the bosom of the Graves family. It was far too soon even to attempt to explain her motives in assisting Chuck's escape.

She could see no reason to believe that they would honor the simple fact of her debt to the person who had saved her life a few hours earlier. They were obviously the sort to give vindictiveness precedence over any secondhand emotion. She was only an in-law: her rescue might provide a kind of relief, but it was hardly comparable in force to the sense of injury of which Chuck was the ongoing occasion.

To acquire full forgiveness she would probably have to recapture Chuck singlehandedly, an achievement unlikely of accomplishment at best: as it was, she had no idea of where he might be found.

The Graves family was now moving towards the house, the two men leaving a trail of water. They were also bickering futilely as to the relative fault to be assigned to each member with regard to the latest debacle. Lydia of course shared maximum infamy with Chuck himself, for it appeared conclusive that she was a full co-conspirator. But not even Audrey was declared blameless, failing as she had to maintain surveillance on the switch that controlled the floodlights.

As to Bobby, according to Doug he had dropped Chuck's feet too soon, else despite the darkness they could have carried to fruition the project to hurl the houseguest into the water. To which Bobby's counter-charge was that if his father had not too long kept a grasp on Chuck's shoulders, they could have lowered their captive to the concrete and merely waited out the brief period of darkness, resuming once the lights were on again.

It took all of Lydia's strength to withstand the awful suspicion that she would never succeed in making common cause with her in-laws, lacking as they were in fundamental values. Their moral tackiness was unbelievable. They had been ready to take human life, but they were apparently incapable of dealing in earnest with any issue of the spirit. She was continuing to discover what it meant to be utterly alone. The personal sense of uniqueness she had cultivated when amidst her own family was hereby revealed as pathetically naïve. She had been special only through the indulgence of those dear people. It was chagrining to reflect that in her own context she had been quite as spoiled as Bobby was in his.

From her place of concealment she now watched the Graveses walking in silhouette against the illumination coming from the house, a house that seemed much more radiant than that which they had left: every interior light must be on. Lydia had only too recently learned that anything unusual was much more likely to be sinister than charmingly eccentric. Her family-by-law, however, continued to plod homewards as if nothing were out of order but their plan to drown the houseguest. If she sounded an alarm that proved false, they might well take out their frustration on her. Perhaps they had no limits whatever and would find her a convenient substitute for Chuck.

These self-pitying projections were brought to an end by the sudden extinguishing of all electric lights on the property. The house joined the pool area, the woods, and the sky in one unconditional medium of blackness so assertive as to be palpable: it seemed as though you could grasp a handful of it, like snow, and pack it into a hard ball and hurl it at —

She shouted at her family and ran after them, miraculously failing to encounter any of the obstacles that might have tripped her up.

"Get down! He's inside! Don't give him a target!" She then collided with a person but stayed on her feet.

It was Doug. He spoke unevenly. "You've got your nerve."

"We can't go into that now," said she. "He must have doubled around and got into the house."

Bobby's voice came from nearby. "Is this another of your filthy tricks?" His overemphasis of the final consonants led Lydia to understand that his teeth were chattering. Both of them had been soaked to the skin, and nights at the shore could be colder by many degrees than the days, especially, as now, when the wind had risen.

"I just didn't want him murdered," Lydia said. "I don't want him to win."

"I can't stand being c-cold," said Doug, as if speaking to himself. "It's the only thing that gets to me."

"Here, dear," said Audrey. She moved past Lydia, bumping her slightly. It seemed as though she might have embraced her husband. Lydia could now begin to discern some slight differentiations in the darkness. She tried to find her own husband, however, without success, perhaps because he could see better than she and intentionally eluded her.

She said, "He'll be watching for us on this side. So you stay here and keep his attention on you. Meanwhile, I'll slip around to the other side of the house, go in and bring back warm clothes for everybody."

"Don't listen to her, Dad," Bobby said heatedly. "It's just another dirty trick. She's been behind this whole thing, I'm convinced."

Lydia moved swiftly to challenge him. "Oh, are you really, Bobby?"

Already doubt could be heard in his voice. "Well, dammit, it's going to take some explaining."

"Listen here," she said to the now dim suggestion of her

husband's figure. "I heard you before. *You* wanted to call off the whole thing. *You* didn't want to drown him."

Bobby's tone turned hangdog. "I was under pressure. You don't understand, Lydia. This is something new here. Ordinarily we don't have any problems with a houseguest, do we, Mother?"

Audrey responded. "But those are the ones we *invite,* Bobby! That's the difference."

"I'll tell you," Doug said, shivering audibly, "I'm just about ready to c-capitulate. L-l-let's face it, he's whipped us. That happens. I don't know what it is, luck or fate or something. G-goddammit, I'm cold! I'm going to give myself up and get into a sweater and drink hot chocolate."

His tone was that of a wanted criminal under siege by the police, and he spoke as if surrendering to Chuck would bring him the approbation of all right-thinking people.

But Bobby surprisingly proved of sterner stuff. "No time to let down, Dad! Is he going to be more decent than he was before we almost drowned him?"

"I have it," said Audrey. Apparently she was still hugging her husband, though to little effect. "Hugo's old blanket is still behind the back seat in the wagon."

Lydia recognized the name in reference as that of a pet Weimaraner, deceased as of a previous summer or two. Bobby claimed to have been fonder of the animal than it had been of him, but Lydia pointed out that dogs cleave to those whom they live amongst, less to occasional visitors to a household: he had spent most of his time at college or in summer pursuits like tennis camp.

"I'll go get it!" he nevertheless said now, and plunged into the even more profound darkness in the direction of the car-park.

"The hell with that!" Doug said desperately. "I'm going

inside." But Lydia could now see well enough to discern that Audrey was struggling to restrain him and if unaided would soon lose the contest. She allied herself to her mother-in-law and hugged the wet Doug from the opposing side.

"Damn!" he cried. "Damn you women!" But he was not proving to be as strong as Lydia had assumed: the ladies were winning now, and fairly easily.

No sooner had she made that assessment than Doug ceased all resistance, and naturally she and Audrey relaxed their grasps — at which their captive burst from them and dashed towards the dark house along the path of flagstones.

Lydia pursued him, catching up at the door that gave access to the pool area. "Doug," she pleaded. "Don't surrender. We can win this thing. You'll see."

He was trying unsuccessfully to turn the knob. "It's locked," said he. "I'm locked out of my own house!" He turned to her, as if she might actually have an answer. "This is the ultimate in degradation. He's in, and I'm out."

"Well, so are we all."

"So far as I'm concerned," Doug said icily, "your right to include yourself is highly questionable. If it weren't for your intervention, this devil would be safely drowned by now and we'd be back indoors, warmed by a blazing fire, once again in possession of that which is ours. And no grand jury in the world would indict us for what was so obviously an accident. All the unpleasantness would soon be over, and the rest of the summer would lie before us, to be enjoyed in the usual way." He pincered his thumb and forefinger. "We were *that* close — and *you,* and nobody else, made the difference!" He had forgotten he was cold.

"But now he and I are even," Lydia said. "Don't you see that? I have paid him back the life I owed. He's fair game to me now. Can't you understand?"

"I don't give a damn for your moralizing!" cried Doug. "He's taken my house!"

She saw that no verbal argument could earn her reinstatement. Once again, action was called for. Though ordinarily she resented aggressive maleness, she would have welcomed it now. Instead of blaming her for his inability to cope, why did he not handle it with the virility that was his by natural definition? Why did she once again have to prove that she was not helpless?

As usual she derived energy from resentment. She started around the house towards the bathroom window by which she had lately left it.

All five doors of the station wagon were locked. The vehicle stood lower than normal: then with his improved night vision Bobby saw the slashed tires, and next those of the car parked alongside. This vandalism struck him harder than anything yet. It was so wanton. They were up against an implacable enemy. To be so savagely punished for committing no crime! He swore that after winning this war — and they must!— he would be merciless henceforth. Woe be to the person who crossed him. Not until he had lost his innocence was he aware that he had had so much. He understood that it was not necessary for him utterly to believe or to disbelieve Lydia's arguments — on any subject, but especially with regard to personal relations: after all, even though being his wife, she *was* someone else. Giving her the benefit of the doubt (as he should in view of their yearlong connection if for no other reason), she would surely emerge with a decided advantage over everyone else he had ever known, even if she would never again be seen as exactly perfect.

Meanwhile here he was, frustrated in his purpose as usual: he absolutely could not return to his father with another failure. He searched the edge of the parking area for a sizable stone, found one, removed his shirt and wrapped the rock in it, and in what took several blows against the shatterproof glass, finally battered a hole in the back window of the station wagon of sufficient size to admit his hand. He unlocked the cargo door and claimed the ex-doggy blanket, which still smelled of the late Hugo, with whom, though not for lack of trying, he had never developed a rapport. Indeed Hugo was quite capable of barring his entrance into either of the Graves residences unless one of his parents was present. In the current situation, it could have been predicted that a living Hugo would have shown marked partiality for Chuck Burgoyne.

Having snatched the blanket, Bobby crouched in silence for a while to determine whether his sounds of forced entry, though muffled by the shirt, had alerted the enemy. But when nothing happened he was emboldened to enter the wagon and crawl forward to the glove compartment, where he found a flashlight with, incredibly, fresh batteries. Armed so poorly, and though Chuck remained in command of the house and all vehicles were immobilized, Bobby was convinced that the tide of battle had now turned in favor of his family.

He returned to his wet father, who was unprecedentedly being hugged by his mother. He gave him Hugo's blanket.

His father was not so demoralized as to refrain from saying, "Phew. This thing is pretty high!"

Bobby looked around. "Where's Lyd?"

"Who knows?" said his father. "She's gone again. Maybe joined *him* once more."

"No," Bobby said firmly, though he admitted to himself that it could well be true. "No, she's helping us now. Take my word for it." Now that he could see better, what he observed were all those windows that reflected only the black of night and forest: a darkened house, irrespective of tenants, seems a sinister place. "She's gone around the other side to sneak in someplace. What we should do here is create a distraction, to occupy Chuck so he won't hear her."

But his father was still obsessed with regaining bodily warmth, stamping the ground and mumbling. Finally he said, "The smell is really something, after all this time. Hugo must have puked in this blanket." He glared at his wife. "Why'd you still keep it?"

"So that it would come in handy now," was her waspish answer.

Bobby thought it essential that the good feeling that had been established between them, as exemplified by the hugging, should not be allowed to dissipate.

"I miss him!" he said. "And he never even liked me."

"No, Bobby," his mother replied. "He never really got to *know* you."

"Oh, he was a fine old fellow," said his father, who surprisingly enough had been close to the dog: at dinner Hugo might come and insert a heavy head between the table and his lap and be tolerated.

Suddenly his father was sad. "I am not as I was in the reign of good King Hugo."

"Why do you say that, Doug?" Bobby's mother asked sympathetically.

"Please," said his father. He dropped the blanket, knelt,

picked up a rock, and threw it at the sliding door before them. But the missile merely bounced off the stout plate glass, almost striking Bobby on the return flight. "How do you like that!" his father said bitterly. "Now I can't even break my own glass door with my own rock!"

"Well, Chuck's not to blame for that," said Bobby. "It's just a matter of physical laws. You shouldn't take it personally." With his fingertips he prized up one of the flagstones from the walk — they were set in loose sand — hefted it, then hurled it against the door. This action was effective. The large pane became several wicked-looking shards that shimmered briefly in the available light before plunging to the earth.

The destruction was so uncompromising that the Graves-es were chastened for an instant, and the sound too was startling. They took *ad hoc* places of concealment behind the ornamental trees that grew from round islands of soil near the pool, though these were for the most part slender saplings. But when a few moments had passed without response from the house, visible or audible, the trio reunited and advanced on their home, the control of which had been taken from them and not really by force.

Bobby kicked out the remaining fragment of plate glass and led the way through the now vacant frame of the door. Once inside, he illuminated his flashlight, even though Chuck would thereby be given an easy target.

When they reached the utility room, Bobby's father found the main electrical switch and threw it on. The house was alight once again, and they proceeded to search its entirety, growing bolder as, room after room, Chuck failed to appear. But what should have been a satisfying experience was not, for neither could Lydia be found. Which meant one of two things, each sorrier than the other: either Chuck had taken her prisoner or once again, in her perverse way, she had joined him — perhaps temporarily, as usual, and would later on return to the fold with still another argument that she would insist was plausible.

Bobby made no reference to his wife until they had completed the search of the semidetached guest wing and he could at least put aside his dread that she and Chuck might be discovered in bed back there — which of course she would subsequently explain as having been a means to distract the houseguest while the others recaptured him.

"I'm worried about Lyd," he said as they were passing Chuck's room on the way back. "Do you think he could have kidnapped her?"

"Let's hope not," his father said curtly.

"No," said Bobby's mother. "He's gone. I know it. I feel it. He finally got the idea that he was not wanted. At long last. But what a struggle it was!" She chuckled. "I've heard of persistent guests whom you couldn't get rid of, but this was a special case. I know people who will find it hard to believe." She sighed. "We never should have let him talk us out of the annual season-opening party. Now no one will have met him. Nobody will be aware of how charming he could be when on his good behavior."

His father grimaced. "I find this whole thing humiliating in the extreme. I'm glad no one's met him. That is, no one we *know*. Of course the Finches are only too well aware of Chuck Burgoyne, but they really don't matter if we can emerge unscathed. In fact, they will be taught a lesson."

"Which is?" asked Bobby.

"That there are limits," his father said soberly, "and you must know what they are if you expect to be taken seriously in life."

"Well, we don't really know how far Chuck represents the Finches as such, do we?"

"But you see, Bobby, we must proceed as if he does. It's not our job to puzzle out every subtle discrepancy. Look, it was he who invaded our property, not the reverse. The burden of proof's on him."

"Good grief," said Bobby's mother, looking at her wristwatch. "Look at the time. This Sunday's certainly been a waste from start to finish."

"You know, Dad," said Bobby. "I wonder if maybe we're being too smug too soon. We might have missed him in this search. Maybe he's just stepped out one of the many exits and has been watching us through the windows as we went around."

"But," said his mother, "that would contradict this very definite feeling I have that he is no longer on the premises. You know, he does exude a certain energy when he's around: that much must be granted to him."

His father snapped, "Are you still enamored of that little rodent?"

Bobby stepped in quickly to prevent a squabble. "All I'm saying is it might be too early to declare unconditional victory for our side."

By now they had returned to the kitchen, which had without formal declaration become their headquarters.

"There's something in what you say," his father told him, with obvious concern for his sensibilities, "but what we need most at this point is something that builds morale. We've suffered one reverse after another, all day long. If occasionally we had a little success, it's been short-lived. This is the longest period yet in which Chuck has been out of power. That might be worth celebrating. If you'll get a *blanc de blancs* from the cellar, I'll provide the ice."

The wine cellar was not subterranean in this house without a basement, being rather a long cabineted series of shelves beneath the bar in the butler's pantry. Several hundred bottles were maintained there at a constant temperature of 55 degrees. One of the many things Bobby did not share with his father was a special taste for wines, but he knew where the different kinds were kept, and he went now and pulled out champagnes until he found the appropriate label.

When he returned to the kitchen, his father had at last discarded Hugo's blanket. Both of them had forgotten the matter of exchanging their wet clothes for dry. Bobby was about to remind his father when he saw, through the windows over the sink, that the headlights of a car were just entering the parking area.

"Dad," he said, lowering the bottle to the counter, "I think Lyman's come back."

§ 11 §

Lydia was still trying to find a means by which she could reenter the house when to her surprise the lights had gone on and she saw the three Graveses on their inspection tour. It would have been natural for her to go knock at the nearest door to their current position, but before she could do so, she saw a shadowy figure emerge from one corner of the building and steal out through the parking area and onto the gravel lane that led to the public road.

Chuck Burgoyne was making his departure, slinking off like a whipped cur. She found it difficult to abstain from sounding derisive applause, perhaps even a raspberry. He was the type to whom it would be heaven to rub it in, and now that she had evened the score by saving his life, she had no motive for restraint. But what revenge *would* be appropriate for what he had done to her? All she could think up was something obsolete, like public shaming in the pillory.

But her sense of triumph was soon moderated by the realistic reflection that it would be utterly unlike the Chuck she knew to leave permanently at this point. He had not long before won exclusive possession of the house, having, in a way that might seem magical to him, survived a savage attempt on his life. Why, when things had again turned his way after a short-lived reversal, would he make a surreptitious exit into the night woods?

Lydia saw it as her duty to follow him as far as the road, if such was his destination, but she could not walk on the gravel, for, though at the moment the sound of her footsteps would be obscured by his own, if he stopped without warning she would be audible at a great distance. She therefore took the verge, in this case a terrain in which parts of dead trees, pine cones, and boulders were routine, and scratchy, even stinging bushes not uncommon. Mosquitoes too were at home in places. A hundred yards of this course left many marks upon her, and soon after leaving the car-park she encountered dense darkness as the lane became a corridor through the woods, too narrow to be penetrated by such feeble light as the sky offered. Yet every time she halted she continued to hear Chuck's regular crunch up ahead. He had no flashlight. If she quit now, he would have proved he was the more competent night navigator. She had long since determined she would never again surrender to him in any area of human enterprise.

The lane may have been as long as a quarter of a mile. Every time Lydia stubbed her toe on an invisible obstacle, or was again slashed by a thornbush or bitten by another insect, she told herself that this would be the last, that she had earned an easy passage from here on, and on each occasion she was immediately proved wrong. Once she fell outright, and her *hair* caught in a spiky bush. It was only after her hopelessness had been established that relief arrived.

The lights of an oncoming car became visible, silhouetting Chuck's figure in the lane. Lydia now plunged to the ground on purpose. It was a nasty place for this, and her right hand encountered a soft, damp mess of something with the texture of excrement though fortunately with an odor no worse than that of mildew.

Chuck was waving in the jovial style in which vehicular friends are hailed, and when the car stopped, he went out of sight behind the headlamps and, as the slam of the door would indicate, climbed on board.

The car stayed where it was; the occupants sat there plotting their tactics for the final assault. Now what she had to do was return to the house as quickly as possible and sound the alarm. Secrecy no longer had a point. She took to the middle of the lane and ran full speed through the gravel, expecting to be immediately pursued by the car and in danger of being ruthlessly run down.

But whether or not the men had seen her, her backward glance when halfway home told her they were staying in place.

At the parking area, the end of her run, she checked again, but now the headlights could not be seen at all. This could have a sinister implication; maybe they had launched an invisible, silent advance. She could identify all three members of her adopted family through the kitchen window, could easily have picked them off with a target rifle. They were more vulnerable than she.

Both screen and inner doors were locked. She banged on the frame and loudly identified herself. Bobby answered the summons, after having peered out apprehensively under a horizontal hand. Yet when he let her in, he pretended to have difficulty in recognizing her.

"Don't bother with how I look," she said, gasping from her expenditures both physical and emotional. "They're coming! Get these lights out!"

"More divided loyalties?" he asked skeptically.

His father came forward. "Let's get this straight," Doug said. "Has Chuck really decamped? By coming back like this do you mean you've broken with him for good?"

"I was never with him!" she shouted. "Will you listen to me? They're out there, in a car with the lights out. They're probably all armed to the teeth."

Doug's expression changed from dubiety to fear. "Oh, my God," he muttered, and then, in a louder voice, "By 'they' you mean his gang?"

"Tedesco was one name, I believe," said Audrey, "and then you claim to have spoken with a Mr. Perlmutter."

"When Lyman left, he threatened to come back with a carload of other relatives who have been drinking all day," said Lydia, looking for the light switch that ought to have been on the wall near the door. "I haven't had time to tell you that."

"And ransack the house?" asked Audrey. "I *thought* we were getting off too easy."

Doug nodded. "Those Neanderthals who hang around in the back room of the gas station. They've been doing that for years, generation after generation."

"Goddammit," Lydia said. "*Will* you turn the lights off!"

Doug went to more or less the same place where she had been looking in vain, found a switch, and put the kitchen into darkness.

In the dark he said, "We've got floodlights out there in the car-park."

"No," said Lydia. "Lights will keep them away from where they can be seen. They'll just keep the car out in the lane, or they'll shoot out the bulbs. In a minute when our eyes get adjusted, we'll be able to see as well as they, and they might not know at first that we're onto them."

"I think we might suffer less damage in the long run," said Audrey, "if we simply surrendered at least some of the items they want. Make a deal of some sort. It has been determined that some of the worst people will often negotiate. Compromise seems to come naturally to human beings."

"Not to Chuck. I begged him at the pool!" Doug said with emotion, and then turned hard. "If they come for me, they'd better be ready to shed blood — their own as well as mine."

Bobby's voice came from near the door. "I agree. For everything they are given, they'll want something else. This is war."

"They don't want your possessions," Lydia said to the others, whose presences were becoming discernible. "They want me."

"You?" Bobby asked, in the kind of voice that could be taken to imply the unspoken question: *For what reason?*

"I'm hardly making it up," she said testily. "Chuck told me."

"They want *you*," said Bobby, putting it as a statement of dubious authenticity.

"I don't intend to stand here in the dark repeating it. That's what I was told."

"You mean to say . . ." Audrey began to speak, her voice falling away.

"Look here," said her father-in-law, in almost a parody of the avuncular tone, "look here, Lydia, we're certainly not going to expect you to make such a sacrifice for the family. Why should you? You've just joined it. Please believe me, you can rely on us to stand back of you one hundred percent on whatever course you choose. That's what a family's for."

Even after the experience of this half a day, she remained shockable. "But you *are* asking me, aren't you?"

"He just said he wasn't." Bobby was speaking. "What more do you want, Lyd? Why make any more trouble than we've got?"

"Will there ever be a way out of this whole thing?" Audrey asked rhetorically. "Short of total ruin? That's all I'm saying. I just wish I had the answer."

Lydia asked bitterly, "You really want me to go out there, don't you?"

Doug said, "I don't know how I could put it in any other way than I already have. I specifically stated I didn't expect that of you. If something's beyond someone's capacities, it's unfair to criticize them: that's always been my policy."

"Now you can't say that's not fair," said Bobby.

Lydia tested them. "Okay, I'm going."

"Uh-huh," murmured Bobby.

"No," said Doug.

"Excuse me?"

"I said I wouldn't ask it of you, and I'm not."

"Is that your response?"

"You're really being a pain, Lyd," said Bobby. "Just let me ask you: Do you really want to go? Because that's what it seems like when you keep asking the same question."

"Do you know what a shit you are being?"

"Sure," Bobby said, "you can abuse me. That's always one way of avoiding the issue."

Audrey came to her side in the darkness. "Don't let

them bully you, dear. They can't take away your dignity."

Lydia suddenly understood she was speaking of the gang in the car, not her son and husband. "You're a traitor to your own sex."

"Sex has nothing to do with this," said Audrey, in apparent, perhaps even genuine innocence. "Survival is what's at stake."

"*Your* survival."

Audrey sighed. "I could hardly speak with authority on anyone else's."

"What gets me," said Lydia, "is that earlier you kept suspecting me of being in collusion with Chuck. Now you are urging it upon me."

"Lydia," Doug said, coming nearer, "the situation's always changing. You'll learn that when you get a few years older. Nations soon go to war with their former allies. After acquiring power, revolutionaries invariably begin to execute their old comrades, and starving persons cannibalize their nearby friends. This is beyond right and wrong: it is simple reality."

"No it isn't," Lydia said with more conviction that she felt. Indeed she suspected he might well be correct, but it would have been unconscionable for her spinelessly to acquiesce, and anyway, just because something is true is not sufficient justification for it to be stated in so many words, thus discouraging those souls who live on hope. "Oh, maybe it is for you," she went on, "and for them out there. But I'm better than you. I'm better than them." Having said which, she realized she would now have to make her claim good, else be disqualified forever.

She breathed deeply and left the house. She was halfway to the parking area before the men in the darkened vehicle were aware of her approach and turned on not only the headlamps but also a row of spotlights mounted on the roof of the jeep. It would have shown a weakness if she had covered her eyes, but she could not help wincing.

To show disrespect for Chuck, she went to the driver's side and spoke presumably to Lyman. She would continue to be blind for a few moments.

"Chief," said she, "I want to file formal charges against someone for criminal trespass, malicious injuries, possession of a concealed weapon, sodomy, and *mala in se*." She impulsively threw in the last, so to speak a catchall, because the penultimate charge was more than a bit doubtful, Chuck's not having performed unnaturally in bed, and in fact the previous one had slim support, for she had never seen his gun if indeed he had one.

The window was rolled squeakily down. With it closed, he had probably not heard her statement of charges, and she had now lost the fine edge of energy that had produced it. To make one good attack is within anybody's power, but consistency is the mark of the champion.

Before the window was fully open she could smell, in the clean air of the shore, the stale booze-fumes emanating from the interior of the vehicle.

"Lady," said Lyman's voice, "you think you can come up here and do anything you damn please, shake your little ass around in shorts without any underpants under them, wear shirts with the nipples of your knockers sticking out, you talk worse filth than any of the hardworking men I know, I've heard your kind in the village, with your *fuck-this* and *fuck-that* and *shit-on-it* and so forth, and we're supposed to clean up after you and bow down like you're royalty or something, but I tell you we get sick of it. We're gonna teach you a lesson you'll never forget." He threw the door open, and had not her vision by now improved sufficiently to see it coming, Lydia might have been struck.

But she stepped back and waited for Lyman to emerge, which he proceeded to do as if he had acquired another hundred pounds of flesh since last seen. It was perhaps unfair of her, considering his current state, in which the chief was obviously incapable of giving more than a symbolic performance, but that was the pleasure of it: she kicked him in the groin with all her force. She was amazed at how effective this blow proved: she had never previously delivered one except against a soft dummy in a two-session female self-defense course at college.

Lyman actually howled in anguish, clutched himself, and sat down heavily in the gravel.

Figures emerged from the jeep, but before they reached her Lydia had claimed the chief's revolver from his holster. It was much heavier than she had assumed it would be, took both hands to hold and was not so steady even then.

"Lydia," Chuck said, coming from around the rear of the vehicle, "do you realize what you've done to an officer of the law?" He was by far the smallest of the four standing men. The others were submissively holding their hands in the air, as if victims of a stickup.

"Now you guys," she said, in a voice that started uncertainly but grew more steady as she spoke, "you guys pick up Lyman and put him in the jeep."

Chuck slowly advanced. "Lydia," he said, "can't you see it was just a joke? You're going to get into trouble if you keep this up."

She waved the pistol at the largest of the big men. "Get going."

He made a little bow of acquiescence and bent to take the crumpled chief under one shoulder. Another man took the other side, and the third seized the ankles just above the hightop shoes. The task looked heavy even for three large porters: Lyman hung between them like an overfilled sack.

Chuck said, "So he goes a little far, but he *is* the duly constituted authority. He can't be deposed just like that, at *your* convenience."

Lydia kept the gun on him. "Why is your name Burgoyne and not Finch?"

"My mother got married." He stepped closer. "I'm glad to see you're coming to your senses, Lydia. Now put that gun down."

Lyman uttered a new groan of pain. His hat had fallen off: perhaps the men had banged his head trying to insert him into the jeep.

"Don't come closer," Lydia warned Chuck. "I know how to shoot a revolver. My uncle showed me."

Chuck said knowingly, "And who would know better than a mobster?"

"He's a veteran police lieutenant," she lied.

"Go on," said Chuck, but he stopped where he was. "Put the gun down, Lydia. Let's talk this over."

"I want you out of here. You've become an embarrassment."

"You can't mean that. We saved each other's lives today. That must signify something."

"One person naturally helps another in an extreme situation: that's only human. It doesn't mean anything else."

"I just wish you could bring yourself to admit it," Chuck said, in a wheedling tone. "You're in love with me. God knows, you've done everything you can to show that, but you simply can't say it. Okay, then don't! But just put the gun down, and we'll forget this little incident ever happened. Am I right, boys?"

The other men had by now installed Lyman in the back seat of the jeep and were presumably awaiting instructions. They grunted inscrutably in response to Chuck's question.

Lydia waved the pistol. "You guys get in."

Chuck pretended to be part of the current directorate and added his own orders as the men were complying with hers. "Go on back to the village. This is it for tonight."

"You're going with them," said Lydia. "Get in."

"Naw," he said in a lowered voice. "That wouldn't work at all. I don't have anything in common with these guys. I left and made something of myself. I didn't come back to *them*. I've got an education. I've got good taste. I know how to act. I can go anywhere."

"That's what you think," said Lydia, waving the gun at him. "Get in the jeep. We don't want your kind here."

Chuck hung his head for a moment. When he brought his eyes up, he said, "You think your fancy in-laws give you the right to take the law into your own hands?"

"Yes." Despite the complexities of reality, or perhaps because of them, the simplest answers are often the most effective: she was learning that. "I could give lots more in the way of justification, but it would probably come down to that simple fact in the end."

Chuck stared at her. "You're my biggest disappointment. I can't really see you getting anywhere in the long run. You're living in a fool's paradise. You think you're clever now, but they'll eventually destroy you."

"I was hoping I wouldn't have to do this," Lydia said, "because it sounds so phony, but unless you get into the jeep before I have counted to three, I'm simply going to shoot you. *One*."

Chuck shrugged, said, "You're in charge," turned and took a step towards the vehicle.

Lydia felt ridiculous, but she went ahead and said, "*Two.*"

At this point, Chuck whirled around and leaped at her. She had no choice but to fire.

§ 12 §

"Good God," said Doug, at the kitchen windows. "Who's been shot?" He had seen nothing yet but the shadowy figures of the men who had deboarded from the jeep on the side facing him. The action was on the far side.

"Put on the lights out there!" cried Bobby, though he made no move to do so himself.

"Would that be wise, with guns being fired?"

"This is *exactly* what I feared," Audrey moaned. "Just *exactly*."

"Well," Bobby said, "I think my place is with Lydia."

His father asked, incredulously, "Unarmed?"

"There must be something we can do!"

"We're doing it, Bobby," said Doug. "We're here. We're standing fast. We're not running. It would make no sense to go out there and get killed. How would that help?"

"Still," Bobby said, "I don't see how anybody else is going to understand afterwards."

Audrey spoke. "If we emerge from this unscathed — and I think it's possible that we will, if what they really did want all the while was *her* — we have no business in mentioning anything about this episode to anyone else. Not even, for example, to Mrs. Finch when she comes tomorrow morning."

"Uh-oh," said Bobby. "The jeep is leaving."

"Is someone on the ground?" Doug asked eagerly. "I can't see a thing." Except of course the parallel shafts of the headlamp beams as the vehicle swung around, and then its red taillights as they diminished in departure.

Bobby said, "I'm going out there!"

"An ambush may be just what Chuck has in mind," Doug told him. "Better wait."

Suddenly someone entered the kitchen and authoritatively threw the switch that illuminated the ceiling light.

It was Lydia. She held a large revolver.

"Now just think this over," Doug said urgently, holding up vertical palms. Both he and she were squinting in the bright light. "Don't do something you'll be sorry for."

"Lyd!" Bobby shouted, but he kept his distance from her. "Did you get him? Is the body out there?"

"I take it you mean Chuck?" Her hair was tousled and she appeared otherwise the worse for wear, sweaty, soiled, scratched. She was not the kind who looked good without grooming, was nowhere near being a natural beauty, but then Doug had never had a taste for dark brunettes. On the other hand, this was the first time since seeing her in the swimsuit that he had been sexually stimulated by looking at his daughter-in-law. Perhaps it was the gun. "No," she said in answer to Bobby. "He left."

"Did you shoot *anybody?*" Bobby sounded as though prepared to be disappointed.

"I fired once between Chuck's feet. That's all it took. He won't be back."

Doug peered at the weapon. "Is that Lyman's gun?"

"He won't make any trouble. He won't want the world to know it was taken away from him by an unarmed woman he and his male relatives, four of them, were going to rape."

Bobby turned away with an expression of disdain.

"Go get some brandy," Lydia said to Doug.

"Hadn't you better put the gun down?"

She waved it at him. "Get going."

"You're a real heroine, dear," Audrey said. "This is your moment."

"Sit down right there," said Lydia, pointing the pistol at a chair.

Doug fetched a bottle of cognac, as ordered, and included a balloon glass: just one. He intended to drink nothing, for he saw a need to keep his wits about him.

But having directed him to pour — which he did, generously, on the assumption that it would be swallowed by her — Lydia asked him to drain the glass into his own throat. He had no intention of denying the request of an emotionally overwrought young woman holding a firearm. He complied.

On her command he poured a second glassful of brandy and gave it to Bobby.

"Oh," Audrey said, reaching, "I believe that's mine."

"No," said Lydia. "We're going to cure you. We're going to make good use of the rest of the summer, despite this bad start."

Bobby took the glass. "All right, I'll drink it for your sake, Lyd. There's no need to keep holding that gun, for God's sake. We're just family now, and we're proud of you."

"Drink the brandy, Bobby. You've just had a narrow escape."

"Me?"

"Just think what would have happened to you if Chuck had stayed."

Doug thrust his chin forward. "Now aren't you going a little too far? It's true that for a while we assumed you were in some sort of conspiracy with Chuck against us. We were wrong. What more can I say? But look at it from our perspective. No offense, but you both were strangers."

Bobby lowered the globular vessel and said, "Wait a minute, Dad."

"I'm just admitting our error, Bobby. We've got to clear the air."

He looked at Lydia and was surprised to see her burst into tears.

"I'm not used to violence," she said. "I never did that kind of thing before. I never even really believed it would work."

Now was the moment Doug should have gone for her gun: he knew that, but he failed to act.

"There were a whole lot of them," Lydia said, still weeping off and on. "I beat 'em! I won!" More tears. "You know what really made me mad? That hog of a Lyman claimed he heard me using foul language in the village. That's not true."

Audrey said, "He was thinking of the sightseers, tourists. He was wrong to include you, dear. Now may I have a sip?"

Lydia stopped crying. "Don't you understand that now it's up to me to make something of you people, now that I've saved you from Chuck?"

"But can't we begin that tomorrow?" asked her mother-in-law. "Bright and early on a Monday morning? And by the way, there's no point in mentioning any of today's events to Mrs. Finch. If Chuck is really related to her, then no doubt she'll have heard *his* version. But let's leave it at that. It would only demean us to plead our case with someone who works for us."

"You see?" asked Lydia. "You forget about drinking as

soon as you have something else to occupy your attention."

"No, I don't," said Audrey.

Lydia disregarded the statement, if she heard it at all. She said, "But don't concern yourself about Mrs. Finch. We're going to fire her. And we're also going to turn away those women who come to clean. There's no need to hire anybody: all of us are here, doing nothing of value as it is. You can cook. Bobby will wax the floors, and Doug can handle the yardwork."

She laid the pistol on the kitchen table, as if tempting her father-in-law to seize it, but of course he did not.

"You'll see," Lydia went on. "You'll all have something to give you self-respect, for a change."

"By doing housework?" Audrey asked, more in amazement than resentment.

"You shouldn't look at it that way. Anything can be disparaged. Law can be called merely the cynical means by which some people claim the right to dominate others. And do you think scientists consciously work for the good of the human race?"

"For the life of me, I can't see what's evil about giving people employment." Audrey sighed. "I know that I'd be grateful if I needed work." She sighed again. "You must be exhausted, dear. You won't mind my saying you could use a good cleanup after all your trials. You've got burrs caught in your hair, and your arms are all scratched. If you'd like to borrow some clothing — I know you haven't brought much along. And we're just about the same size."

"No," said Lydia, "you *can't* have anything to drink. I'm nailing the liquor cabinet shut, and when the secret supply you must keep in your room is gone, that will be it. But you won't need any, you see. Doug will be staying here all summer. And Bobby won't even be going to the club."

"And *you?*" Bobby asked bitterly, having at last drained the brandy glass. "What are you going to be doing, Lyd? Just waving that gun around?" Already feeling the effects of the alcohol, he added, "You don't know how silly you look."

"Me?" Lydia asked, smiling. Her face was dirty, but her teeth sparkled. "I'll be enjoying your flawless hospitality."

"Oh, come on," said Doug. "Aren't you being a little self-pitying? You're family, and you know it. This experience has brought us all closer together. In the years to come, we'll undoubtedly look back on it as something that worked for the good of all — even the Finches, or in any event, the more reasonable of them, who must surely appreciate that we all have to live together. Which doesn't mean we have to like one another." He yawned and stretched. "Well, I don't know about you people, but *I'm* exhausted. I don't even want to think about any more problems. Tomorrow we'll deal with the cars. Maybe the phones will be back on by then. If not, someone can hike to the gas station: it's only about two miles."

"Yeah, Lyd can go," wryly said Bobby. "She's the one with the gun."

"Mark my words," said Doug. "No Finch nor anyone remotely connected with them will remember any of today's events. They've lost face, you see. That's mortal for people of their kind. You think they don't have feelings? They do. They don't want to be reminded of the trouncing we gave them out here."

Lydia at last lowered the gun. "Yeah," she said, "you really showed 'em." She seemed to be running out of steam now, and therefore was once again not terribly attractive to Doug.

He said to Audrey, "C'mon, I'll walk you back."

"Oh," said she, as usual thinking exclusively of herself, "I'm not afraid."

"Just be sociable," said he. He bade Bobby and Lydia goodnight. He believed his daughter-in-law must eventually be persuaded to return the gun to Lyman, but that could wait.

He remembered all the disarranged furniture in his quarters only when he returned and saw it. On leaving the hastily constructed fortress they had merely moved the desk and thrown the mattress aside. Everything was still in disarray.

Audrey was just entering her own doorway.

"Look," said he to her back. "Don't worry about what that kid was saying. She's all worked up. She'll be back to normal tomorrow."

His wife turned. "I can't say I like her, but she's not all wrong. She's the only one of us who could have gotten rid of Chuck."

"You mean she may be a necessary evil, like a policeman?" He grimaced. "Mind if I spend the night with you? I think we're all a little lonely after a day like this."

"Speak for yourself," said she. She entered her room and closed the door.

"Go on to bed," Lydia told Bobby.

"Alone?" he wailed. "Are you still mad at me?"

"I can't sleep," she said. "I'm too wound up." She gestured at the pistol. "I feel like shooting this, but I don't know at what. I don't want to hurt anybody, but it seems unfinished, somehow."

Bobby raised his hands and let them fall. "I really think you ought to get some rest, Lyd. Sleep with the pistol, if it will make you feel better. I'll take one of the couches."

"Go away, Bobby." Finally he did. Lydia wandered through some of the rooms overlooking the now invisible ocean. At last she sat down in a chair so soft and capacious as to be a complete environment, and she fell asleep. . . .

The first thing she noticed when she awakened was the revolver in her lap. In the light of morning it was an embarrassment, and she hid it within the chair. The sun was shining, but the sea, full of whitecaps, was obviously being agitated by an offshore wind. She was far from finished with that ocean, with which she had a score to settle.

All at once she smelled the delectable aroma of coffee, and went without delay to the kitchen.

Chuck Burgoyne was peeping into the oven, through a door slightly opened for the purpose. He was dressed in the same clothing he had worn since his first arrival: the chino trousers, navy-blue knitted shirt, and loafers, none of which seemed the least soiled by incessant use. Materially he was of a stainless character.

"Morning, sleepyhead!" he cried before he had turned far enough to identify her by sight. "Though I shouldn't pick on *you:* the others are still dead to the world." He gestured with a shoulder at the stove. "Go get yourself a cuppa. Give me another five minutes for the muffins."

"You came back?" Lydia asked incredulously, though she realized it made her sound naïve as ever.

Chuck had the same beautiful rosy complexion. No doubt he had had a night's sleep in good conscience. "I thought I had a certain investment," said he, "and shouldn't just write it off. I'd never forgive myself."

"There's nothing here for you."

"That's a matter of interpretation."

"Yes," said Lydia. "Mine. I'm in charge here now."

"Forgive me for saying this, but you look *awful*." Here he had made a grievous error: he had turned trivial.

"I'm also just getting my period."

When he looked revolted, she knew she had him on the run. "I just want to ask you," he said mournfully. "That bullet last night nearly hit me in the groin. Were you aiming there?"

"If I had been," said she, "you'd be a soprano today." This was not true; she really didn't know how to shoot a pistol, let alone aim it. In desperation she had closed her eyes and pulled the trigger.

"You're one tough chick."

"You're an amusing little fellow."

"You don't want a blueberry muffin?"

"No," said Lydia. She was backing him to the door.

He showed his famous grin one more time. "I'll admit I underestimated you, but I can change."

"That may be true," Lydia said, "but you'll never really make a go of it. You're all resentment. You have no vision."

"I suppose *you* do?"

"I'm trying to accomplish something here," she said. "*You* are the cheap hustler, not me."

"All right," Chuck said bitterly. "You don't have to pull a gun on me again." He turned and left the house. She watched him until he had trudged through the parking area. Apparently he had come on foot from wherever he had spent the night. He was, perhaps intentionally, something of a pathetic figure. She regretted not having been able to tell him that all in all he had helped her establish herself in this alien place, but she did not yet have the skill to deal finely with someone so lacking in moral discrimination.

She might have stayed longer at the window had not dark smoke begun to issue from the oven. She found an insulated mitt and removed the muffins from the heat. They were badly singed, the bottoms positively blackened. Her mother would have trimmed them to an edible state, then eaten them herself or crumbled them for the wild birds, would never have tried to pass off such on the family. But that was another kind of family.

When the Graveses appeared — first Audrey, then Doug, and finally a groggy son — they ate the muffins with enthusiasm.

"Delicious," said Doug, on his second. "And I thought you said you couldn't cook!" He waggled a fake-chiding finger at her: its nail looked freshly manicured, though he had not been in the city for three days now.

Bobby, obsessed with his third muffin, buttered its latest surface after each bite.

Audrey wore lime-green slacks and a sparkling white blouse. She smiled at Lydia. "Have you slept at all, dear?"

"What I haven't done is wash or change my clothes," Lydia said in as civil a tone as she could manage when she really felt like snarling. "If you'll excuse me now . . ." She drifted towards the door but eventually stopped and said, "Look, I can't take credit for the muffins. Actually, *Chuck* sneaked back and baked them while I was asleep. Maybe he thought something like ʼ that would be atonement! Naturally, I ran him off."

Audrey's expression did not change. "Naturally," said she.

Doug nodded amiably and took a sip of the instant coffee each had prepared individually.

"Did you hear me?" Lydia demanded. "*Chuck* had the nerve to come back!"

Doug swallowed with care. "I don't find that surprising. Do you, Bob?"

Bobby shook his tousled head and plucked up some fallen muffin crumbs. "I even expected it, to tell you the truth. He's hard to discourage."

Audrey made a sort of tulip of her hand. "Such persistence," said she. "It can even be seen as flattering. He went through an awful lot of abuse."

Lydia looked from one to the other. "What is going on here?"

"You have to admit," said Doug, deploying his butter knife, "that he went to a good deal of trouble. Those telephone voices, for example: I admit I still can't quite explain them. I did speak with someone claiming to be named Perlmutter, with Chuck standing right beside me. Therefore he could not have been faking *that* voice. On the other hand, it might well have been he in the case of the *first* —"

"Goddammit," cried Lydia.

Bobby had seized another muffin. Notwithstanding that its bottom was black and hardened, he chomped on it with relish.

"He did not always know his place," said Audrey, "but that's true of many people who make something of themselves. They err on the side of zeal, but that's not necessarily something to be deplored."

Lydia let them go on eating and drinking for a few moments, which they proceeded to do without looking towards her. What she resented most was their aplomb.

"All right," she said eventually. "Where is he?"

Doug smirked. "You anticipated us. We thought it would take a lot more preparation."

Chuck came in from the butler's pantry. "Sorry about

those muffins," he said to Lydia. "They wouldn't have burned if I hadn't been distracted at the time."

Lydia's glance made a tour of the Graveses. "You want him back, don't you?"

Audrey shrugged, though with no suggestion of apology. "He could be mighty useful. Mrs. Finch is not as young as she once was."

"Neither am I, for that matter," said Lydia.

Bobby spoke eagerly. "He's going to get the cars running and put the phones back in shape."

"Also," said Chuck, "I have to replace the broken glass in the door to the pool. There's more than enough to keep me busy." He walked briskly to the refrigerator. "Now, who wants what for the next course? I think you all deserve a big breakfast, to start the week off with a bang."

"I'm willing to pay Lyman for the gun," Lydia told him. "But I'm keeping possession of it."

"I can't say I blame you," Chuck said blandly. "With all you've gone through."

She stared at her in-laws. "Listen to him. *He's* the one who's responsible for the damage he's now allegedly going to repair. *He's* the reason I intend to keep the gun." None of them returned her gaze, but neither did they seem concerned by what she said. "He *despises* all of you."

Audrey chuckled. "He made that clear enough!"

Doug's noble forehead showed a frown. "Which of course has nothing to do with the quality of his work. There's no reason why we have to love everybody with whom we deal in life, or even to regard them in a personal way. We simply want the job done."

"Then he's an employee now?"

Doug smirked. "He could certainly never get back in here as a guest! That was the trouble before: the basic arrangement was wrong."

"Putting him on wages takes care of everything?"

"That's right, Lyd," said Bobby. "It's the perfect answer."

"And," said Doug, as if Chuck were absent, "you can be sure I'll keep after him until I get an explanation of those puzzling phone calls and also the matter of the gun in the ankle holster."

"And," Chuck said with verve, "you can be sure I'll come up with plausible answers!"

Lydia put her head down and deliberated for a moment. The knees of her jeans were muddy, and she still carried burrs and other foreign matter here and there on her clothing. She had never been so filthy or exhausted in her life, yet she was far from being contaminated.

She looked up. "It makes sense."

"It does?" Bobby asked happily, and the others, including Chuck, showed their pleasure.

"I don't think I've ever before understood what manners are," Lydia said. "And I'm not at all sure I do even now. But I'm going to give you *my* condition: the only way I'll put up with the new arrangement is if *I* become the houseguest."

The Graveses looked at one another, and then Doug said, "I can't see any objection."

"With all the privileges of that situation," said Lydia.

"Of course," Audrey said grandly. "That goes without saying."

Chuck was holding a spatula. "Now, who would like flapjacks?"

Lydia pulled off her dirty sneakers. "Here," she said to him, "go scrub these someplace."

"I'll pop them into the washer," said he, accepting the

shoes. She could identify no irony in his speech or expression. "And then I'll take Bobby to the club and Doug to the airfield for the ten o'clock flight. Then back here to do the rest of the week's wash, and if time permits, to draw up a guest list for the annual party. Then I'll prepare lunch."

"Something special," said Lydia. "I'll never eat another frank or bean or a forkful of cole slaw in this house."

"As you wish," said Chuck, with an inclination of his smooth head. "We'll do anything we can to assure you a pleasant stay."

She could not resist saying, "That's the slogan of a chain motel."

Chuck's response to the gibe was in the same idiom and could be heard as either submissive or ominous. "We'll stop at nothing to please you."

Whether or not that "we" included her relatives-in-law, all four people in the kitchen were smiling benignly upon her.